Love Me Again

Love Me Again

J.L. POLANCO

First Printing, 2022

This book is dedicated to my loving and supportive husband.
Jason, without your love and support, there would be no words on these pages.

I would also like dedicate this book to the lovers; the ones who have found their soul mates and those still looking.

1

Jovi

"I want a divorce and I want it now!" The words fell out of my mouth like lava spewing from a volcano.

And boy did it burn.

I've always imagined that I would say those words, but I never really thought I'd actually say it. I am a thirty-three-year-old mother and wife. Just last year we were talking about reproducing for the second time.

I mean, the first kid turned out to be awesome, why not have a second?

But lately I felt like things were spinning out of control.

I stared at my stunned husband.

Scott looked like one of those Bugs Bunny cartoons where Elmer Fudd is so mad you can see it in his eyes, resulting in comical steam coming out his ears.

That was my husband, but without the genetic baldness and speech impediment. Most people would say that my husband was handsome; Dark hair, tan skin, full lips.

Coming in at six feet, five inches— he was a giant.

Most people were thrown off by the tattoo sleeve he wore proudly, but he was honest to God, a gentle giant; like the ones that try to get you to eat vegetables. It was one of the reasons I began screaming at the top of my lungs like a banshee.

"You what?" he asked through gritted teeth.

"I want a divorce! I want a divorce!" Every time I said it, my voice just kept getting louder and louder, as if I had no control of the volume.

I was out of breath from my heart beating faster and working overtime, trying to prevent a panic attack.

"I heard you the first fucking time, Jovi!" He still hadn't gotten up from his seat at the dining table. I could see his temples throb and the vein pop up on his forehead.

I could imagine Scott silently regretting letting me become a Garcia in holy matrimony.

All those years ago, we were so infatuated with each other that we pretended that morning breath didn't exist. All those years ago, when everything on my body was tight and I had the ability to wear skinny jeans without the clasp digging into my belly button; back when high waisted jeans weren't a necessity.

Oh, how things have changed.

Tonight, my parents were babysitting our daughter because we wanted to have a date night, but my husband at the last minute decided to cancel our plans so we could *Netflix and chill.*

A lifetime of being with this human told me that that was code for *start a movie but fall asleep right before the opening credits.*

I may sound like an ungrateful bitch, believe me I know, but we never go out anymore. I've forgotten what ordering from a menu that wasn't stuck together with syrup was like!

I had a job as a reporter with long, unpredictable hours and Scott's job as an elementary school gym teacher often made him too tired to want to go out. But damn, there were times that I wanted to dress up and be cute. I wanted us to be cute together.

"You don't think I heard your psychotic cry? You're two feet away from me!" His deep brown eyes glared at me.

"Scott," I said his name as a way to start my sentence, but I was at a loss for words.

"What, Jo? What the hell you gonna tell me now? You have a boyfriend?" His face flushed with anger.

He had the audacity to be angry at me?! I put my hands on my hips to keep from choking him. "Yes, that's what this whole thing is about! There's this one guy at work..." I began only to stop when I saw the blood drain from his face. The tick in his jaw warned me that I hit a raw nerve. "Oh my god, Scott! It was a joke!"

He threw back the beer he'd been babysitting, swallowing hard. "Were you joking about the divorce too? Because that's not funny."

I couldn't meet his eyes. "No, I wasn't joking," I said quietly.

With the hysteria in my veins calming itself I began to shake, the gravity of what I had yelled was starting to sink in and I couldn't take it back.

My eyes glanced around our beautiful apartment; we had to go through so much to get it...or at least that was what the broker said, because it was in the nice part of the Bronx, where gangs were nice to the elderly and didn't bother you if you didn't bother them.

I cleared my throat and continued, "Scott, I want a divorce." This time I met his eyes.

My big, strong husband, the provider and protector of his clan, looked defeated.

I did that to him.

There were two times that I've seen Scott cry; the first time was when the original *Yankee Stadium* closed down and the second time was when our daughter was born.

Tonight, might be the third.

His eyes shone bright from the moisture.

Scott stroked his beard and looked away, probably wishing he could kill me and get away with it. He shook his head. "Why?" he asked.

How could I answer such a loaded question? How could I tell him "It's not me, it is in fact you" and not sound like a lame person?

It's not that I wanted the divorce; I felt as if I *needed it.*

"Because I'm just your roommate," I finally answered. That just sounded lamer.

Truth be told, I've been keeping close tabs on Scott's phone since I met his secretary at a school function last year. The way she looked at him tore at my heart. He would never admit it to me but I knew he was attracted to her just by the way he stood when they were near each other. That slight lean you do when you want to touch but don't want to make it obvious. My suspicions turned out to be true. They've been having deep meaningful conversations through text, the kinds that we use to have.

It also didn't help that this secretary sent a picture of her bare tits as if it were no big deal. Just a few minutes ago I heard the chime of his phone and asked, "Who was that?"

All he said was, "It's work."

No other explanation.

I stomped to the room and checked his watch that linked to his phone. When I looked at his messages, there they were; two perfectly round breasts staring back at me. I wouldn't be surprised if she didn't have any kids. They didn't look like tits that had breastfed...unless she was a Kardashian.

And I knew for a fact that she wasn't.

So here I was giving my husband, a lame fucking excuse.

"Bullshit, Jovi." His voice was low, and I just wanted to sock him in the face.

"What do you want me to say, Scott."

"The truth!" he yelled.

Oh, he wanted the truth? I was going to give it to him. "Okay, here it goes. I want a divorce."

"You already said that, Jo." Irritation prickled in his voice.

"And I want it because I saw it!" Hysteria made my voice rise again. I couldn't stop yelling, my voice was going hoarse from the strain on my throat.

"Saw what?" he hissed, growing impatient.

"It! Them!"

"Full sentences, Jo."

"I saw the tits on your phone! The perfect round ones that that bitch sent you!"

He sat stunned. He didn't expect that answer. While Scott fumbled for words, I ventured forward. "I've been looking through your phone and I saw them." My tears began to fall, and he got up to reach for me. "Don't touch me, Scott! I swear I'm crying but it's only because I'm that angry. Does the name Lorena Bobbitt mean anything to you? Because that's where my mind is headed."

"Jovi, I didn't do anything with her." His voice grew soft as he dropped his arms to his side.

"Yes, you did." My voice cracked; my anger was tiring me out.

"Jovi, I swear on our daughter that I didn't have sex with her."

I shook my head. "Really? Why did she feel so comfortable to send you that?"

"I don't know."

"You told her things. I didn't just see her tits, Scott. I saw the things leading up to it. The things you told her. Things that I didn't know about until I read the messages."

I could see the little hamster in his mind, running on the wheel trying to get to nowhere fast.

"I want a divorce," I said one final time, before I walked past him and locked myself in our bedroom.

******

Scott

I don't know what the fuck just happened.

We were sitting in silence, enjoying our takeout and then a wail came from the bedroom. The cry of a maniac.

We weren't the family to cause a scene. In our apartment building we were the family with no drama. That usually lasted until Jovi's family came to visit.

We were the ones that everyone wanted to be. Holding hands, perfect kid skipping and playing between us.

We were the dream.

I shook my head in disbelief. I can't believe she's been looking through my phone. I felt a deeper sense of hurt at the mere fact that my wife had no faith in me. Where was the trust?

I wanted to know what she read and why she read it.

I definitely knew that she saw the naked picture Kim sent. I didn't ask for the picture. I didn't think our conversations showed any indication that I wanted more than friendship!

It was just nice to talk to someone who didn't nag at me about doing laundry or cleaning. I like conversations where the other person isn't silently stewing in anger or disappointment because I bought Valentines chocolates for our daughters pre-K class when I was told to bring baby carrots and vegetable chips...who brings baby carrots to a Valentines day kiddie party?!

It was nice to just sit and relax and shoot the breeze.

Maybe it was wrong to talk and bond with someone else who wasn't Jovi, but a divorce is not what I wanted.

It didn't even cross my mind.

I could see where we may have had a little friction; Jovi went through a difficult time when Clara was born. She went through an emotional rollercoaster that the doctor chalked up to sleep deprivation, which was normal with a newborn.

One day Jovi would be happy and the next she'd be on the kitchen floor crying and I didn't know what to do.

I would be the one taking care of our newborn daughter, along with everything else and I had had enough. Back then, I told her if she didn't shape up, maybe we should consider a separation. During that whole scene, I told Jovi that I didn't feel like Clara and I were priorities, that sometimes I thought about how it would be to be with someone else.

The tears began to fall; I felt like a complete asshole for saying all that stuff out loud. Since then, I've been a little bit reserved with my wife. Things that I would feel comfortable talking to her about, was left untouched because I didn't want to stir the pot; triumphs, disappointments, anxiety driven madness were all topics kept to myself.

Things between us got a little better and Jovi picked up the slack with Clara. But other things were still lacking like...sex was almost non-existent. She was always tired, or I was always tired...it's crazy how many headaches and migraines or body aches one person can have.

Then, we had a big blow up because I couldn't pick Clara up from daycare and Jovi was completely unreachable, she was on deadline and had put her phone on silent. I vented to Kim. She was always friendly with me. After my frustrated outburst, our conversations switched from just casual greetings in passing to mutual interests, inside jokes...it didn't feel wrong to talk to a friend...until she sent that picture.

But a divorce?

I loved Jovi.

Jovi and I have been together almost fifteen years. In a lot of ways, we became adults together.

I looked around the room of our beautiful apartment; at the soft grey paint that we chose for the walls, the lamps, rugs, plants and pictures that Jovi expertly chose to decorate our apartment to make it feel like a home. The wooden dining table that we found in the trash and restored.

Was this all really over?

I heard the bedroom door open and stood to attention. "Jovi I—"

She held out a duffle bag. "I packed you a bag, this should hold you over until the end of the week."

"Where am I supposed to go?" I kept my voice even, although I wanted to scream until she came to her senses.

Jovi's eyes narrowed in my direction as she shrugged her shoulders. "Why don't you ask big tits McGee?"

"Jovi..." I said through clenched teeth.

"Scott! I don't know where you go but you can't stay here, or I will kill you with my bare hands!" Her manic cry came back in full force.

"This is my apartment too!" I could feel my blood pressure rise.

Jovi was never an easy woman. When we met, she was wild and crazy. She was the kind of woman people warned you about; the kind that would make you fall in love with every part of her and then break your heart. She was vibrant, loud and passionate. Jovi was different; it was the reason I fell in love with her.

Jovi had calmed down when we had Clara; maybe it was the strains of parenthood.

This woman standing in front of me with her short brown hair all over the place, face red with anger, was a completely different woman.

This was a woman who apparently has had enough. "It's your

apartment but I don't want to go to jail, so it's best if you just go." Her voice cracked and that's what did me in.

My wife was standing in front of me telling me that I had to leave, or she'd kill me; looking at her, I believed it.

"Jovi, I don't want to go. I don't want to get a divorce. We need to talk about this."

She shook her head so hard. "No, Scott." She held out my duffle bag and I finally took it.

I threw on my jacket and looked back at my wife before leaving. "I'll be at my mother's if you need me."

The calm fall night was a contrast to the chaotic, emotionally charged bubble of our apartment.

Maybe a couple of hours at my mother's wasn't a bad idea.

2

Jovi

"And what did he say?" my brother, Tommy, asked.

We were sitting at my massive mahogany dining table while our kids played in the living room.

I shrugged. "What do you think he said? He said bullshit. That I was trying to create drama because that's what my side of the family is all about."

My brother laughed. "Just because mom and dad called a priest, rabbi and bruja because Titi Lucy had an ingrown hair the size of Texas and they thought it was cancer, doesn't mean that they're drama."

I smiled at the absurdity of the memory. "Maybe because of them it turned out to be an ingrown hair," I added.

"Exactly."

I let the small bit of amusement settle in my bones as I sat back and finally noticed Tommy's thinner frame; it was intensified by his curly brown hair that was all over the place, making his face seem sunken in. "Tommy, you okay? you look like you lost a lot of weight."

The dimples, that only he and our mother possessed, were

prominent as he smiled. "I'm on this new diet where you don't eat anything but broth for eight hours. But when that time comes, I'm so tired I just fall asleep."

"So, you're eating nothing?" I suppressed my worry.

"I have broth," he said around a mouth full of his bacon, egg and cheese sandwich. I hid my giggle behind my massive cup of coffee.

I called Tommy this morning and told him the news, he came over in record time and he brought along breakfast.

We watched our daughters play tea party while we ate in silence. They felt like the only bright light in such a sad, soul shattering time.

After he washed it down with coffee, he leaned over and whispered. “Jo, tell me for real, are you okay? You’re sure this is the right thing?”

I sighed instead of answering.

I wanted to say, *Yes! I’m doing the right thing, it’s something I needed to do to save myself*. Scott definitely had sex with that woman. On top of that, he emotionally cheated on me with her, which just felt worse. It’s like watching a show that you and your partner wanted to see together and then one of you go and watch it without the other...it’s a betrayal!

It’s probably absurd to compare my marital issues with a hijacked Netflix night, but my brain isn’t functioning properly these days.

I didn’t want to lie to my brother, because in all honesty I didn’t know if this was the right thing to do.

I cried all night.

I know it was my decision. I’ve been feeling like this for a while, ever since that infamous lecture that Scott gave me about how I’m not carrying my weight when it came to raising our daughter; basically, calling me a bad mom. He even went so far as to say he imagined being with other women! Who says that to someone who is going through a tough time?! Scott Garcia, that’s who.

But to say that divorce is the right thing and to continue with life as if none of our time mattered, would mean I have no heart.

We met when I was twenty-one.

I was working at a retail store to pay for the astronomical cost of college textbooks and my co-workers decided to treat me for drinks. I mean, I wasn't one to turn down a celebration especially if it was celebrating me. After one too many drinks, I couldn't walk straight, let alone take the subway by myself. My co-worker suggested her friend drive us all home and her friend happened to be Scott. In the dim light of a red *Honda Civic*, I only saw his afro. As he drove us home, our eyes kept meeting through the rearview mirror, but we didn't say a word to each other. I guess, I was too drunk, and he was not the type to talk to shit-faced girls.

Even in my drunken state, I began to feel butterflies.

"Jo, can you be honest with me?" Tommy brought me back to the present.

I eyed him wearily, afraid of what he might ask. When he took his time to continue, my frustration surfaced. "Ask your question! Geez, man!"

"Alright, relax!" he yelled back.

Clara looked over at us from the living room. "Mommy, why are you guys yelling?"

"Sorry, baby, Uncle Tommy is being an ass," I said, lightly kicking him under the table.

The girls giggled. "Mom, you said ass."

I took a deep breath to center myself; I usually wasn't into hippy dippy stuff, but I'd do anything to release the tension in my neck...even if it involved *centering* myself. "Ask your question, Tommy," I said calmly.

"I wanted to know...is there someone else?"

"NO!" I couldn't keep myself from shouting. He should know better, I'm not that type of person. I wasn't made to cheat. It involved lying which I wasn't good at. Also, if I didn't want someone to do that to me, then I shouldn't really do it to anyone. Even this non-hippy dippy person believed in karma.

"Maaaa, you're yelling again," Clara said.

"Sorry, baby!" I yelled back.

I turned my full attention back to Tommy. "There's literally no one else," I whispered.

Tommy tilted his head, giving me a look that said I was full of shit.

I began to shake my head. "Why is it difficult to believe that there is no one else?"

"Because there has to be a reason as to why all of a sudden you want a divorce."

I looked down at what was left of my breakfast, to hide the sheen of moisture that clouded my eyes. "Who said it was all of a sudden?"

I looked up in time to see his eyes widened with shock. "You've been thinking about this for a while?"

I nodded. For some god-awful reason I couldn't tell my brother, the person I told everything to, the reason behind my final decision.

It would be a hard thing for Tommy to grasp. His life was perfect.

He was the oldest out of the three of us; he was the calmest. I knew that I could depend on him for anything. But I rarely did—that was our baby sister Liz's job.

Tommy had a loving husband, Frank, who was this big bear of a man. Frank was very lovable and the complete opposite of my brother. Where Tommy was calm, Frank stressed out over the smallest thing, but they were perfect for each other.

After opening up their own barbershop in East Harlem, they adopted my niece, Daniella, a year later.

It was no secret that Tommy loved Scott like a brother, so even though he didn't show it, I knew that the news of the divorce hurt.

The silence was deafening as we tried to get our thoughts together. I had no intention of telling Tommy that Scott cheated. Or about the text messages and pictures.

In disclosing that information to my brother, there would be a trickle effect; Tommy would tell Liz, who would tell my parents and they would make this a bigger deal than what I wanted it to be.

It was embarrassing. Also, if my parents found out, like they eventually would if I told either one of my siblings, who knows what would happen. I can only guess that my mom would pray for Scott before jumping out a window and my dad would hunt him down with a baseball bat. I had to be strategic about how I dropped the news to everyone.

"Jovi!" My brothers voice cut through my thoughts.

I jumped up in surprise. "Hmmm? You say something?"

Tommy gave me a half-hearted smile; Treating me like a scared deer that would run at the sight of human contact. I hated that.

"So, what's the plan?" he asked, his whole demeanor showing how flabbergasted he felt.

I glanced over at our daughters playing quietly on the floor. "At the moment, there is no plan. But when I come up with one, you'll be the first to know." I kept my voice even, although I felt like curling up in a fetal position and crying.

He reached for my hand and squeezed. "Or we can come up with a plan together."

Oh, no! My eyes began to well up!

Tommy squeezed my hand tighter and I winced. "Ow! That hurt." I narrowed my eyes at him, shaking my hand as he released it.

"I'm sorry, I just...I want to be there when you tell mom and dad," He said.

I shook my head. "No, definitely no."

He clasped his hands together and continued to beg. "Pleeeease."

"No, you know she gets dramatic when she has an audience."

He clucked his tongue at me. "She's dramatic without one too."

"You have a point."

We continued to sip our coffees. The traffic noise and the sounds of Cookie Monster going to town on some freshly baked goods was kind of comforting.

Tommy cleared his throat to get my attention. "Did you tell Liz?"

I let out a big sigh at the mention of our younger sister. "You know I didn't," I answered.

He nodded his understanding.

Although Liz was our sister, she was the biggest troublemaker and instigator the world has ever seen.

There was this one time we were all in church for our niece's baptism and she stirred up a thirty-year old fight between my aunt and her ex-husband...who happened to be the priest!

It was chaos and Tio Robby was arrested. But my aunt dropped the charges, and all went back to normal.

"Have you spoken to her at all?"

"Mom! Can we have an icy?" Clara asked from her spot in the living room.

"Are you crazy? It's not even 10 in the morning."

"Pleeeease, Titi Jo." Daniella begged.

"If you guys eat a whole plate of broccoli right now, you can have an icy, deal?"

Tommy and I smiled at each other, while we waited for an answer. Four-year old's loved to negotiate but thankfully they were really bad at it.

I loved the bond our daughters had. They leaned their heads close to each other; two messy mops of hair, whispering and then...silence. They exchanged a conspiratorial look.

"Girls, do we have a deal?"

There was more whispering and then, "No!" they answered in unison.

It felt good to laugh, even if it was for a little bit. "I spoke to Liz two weeks ago. She told me that she met the love of her life," I said, finally answering Tommy's question.

Tommy looked skeptical. "Two weeks? That means it's already over."

Besides our baby sister being a shit-stirrer, she was also a hopeless romantic with her relationships usually lasting two weeks...three if she was thought the sex was great, and unfortunately Tommy and I would hear about it.

Tommy wore this sympathetic expression that I just didn't care for. "What?" I asked, my temper getting the best of me.

"It's just weird."

I felt my eyebrows lift in question. "What's weird?"

Tommy let out a sad smile. "I thought if anyone had staying power, it was you guys."

"Funny, I thought so, too." Tears slipped from my eyes.

"Mom!" The girls ran over to us. I sucked up my feelings and looked toward my daughter and niece. "Yes?"

"If we can't have Icy, can we have donuts?"

Tommy reached over, patting my hand. "I got this," He whispered as he corralled the girls into the kitchen. "Come on girls, let's see what's in the kitchen before we start more negotiations."

I was thankful that my brother gave me a couple of minutes to alone to compose myself.

3

Jovi

I laid there in my bed with a sleeping Clara next to me. It's been a week since I told Scott I wanted a divorce and I still hadn't told anyone but my brother.

Liz was not reachable, and I was too scared to tell my parents. Fear was keeping me mute.

In the still of the dark room, I began to question myself again; Am I making the right decision? After all the years that we spent creating a family, it began to go downhill a couple of years ago. We began to share a living space rather than connecting on an intimate level.

"What do you wanna do?" Scott asked as we laid in our underwear on a mattress in our tiny, empty apartment. I don't know why we decided to move in the middle of summer. Even with all the windows open, it was stifling.

"I want to write books. I want to be able to make enough money to buy us a house, work from home and not to worry about a thing." I admitted to him in the dark.

"Can you imagine when you're this big-time writer and I'm the man candy hanging around holding your purse?" he joked. Even in this

humidity, I wanted to be close to him. I came alive even as our sweaty arms stuck to eachother as we laid side by side.

"You don't have to do my thing. What do you want?"

"I want us to be happy."

I rolled over to stare at his profile. His beard started to grow in; I begged him not to chop it off. "We are happy," I told him. I ran my hand across his face.

We could hear the noise of the neighborhood; The reggaeton playing from the cars below, the smell of every type of dish that the Cuchifrito downstairs had to offer making my stomach growl.

"It wouldn't hurt if I was picked up by an MLB team," he confessed.

"It can still happen."

He grabbed me by the waist, rolling my sweat soaked body on top of his. "But I'll be okay if it doesn't. If we're together..." he kissed my nose. "...and we're happy..." he kissed my neck. "...then I'll be good." He kissed my lips.

Clara moved in her sleep bringing me out of the memory.

Just as easily as the good memory came and went; the bad one wasn't far behind.

"What's with you, Jovi?!"

"Don't yell at me, Scott! Don't you dare yell at me!"

"That's the only way to get through to you! She was crying!"

"I know! I can hear her from the bathroom!" I stomped away from him.

"You locked the door! What if something happened to her?"

I spun around, fire coming out my ears. "Nothing happened to her!"

"But what if it did?! Monday, I come home and you're crying on the kitchen floor, so hysterical that you don't even hear me. Tuesday, you're bouncing all over the place, but Clara was left in the crib for God knows how long."

"She was fine! I'm in the middle of writing a—"

"A book! The same fucking book you've been writing for a million years."

"Scott! At least I'm not playing in some dinky city league because I was too scared to go try out for the majors!"

"I gave it up on it for you! For us!"

Clara's cry penetrated our screams. Scott stomped to the room, picked our daughter up and bounced her, calming her almost instantly. "Jovi, you need to do something, pick up the slack. As soon as I walk home, I have to be super dad...I have bad days too."

"Don't compare what you feel with what I'm feeling."

"What are you feeling, Jo? Because it's getting harder to tell. Do you know how scary it is to see my wife zoned out on the kitchen floor? You need a doctor."

"The doctor said it's just sleep deprivation."

"How?! All you do is sleep?"

"Scott, if it's a problem for you just go," I stormed out of the room back into the bathroom making sure to lock it behind me.

"I don't need this, Jo."

I dropped to the floor, letting out a flood of tears.

A soft knock sounded but I didn't move. "Jovi, we need to talk about this."

I didn't say anything. I heard him clear his throat. "I think...I think you need to pitch in more. I can't keep coming home, finding the baby in her crib hungry, crying, and the house a mess...whatever. I don't need this, Jo." I covered my mouth to keep him from hearing my sobs. "There are days I dread coming home. Not knowing who's going to greet me...sometimes I imagine what it would be like to be with someone else."

I swallowed the sob that was on its way out. "Scott, give me a minute alone...please." My voice cracked and I could tell by his silence that he knew I was crying.

How do I explain to him that my senses are so overwhelmed with everyday noise and life that I don't have the energy to move; to do the most menial tasks. I didn't explain. Instead, I cried alone on the bathroom floor; struggling with my demons, unable to unlock the door and embrace my husband like my heart wanted me to. My fears, doubts and insecurities won out.

A big fat tear escaped my eyes, dropping onto my hand. After his serious talk with me about how bad of a mother I was, I began to consider marriage counseling. Four years passed by and I never brought it up because my mind kept going back and forth on the issue. It seemed as if I was the problem. I was afraid to stir the pot. I was afraid to cause my husband anymore pain.

Up until last week, I convinced myself that we could fix us. Then that picture appeared.

I focused on our daughter's little cherub face, hoping to erase that image in my mind that didn't want to die. With every flash of that picture, it was like God punishing me for every Kardashian joke by showing me that perfect tits actually exist. This whole thing drove me mad!

Jovi! Look at Clara! My mind screamed at me.

Clara was the best thing to happen to me...to us. When I found out I was pregnant, Scott and I were so excited.

Ok good, see? That wasn't so hard

I'd be lying if I said Scott was a bad father; he always made sure Clara had everything she needed; he made sure that he was there.

Why did he have to cheat?! Every one of my insecurities began to slowly come into the focus, flooding my brain.

Oh, no honey...I didn't say do that, my mind yelled.

I finally came to the realization that I wasn't good enough for him. I let the tears fall, making sure to be quiet as to not wake up Clara. To preserve my mental, I conjured up more of the good times.

I looked at the stick while Scott stood in front of me biting his thumbnail.

"So? What's it say?" He was trying to play it cool, but I knew deep down he was just trying to be chill. We've been through this before. The waiting game.

We've been trying to get pregnant for a couple of months now and every time I took a test I was faced with disappointment.

"Jo! What does it say?"

I smiled big and flipped the pregnancy test around. "I'm pregnant!" I yelled.

Scott scooped me up, spinning me around in his arms in the tiny bathroom. I let my head rest in the crook of his neck as my emotions took over. Happy tears slid down my cheek, soaking his t-shirt.

"Babe? You okay?" I could hear the emotion in his voice, but he wouldn't let a tear fall in front of me.

Scott pulled back slightly, his eyes searching my face. "Are you happy?" he asked.

I stood on my tip toes and planted a soft kiss on his full lips which immediately turned into need. I clawed at his belt buckle, eager to get my fill. Scott took me by the waist, carrying me to the bedroom.

I shook my head at the memory. My head knew that Scott and I were no longer together, but my body was taking a little longer to adjust. Sex turned into a once in a blue moon occurrence. The realization of that fact began to bring about my sadness that I knew would send me into a deeper spiral.

I immediately switched my thoughts to what was going down the next evening.

Okay, good...that's good.

Because I couldn't prolong the inevitable, I invited my parents over for a pow-wow. The plan was to ease them in; tell them that I was given a great assignment at work, no longer was I reporting on the goings on of the police blotter, I was actually writing full-fledged articles. I'll also tell them that I'm finally trying abuela's flan recipe and at the end of the night when everyone was liquored up and suffering from the meat sweats, I'll mention in passing that I'm getting divorced and it won't be a big deal.

Who am I kidding?

It is a big deal. They would make it a bigger deal and the theatrics will start and my mom will be the one that would need consoling. Not to mention the side comments that they will make for all eternity about how I needed to be a better wife.

My mind was in the middle of resolving a scenario, *a just-in-case mom tries to jump out the window*, when I heard the jingle of keys at my front door.

I jumped out of bed and ran, stopping short of the door. I listened again and...there was someone trying to come in!

It can't be Scott. I wasn't ready to see him. I quickly wiped my face, making sure that the tears and snot were gone.

I looked through the peep hole and there was a mop of curly light brown hair bouncing around.

I breathed a sigh of relief.

I unchained the door and opened. "Hello, Liz." I greeted my little sister with an even tone.

I wanted to kiss her and punch her at the same time.

She stood straight up and gave me a devilish smile that was her signature. "Jovi!" she yelled as I yanked her into my apartment. "Whoa, Jovi, relax!"

"Shhh!" I commanded as I closed the front door. "I have neighbors and a four-year old who is sleeping."

Liz stood back and observed me. I felt her eyes travel from the tip of my toes to the top of my head, finally landing on my face. Her perfect bow lips turned into a frown. "What's wrong?" she whispered, her hand reaching out to touch my shoulder.

"Where have you been?" my voice was layered with an anger that was unexpected.

Her eyes widened. "I had to go away for work, a video set needed a make-up artist last minute." She took a longer look at me. "What's wrong with you?"

"What do you mean?" I smooth a hand down my limp, knotty hair.

"Your eyes are so red and glassy like you just smoked the biggest blunt, your wrinkles are starting to show, the grays are coming out and don't even get me started with the bags under your eyes." Liz's smile disappeared as my façade began to crack. I felt my lips begin to tremble and a ball of emotion form in my throat making it difficult for me to answer.

"Jovi, relax, it's nothing a shower and a ton of make-up won't fix."

When I didn't react to her, Liz's face turned from worry to anger in no time flat. Liz looked around the foyer and I guess she didn't find what she was looking for because she stomped through my dark living room, her head swiping back and forth in search of something. She came to a sudden stop in the doorway of my bedroom causing me to smash into her back. "Damn, Jovi." She hissed.

I crossed my arms. Why was she angry with me? "Liz, what the hell are you looking for?" I asked.

She looked to where Clara slept dreaming about whatever four-year old's dreamt about.

Liz's face softened and her eyes landed back on me. "Where is he?" she whispered.

I gestured towards the living room, so she knew to follow me. I turned the light on and faced my baby sister. "I think you need to sit," I said.

Just like every other person in our family, Liz could be overly dramatic about everything. "I'm perfectly fine just standing here," She said in defiance. She was ready to attack Scott for whatever he did. In the same way that Tommy loved Scott, Liz hated him.

I honestly never knew why but I remember the weeks leading up to my wedding there was a lot of drama and baggage that Liz brought; there was almost no wedding because of it.

I passed my hand through my hair, trying to mentally prepare for her reaction. "I'm filing for divorce."

Liz went still. I've never seen her so still since...never. She let out a breath she'd been holding. "Oh my god, Jovi!" she yelled, placing one hand on her chest.

"Shhhh, What?" I tried to quiet her down.

"You scared me! I thought somebody died." her eyes bugged out as she let out a nervous giggle.

I felt my face scrunch, bringing out every wrinkle on my face. "What do you mean?"

She shrugged her delicate shoulders. "Millions of people get divorced every day, I thought he died or got seriously injured or..." her eyes rolled upwards as she thought of what to say next. "Or I don't know...that he cheated."

I felt a stab at my heart at the word *cheated.*

I walked to the kitchen to grab a glass of water, to be honest I wanted something stronger, but I had to get up super early to run errands and then I was dropping Clara off at my mother in laws, so she could spend the weekend with Scott.

It would be the first time I'd see him since I snapped and demanded a divorce.

I walked back to the living room where my baby sister was already curled on the couch, with the T.V. on mute.

Liz turned to look at me. "So, he didn't cheat, what did he do?"

I laid on the opposite end of the couch, my legs overlapping hers. "Nothing. He did nothing and that's why I want a divorce." I gave an angry sigh because I didn't want to talk about it. Me, telling everyone what was going on only opened the door for them to try to talk me out of it or pity me. I didn't do well with pity.

She raised her eyebrow while I took a sip of water. "What do you mean he did nothing?"

I rubbed my eyes; I was tired from overthinking.

"I was nothing but a friend. This last year I've been the one up at three in the morning to get to work, to come home and take care of Clara and clean the house and do the laundry and clean the house—"

"You already said that."

I ignored her and continued, "And he would get up at 8am and just take her to school. When he got home, he'd have his headphones in and be glued to his phone." Liz picked at the rip on her jeans and said nothing, so I went on, "I just want to be more than a roommate. I miss being in love, I miss being the confidante, I miss the passion...I miss being a partner." I looked at my sister for any reaction but when I got nothing but a blank stare, I sprinkled water her way. "Hello, earth to Liz, what do you think?"

She looked around in confusion. "You wanna know what I think?"

"Yeah."

"I don't have anything to say, you have your reasons and I'm not going to stop you."

It was my turn to be shocked. "Really?"

She gave a quick nod. "Yes."

"It's just that you've never really liked Scott and you know I really thought that you'd be jumping for joy, adding your two cents... bashing the father of my child."

Liz looked thoughtful. "That was the old me."

I braced myself, Liz was not the person who was compassionate and understanding. "The old you?" I asked.

"Yes, I found the love of my life and he—"

I held my hand up to stop her. "Really, Elizabeth?" I felt the fire in my chest as my anger began to sprout.

She folded her arms, like she used to do when we were little, and I told her she couldn't hang with me and my friends.

"What?"

"I tell you that I'm filing for divorce and then you turn the conversation on yourself?" It shouldn't surprise me, but it did.

She swatted at me. "You want me to talk about myself and distract your mind? Or do you want to wallow in the demise of your marriage?"

I looked up to the ceiling, throwing one free arm up; flabbergasted. "I kind of want to wallow."

Liz rolled her eyes. "Come on Jovi! Really?"

"Yes, Liz! I'm going through some heavy shit. I would like someone to just listen. No judgement."

She gave a quick nod. "You're right. Go ahead, tell me everything."

******

Scott

I can't believe I'm lying in my childhood bedroom.

This is rock bottom.

There was that lingering smell of dirty socks in the air, the Yankee logo border that I stuck on the wall when I was twelve was still up. The only difference was that my mother had turned my room into a storage. My mom was in the process of packing barrels to send to our family in DR, I was too lazy to move them out.

Now here I am.

Laying on a dingy, queen sized bed, its origin I knew nothing about.

I never thought that I would be back here getting a divorce.

What has my life become? People at work knew something was wrong, I was moping around, taking lunch in my office, half-assing my lessons. I was the gym teacher at one of NYC's best charter schools; it was not a place to divulge relationship drama, especially when it involved the school secretary.

My mom knew that Jovi and I were separated but I kept the reasons to myself. I knew that she probably told my entire family, and everyone was lighting a candle for me.

My family tended to be a little old school. My parents were married almost fifty years when my dad passed away. My mother never talked about seeing anyone, didn't make any attempt at dating...that I know of. She was the type to be with one man, have his kids, and live happily ever after. They were soulmates. My mom always made me believe that when you find your soulmate you don't think about anybody else. Jovi and I were soulmates.

We met during her twenty-first birthday when she was drunk out of her mind and I, being the ultimate gentleman, drove her and her crazy friends' home.

Why didn't I come clean with Jovi? I loved my wife. I should've told her how I was feeling instead of talking to another woman.

I mean its not like you cheated, you guys were just friends, my mind rationalized.

I'm a fucking idiot; I felt like the world's biggest scumbag. You know *'grab them by the pussy'* kind of scumbag.

There were so many questions I wanted to ask my wife; things that I wanted to tell her, but she didn't want to speak to me yet.

Or that's what her brother told me.

Tommy had called to check up on me; Jovi told him about the divorce. I just apologized to him. I don't why I did. I just needed someone to accept my apology. If there was a chance that Jovi could hear how sorry I was, I'm going to take it.

When he asked why, I couldn't form the words. In my mind, Jovi and I would get over this and be back to normal. There was no point in disclosing all the gory details if we were going to end up together.

I just thought that if any two people in this world were going to last, it would be me and Jovi. We've been through so much together;

college, shitty jobs, shitty apartment, mall jail for starting a riot in a *Best Buy*...was it all for nothing? I didn't want to believe it.

This was all depressing. I groaned into my pillows to keep from screaming.

I could smell the oil from the empanadas my mother was frying seeping through my door as I laid in bed, I knew that it was only a matter of time before—

Knock, knock.

Ugh, I didn't move, hoping she would take the hint and go away.

She was going to ask me if I was hungry, like she did every day, three times a day all this week.

I heard my mother turn the doorknob and I thanked God that I remembered to lock the door before I passed out on the bed.

When that didn't work, she knocked again. "Bebo! *Abre la Puerta*!"

I didn't make a sound; I didn't move, I didn't breathe...no amount of food was going to get me to open that door.

"Jovi called!" She yelled through the door.

I jumped up quickly, looking all over for my cell phone, which I threw across the room because I had to fight the urge to call my wife. Jovi would call me a million times before she called my mother's house; she would call my mom's house only as a last resort.

Jovi and my mom had an okay relationship on account that they are both stubborn, strong, independent women. My mom thought she knew better and Jovi wanted to do things her own way, it was one of the qualities that attracted me to her.

I found my phone wedged behind the bureau...I was right! There were thousands of texts and missed calls. I read a message, she wanted to bring Clara over earlier because her parents had shown up way earlier than expected.

I knew that she was going to tell her parents today and that she didn't want Clara to be around because her parents could be...emotional.

Yeah, emotional was the best word.

Other words that people used to describe Jovi's family? Crazy, dysfunctional, dramatic...the list goes on. But since they were legally my family, I'll stick with emotional.

I text back as quickly as I could:

I could stop by and pick her up if that'll make it easier for you.

I saw the bubbles that pop up when someone is texting back, and I waited. It felt like I stared at the screen for ten minutes when an answer finally popped up.

No.

No? I waited ten minutes for a simple no? Who did she think she was? I began to type with fury:

No?

Again, with the fucking bubbles and another ten minutes.

Listen, it took you almost two hours to get back to me and I know you aren't working and you're obviously busy, so I'll drop her off at the regular scheduled time.

I should be happy that Jovi was still bringing Clara, but she obviously thought she held the power.

I wanted to see my wife. I needed to speak to my wife. Why was I the one that was suffering in a dark, dingy room? If I wanted to pick up MY daughter, then I will go pick up MY daughter!

But I didn't say that, I just text back a simple reply:

Fine

After a few minutes, there was no reply and I immediately began to get dressed to pick up MY daughter.

4

Jovi

I sighed in relief as I placed my phone on the kitchen counter and went back to check on the *pernil* I had roasting in the oven. Even though it wasn't a major holiday, I had enough family over that I needed to roast some type of meat. Reluctantly, I gave in and invited my brother, his family and Liz. It wouldn't hurt to have a little emotional support.

I peeked into the oven, stuck a fork into the pork and was about to savor a juicy delicious bite when I heard my mother clear her throat behind me. I resisted the urge to suck my teeth because I knew that she would give me the biggest guilt trip. Instead, I asked, "Yes, Mami?"

"*Nada*, just wondering where Scott is, I thought he didn't work weekends," She said nonchalantly, as if I was dumb enough to not know she was prying. "Is he going to be here when you tell us the big news?"

I immediately looked behind me and narrowed my eyes at her, while she raised her eyebrows in anticipation.

I thought to myself, how can I answer her question without giving away the news? I was too chicken to just blurt it out. I had to work up the nerve and the night was still young. I'm just going to keep the answer short and sweet. “No, he will not be here.” I stood up straight and stepped away from the oven, only to have my mother check in on the pork.

“It still needs a little bit more time,” she said.

I felt my left eye twitch, which usually happened when I was annoyed. It was like my body decided to have a mini seizure instead of disrespecting my mom. “I know, Mami. That’s why I left it in the oven,” I said smiling over my sarcasm.

I could hear the kids in the living room playing, and my dad, brother and brother-in-law yelling over each other ‘discussing’ the latest Giants stats, while my sister was probably sitting in the corner of the loveseat talking to someone on her phone while the T.V. was blaring; to my neighbors, my place sounded like complete chaos but to us, this was completely normal.

“Jo!” my dad called from his spot on the couch. “Can you bring me another beer?!”

I automatically went to the fridge, cracked open a bottle and walked straight to the living room with my mom following close.

“So, what’s the news? Are you pregnant?” my mother asked, making my father spit out the beer he began to drink. Liz and Tommy's heads snapped up to attention as they waited for my answer.

My mom looked around in confusion. “What? Is it so crazy to think that you’re pregnant? Clara is four and you should’ve had another when she was two,” She continued.

I closed my eyes, willing the conversation to stop. My head felt like it would explode.

“So, then what is it?” my little Puerto Rican mother asked with her hands clasped in front of her. The eagerness in her brown eyes told me she was hoping I would tell her I was pregnant or buying a house and she was moving in with us.

I looked around the room and made eye contact with my brother and sister; Tommy looked at the empty beer bottle he was holding, and Liz shrugged her shoulders, as if telling me it didn't really matter what they thought. I hoped that's what she meant and it wasn't just my own thoughts making things up just so I could get it over with. This was the time I wish I could decipher shrugs.

"Liz, why don't you take the girls to the room?" I asked.

She nodded, getting up and taking the girls without hesitation. "Come on girls, Jovi has a bomb she has to drop, wouldn't want to scar you for the rest of your life so early," She cooed.

My mom watched the girls leave the room and immediately began to panic. "Really Jovi, you're scaring me, what's happening?"

Okay, Jovi, just get it out the way.

I listened to my inner voice and finally let it out. "I am filing for divorce. Scott and I are no longer together." The words felt as if they came out in slow motion. Beads of sweat formulated at my temples.

"Noooooo!" my dad yelled, scaring the shit out of everyone, making me jump out of my skin.

We all turned to him, realizing he was yelling at the game. "Dad, Jovi just said something important," Tommy scolded him.

My dad looked at everyone's faces; his gaze finally landed on my mother. His thick, bushy eyebrows sunk down in worry. "Why are you crying?" he asked my her.

"I'm getting a divorce, dad," I said, this time the words rolled out easily.

My dad had a look of confusion. How could his sane daughter say she's getting a divorce? She was madly in love. She was the one who would provide unlimited amounts of grandchildren...is what he probably thought. Or maybe he didn't.

I wanted to tell him that I was adulting, but he didn't ask, and I didn't want to disappoint him.

The pain he must feel at the realization that his grown daughter, in her thirties, was a hot mess. He expected it from Liz, but not me.

With a slight tilt of his head he asked, "Why?"

My dad was a man of few words, throughout my life he has always given a grunt as a response. My siblings and I have learned throughout the years how to tell the difference between a good grunt and a bad one; facial cues helped. Now, he's asked a monumental question with no grunt and I honestly couldn't find the words to answer.

I began to nod my head like a maniac. "Good question," I started, hoping that me just talking would force a response that they would approve of; instead, I started sweating and fumbling. "The thing is..." I couldn't get the words out, my breathing becoming more erratic. I began to see tiny dots float around.

This moment reminded me of when I was sixteen and I snuck out the house to be with my friends returning home wearing my boyfriend's shirt; in reality I did nothing wrong, we just got caught in the rain and he lent me a shirt so I wouldn't get sick, but in my parent's mind, we banged like bunnies and I was pregnant with their illegitimate grandchild. They went ballistic...so yeah, this kind of felt like that.

At thirty-three years old, I felt like I was about to get in trouble. That was until I heard a knock at the front door.

I thanked God for the interruption; I looked at my mom who had her jaw to the floor from shock. "I'll be right back." I made my way out the room with a speed of an Olympic runner.

I was so eager to get away that I didn't even look through the peephole.

The smile I had planted on my face to show my unexpected visitor that everything was okay and the noise coming from my apartment wasn't means for police intervention immediately dropped when I realized who it was.

"Scott? wha- why are you here?" I managed to ask even though I felt this overwhelming sense of anger take over my body.

It was a shock to see Scott with an overgrown beard; his usual clean-cut hair was overdue for a shape up and the bags under his eyes told me that he hadn't slept much.

My mother's squeal of delight interrupted whatever Scott was about to say. "Nene!"

God, this can't be happening right now.

I looked at mom who managed to wedge herself past us to stand between Scott and I.

"I should've known that Jovi was joking! She has the worst sense of humor." She laid a hand on his shoulder, trying to usher him into the apartment.

"Mom, I wasn't joking," I said low so the neighbors wouldn't hear me but loud enough that she could.

She looked at me and then Scott, for what seemed like a million years. "So, what you're telling me is that you're really getting a divorce?" she asked one more time.

I didn't have the strength to answer. I looked to Scott for some guidance, but he just stood there with a frown on his face.

My ears burned up with the anger that overcame me.

I threw caution to the wind. "Yes! We're getting a divorce! It's what I want!" at this point I didn't care if the neighbors heard everything. It irked me that I felt the need to tip toe around this issue.

My mother crossed herself at my sudden outburst; maybe she was afraid whatever demon that suddenly sprouted in my body was going to overtake her too.

Her sudden show of tears could have won her an Oscar! She reached for Scott's face, pulling him down in an awkward hug. "I'm so sorry that my daughter wasn't good to you but please take her back! I take responsibility! I never really asked her to cook or clean the house when she was a kid...I never—"

Scott pulled out of my mothers hold. "I would take her back! She's the one that asked for the divorce, not me."

Just as quickly as my mom's tears began, the tap suddenly closed up. She slowly turned her attention to me. "You?" she spat at me.

I was at a loss for words. I wished the floor would open up and swallow me whole.

"*Porque*?" she asked.

Before I could answer, I was interrupted by the fire alarm that went off. That's when I smelled it; the burnt pork in my oven.

I ran back inside, stopping short because my entire family had beaten me to the kitchen. Liz had the oven mitts on and did the honors of taking it out and placing it on the counter; Tommy was fanning the fire alarm. The chaos died down and eyes darted as everyone finally noticed Scott.

I should've just told them over the phone like a normal person. My daughter and my niece were both taking in the scene from the kitchen entrance.

My throat burned from the emotion I held back. It took a lot of energy and I was barely hanging on.

"You had this thing turned all the way up," Liz said.

"What? No, I—"

"I put it up," my mom admitted.

"Why?" I asked.

"Because it needed more time!" She yelled. Her curly hair stood on end and her eyes burned red from emotion; It was like looking into a mirror.

Scott cleared his throat. "I just came to pick up Clara."

Clara, just noticing that her dad was there, squealed with excitement. "Daddy!!!"

As shabby as Scott was looking, his smile was just as bright and wide as always when he saw our daughter. "Hey, Kiddo!" he yelled back, trying to put a brave front for her and the rest of my family. "I came to pick you up. We're going to have a sleepover at grandma's house."

Clara's angelic face dimmed. "But why can't we stay here?"

"So, you mean to tell me that you guys didn't tell the kid about what's going on? Her therapy bills are going to be through the roof," Liz scoffed.

I did my best to contain the situation by saying the first excuse that came to mind. "Mommy is working all weekend and daddy thought it would be fun to camp out at grandmas."

"Well..." Scott began. The daggers that I shot at him didn't stop him from continuing, "It was actually mommy's idea that we sleep over grandmas—"

Oh, so we're playing the blame game.

"Daddy gave mommy no choice." I tried to keep my tone as even as possible; he was really putting my nerves to work.

"How, Jovi?! Because of some stupid picture?"

I found myself nose to nose with Scott, my temper at an all-time high. "Scott we're not doing this now in front of everybody," I said through clenched teeth.

"So, when? I need a specific time."

"Scott—"

Someone coughed, forcing me to look around the room at the faces of the people who were closest to me but also the last people I wanted to witness this.

"No, Jovi! I've been trying to call you and you've been avoiding me! Today is the first time since you told me we were getting a divorce that I've seen or heard from you."

"Bullshit, Scott! I text you to set up a pickup for Clara!" I didn't care anymore that my family was witnessing the drama.

Scott ran a hand down his face. "And that's it, Jovi! Nothing else! Just some cryptic message saying you—"

"Okay, guys!" My dad's voice boomed in the tiny kitchen as he stepped between us. "I think it'd be best if Clara stayed with us tonight, we can take both girls and make it a slumber party."

We both looked at our baby girl who eyes glistened with unshed tears. Shock kept her still and all I walked over to take her in my arms.

"No—"

"Dad that's okay—" Scott and I answered at the same time.

My dad shook his head. "No, no, no. I think you kids have some talking to do."

My dad directed his gaze to Scott and although I couldn't decipher what man code passed between the two of them, Scott gave a curt nod in response.

Dad clapped his hands together. "Now that that's settled, we are going to get the girls packed up and we'll get out of here..." he looked at the burnt pork. "I think no one will be upset if the girls have pizza."

My niece began to jump in excitement at the mere mention of pizza, "Yeah!" she squealed in delight, while Claras face was showed her melancholy as she was pulled to her room to pack a bag. My mom and siblings followed them out the door. My dad made his way quietly out the kitchen, back into the living room to watch the game that was interrupted by the burning pork and our drama.

I was finally alone with Scott. "I don't want to have this conversation now and I need you to respect that and let me—"

"Fuck that, Jovi, fifteen years together, and we can't work this out?" He was frowning, making his sunken eyes all the more concerning.

Tommy, Frank, and Liz came into the room. "Listen I think we're going to head out too," Tommy said.

I wasn't going to stop them; my dinner was ruined. I just wanted to pop a couple of pills and go to bed.

I nodded and hugged them before they headed out. "Scott it was nice seeing you." Tommy patted his back on the way out.

"Yeah, it's weird when the attention isn't on me, thanks for the entertainment," Liz added.

I sucked my teeth, a bad habit from when we were kids. "Shut up, Liz."

"Nice see you too, Liz," Scott replied coldly.

She gave a small laugh as she sauntered out the door.

We were left in the kitchen. Just the clock on the wall ticking away.

I ignored Scott and began cleaning up the kitchen while he took off his jacket and sat at our small breakfast table.

I could hear my mom helping Clara pack by making a game out of it.

It seemed like forever when the girls finally came out and said their goodbyes. Scott and I kept the act up. "I'll pick you up from grandma's house tomorrow, okay, boo?" Scott said to Clara, who wrapped him as tight as her small arms could hold him.

"Yes, daddy."

Clara embraced me with the same enthusiasm that she gave to her father, and it almost broke me.

"Bye, mommy. See you later."

I kissed her all over her face. "Bye, baby."

I gave my parents and niece hugs and kisses. It wasn't more than five seconds that I closed the door when Scott said from behind me, "We need to talk."

******

Scott

I hate that I had to practically beg my wife to speak to me. It was annoying as fuck! I wish I could shake some sense into her.

"Talk about what, Scott? I told you why I wanted a divorce, so let's move on," Jovi said as she pushed past me to go back into the kitchen.

"Ahhhhh!" I yelled. I was a pretty levelheaded guy; I am proud to say that I never raised my voice, I never thought of raising my voice, but this woman was pushing me over the edge.

Jovi and I met when I had an afro and she was too drunk to remember anything.

If you were to ask her now, she would say that she didn't know what I looked like; it was the vibe she was attracted to. If you were to ask me— I remembered her; she was as beautiful to me then as she is today; same dark hair, full lips and big brown eyes. She was a bit thinner back then. Although, she would bring up her slight weight gain on the rare occasion that an infomercial broke into her mind, I didn't see anything wrong with it; more of her for me to grab on to.

Jovi back then was wild and a free spirit. Over the years she's settled down; I chalked that up to maturing but...maybe I was wrong.

She pushed her sleeves up, her straight hair standing on end, as if it were angry too, and turned around to face me like a mad woman. "Okay, you want to talk?" she sneered.

"Yeah, I do."

Her laugh was a sinister one, the kind that should have warned me to back off, but I needed to talk. For the most part, I've been a good husband; I kept a roof over our heads, provided for our daughter, played handy man when we needed, I killed ginormous bugs when necessary.

I did my part!

This whole idea of an automatic divorce, without trying to salvage what we built was mind boggling.

"When was the last time we had a real date, Scott? The kind where we have to get dressed up and the napkins are laundered? Where there's no kids menu?"

"So, you don't want to fix our marriage because you don't want to eat at *Applebee's*?"

She turned on the faucet and began scrubbing a ladle with such intensity and focus I didn't think she heard me.

"Jovi!"

She turned back to me, cradling the ladle, soap dripping from her hands. "No, Scott! That's not it. When was the last time we talked? About our dreams and goals? You know I still have them, right? It didn't end because we became adults, got married and had a kid."

"We talked—"

"About bills, about teacher conferences...did you know I started taking creative writing classes two months ago? That I go to book club every Saturday at the library while Clara is at dance class?" with each question she pointed the ladle at me.

"No, but—"

My wife sighed with an indignation that I felt came from deep in her soul. "Scott..." her voice cracked.

I stepped forward, instinctively reaching out.

Jovi took a step back and hurled the ladle straight at my head, missing me by an inch. "JOVI!" I yelled. "You almost hit me!"

"I wish I did!" the veins in her neck became more prominent with every screech. "What makes you think that you can come up to me and think that you can make it better with a hug? Another woman sent you a picture of her bare tits! You slept with another woman!"

"I didn't do anything with her!" I bellowed.

"You say you didn't but I don't believe you! You had an emotional connection with her! I saw the messages before her boobs!" I thought it best to keep quiet, thinking that that was my best option. Jovi continued, "I saw that you would talk to her about life, your goals, aspirations, baseball...all the flirty messages you sent back to her when she was clearly flirting with you."

"I didn't mean for it to be flirty. Things are twisted when it's through text—"

"Bullshit! Just be honest!" she shrieked.

"Why didn't you say anything?" I asked, keeping my voice calm in an attempt to keep her calm.

Jovi took a deep breath. "I tried, Scott. Plenty of times. I'd try to make conversation just to be ignored. I'd suggest a date night, hoping we could talk about everything just to have them cancelled or end early because you were too tired."

I felt the tension in my neck; I just wanted all this to be over. "Jo, I want us to get back to normal." The look on her face made me regret what I said almost immediately.

"Shit, Scott! Don't you get it?" The truth was— I really didn't get it! I didn't want her to throw a pot or something else at my head. "You fucked up! This is not normal!" She said. "We are not normal!" she gestured between the two of us.

I ran my hand down my face, tired of all this...I didn't understand what she wanted from me. "You want me to take you out on a date? You want me to talk to you? I'm talking now!"

"Scott." she shook her head.

"Then what do you want, Jovi?" I sighed.

The tears fell from her face when she answered. "I want a divorce."

Fuck that. In my head, divorce wasn't an option. I was not going to give up that easily. "Therapy!" I blurted out.

She wiped the tears from her eyes. "What?" she asked angrily.

"I refuse to divorce you."

Her eyes widened in shock. "You refuse? That's not how this works, Scott. When one person is done with a marriage, the other person has to be done too. They can't be in a marriage with their self...you're not Carrie Bradshaw!" she said crossing her arms.

"What the hell are you talking about?!"

"In *Sex and the City*, Carrie marries herself and registers at Manolo—"

"So, you're not talking about a real person?" this woman was going to be the death of me.

Her lips were set in a grim line.

I tried again. "Jo, what about therapy?" I would grasp at anything just to keep us going.

Therapy happened to be the first thing that came to mind. I continued to plead my case, "Isn't therapy the step before divorce?" I asked. "We missed a step."

Her eyebrows came in together in either horror or rage...maybe both, I couldn't tell. "We missed a step? There are no steps to divorce, Scott."

I closed my eyes, steadying myself and keeping my anger under control.

"Please stop saying my name like that."

"Like what, Scott? That's your name, Scott."

"You're saying it like you are cursing me for life...like you should be holding a poison apple or something."

She closed her eyes, pinching the bridge of her nose. "Like I was saying...there are no steps to divorce."

"Let's try therapy," I begged.

Her eyes looked up to the ceiling, as if she were asking some divine being for assistance.

"What's so wrong with therapy? Jo, I'll admit we have our issues. But it can help."

Jovi's eyes finally connected with mine. "What if it doesn't work? What if we don't work?"

I shrugged. "What if we do?"

"If therapy doesn't work. Then we get divorced," she said with a finality that turned my blood into ice.

I gave a quick nod, clenching my jaw so tight that I thought I cracked a couple of my teeth.

I turned on my heel and left with the slamming door punctuating my anger.

5

Two weeks later...

Jovi

I bullshitted my way through work today because I was dreading going to therapy. We were supposed to start last week but I cancelled at the last minute.

Did I think therapy would work? Not really. I mean, I believed it worked for those who needed it. Scott and I were beyond the help therapy could bring. It's not like the therapist was a miracle worker.

I just thought that if Scott saw how bad it went, he would be more willing to move on from this. A lot of people fall out of love.

Or at least I thought so.

I was so ready to move on.

I was ready to be one of those women on an *Eat, Pray, Love* journey. I wanted to eat endless amounts of pasta, learn a new language, meet knew people, have passionate sex.

Sex? Where did that thought come from? It's been Scott for the last fifteen years...I definitely wasn't ready to have it with other people.

I sighed. *It would be nice to be touched*...sex hasn't been a priority since we've been on rocky ground. It's been months. Still, Scott knew my body better than I did. *What I wouldn't give to just...snap out of it, Jovi!*

I shook my head as my pulse raced at the mere thought of Scott on top of me. I peeked into the waiting room. I felt the palms of my hands begin to itch from nerves. The memory of Scott rubbing the base of my spine, trying to calm me before our wedding, before my first day at the paper, before I told my parents I was pregnant; that tiny bit of physical connection would've been enough to calm me. That was gone.

I stood in front of the glass doors, deciding whether I should just walk in, sit in this waiting room and look around at everyone wondering why the hell they were there. I scanned around looking for Scott. Of course, I arrived first. This whole thing was Scotts idea; why wouldn't he show up first?

"You look like you're a pervert getting your kicks from peering in that office." I heard Scotts voice from behind me.

I gave him a sideway glance. "Shut up," I whispered.

His attention went to the hand that I was too busy scratching. "Why you so nervous?" he asked with a sly grin.

I turned around to face him. "I'm not nervous." I mumbled. "I just think we're wasting our time."

"You have somewhere else to be?"

"No, I just...look at that woman," I whispered. I pointed to a woman with dark circles around her eyes.

"What about her?"

"Does she look happy to be here? If it's not working for her, it's probably not working for anyone."

"So now you're Sherlock? You can deduce what is going to happen just by observation of the waiting room? How do you know therapy's not working for her?" his anger took over his body; his eyebrows came down as he folded his arms. "Everyone's experiences are different. Do you know her?"

"No," I mumbled.

"I'm sorry, I couldn't hear you." He leaned forward.

"I said no!"

He shook his head. "Have you always been like this? Or is this whole thing a side effect of your mental breakdown?"

"I didn't have a breakdown," I barked through gritted teeth, scaring someone trying to get passed us.

Scott's full lips formed a thin line. "Let's go in," he said. He held the door open for me. I hesitated. I was a grown woman; I had choices. I could say no like I wanted and just head home and curl up with a glass of wine. "You coming?" Scott asked.

I couldn't tell what he was thinking but I heard the challenge in his voice. There was something inside me that needed to go in; I needed to prove to myself that I was right.

I passed Scott, marching straight to the reception desk. I looked around the office; white walls, black chairs that look too stiff to be comfortable. *Is that a fish tank?* It looked like this office belonged to a Bond villain.

"Hello, can I help you?" the receptionist looked at me with her over-lined eyes and giant lashes; with every blink I felt a gust of wind.

"Hi, we're here to save our marriage," I replied with a voice so sweet it could give someone a cavity.

I heard Scott suck his teeth from behind me while the receptionist didn't even bat an eye. "We're the Garcia's, we're here to see Dr. Rubenstein," he answered.

The receptionist dutifully went to work, clacking on the keyboard with her razor-sharp nails. With a final tap, she looked up. "Okay, the doctor will be out in a couple of minutes, please have a seat." She gestured towards the seating area, where the woman I pointed out to Scott earlier looked at us with curiosity.

I gave her a stiff smile.

"Did you have to say that to the receptionist?" Scott chastised.

"What?"

"That we're trying to save our marriage."

I leaned back, folding my arms in frustration. "You honestly think she doesn't know why we're here? Because I hate to break it to you, everyone in this office knows."

"I know she knows—"

"Then what's the issue, Scott?"

He closed his eyes. "I just don't feel comfortable with other people knowing why we're here," he whispered.

I sat up straight. "Oh. So, now it's an issue when other people have the inside scoop on our lives? Kim was other people to me." I shrugged. "She knew more about you than I did."

Scotts face flushed, the vein in his neck popping out. "Jovi. It's not the same thing." He spared a glance at the other patients who were starting to observe us. "I don't want to talk about it now," he whispered.

"I don't know why you're getting so worked up, you were the one who made this mess," I added knowing that it would irk him to his core.

"Jovi..." Scott used his dad voice, warning me to relax my temper.

"What you did is worse than a bunch of strangers knowing that our marriage is over," I whispered. I could feel the tension in my jaw, which was not a good thing for my TMJ.

He shifted in his seat, turning to face me. "Are we talking about Kim?"

"Of course we are!"

He pointed his finger at me. "First off, Kim is not the issue."

I laughed. "You better put that finger down. And she most definitely is."

"No, she is not. *We* are the issue." Scotts restraint was slowly fading.

"Of course we are! But you fucked up and dragged her into this when your penis—"

"I did not!" he yelled.

"You—"

We were interrupted by a polite cough. Scott and I turned to look at the person standing in front of us. I silently thanked the baby Jesus because if given another second, I would've dropped kicked Scott through the glass doors.

"Hi, I'm Dr. Rubenstein. Shall we take this show into my office?"

I eyed the doctor, taking in her disheveled appearance; threadbare grey sweater, frizzy bun with pens poking out...if I had to guess her age, I'd say...no younger than 100.

She looked like she was at the party when Jesus turned water to wine.

She was supposed to save my marriage?

I looked at her wrinkled hands, the blue veins were freaking me out!

Why were my thoughts so bitchy? God, I was in an awful mood.

My mood was so sour; no amount of caffeine or chocolate could save me.

Okay, Jo...be nice! You can do it!

I plastered a giant smile. "Hi, doctor, I'm Jovi." I held my hand out, then seeing the creepy mummy hands, I snatched my hand back. I looked at the doctor who was squinting at me. "Sorry, forgot to wash my hands," I added sheepishly.

She nodded as if she were used to people being repulsed by her crypt keeper hands. "Follow me." Dr. Rubenstein led the way to her office.

I stood frozen unable to move. That's when I felt Scotts hand briefly touch the base of my spine before quickly falling back to his side as if remembering that we weren't together and that there were boundaries now.

I swallowed my resistance and followed Dr. Rubenstein. I found myself relaxing with each step...until I caught sight of the office. I came up short causing Scott to walk into me.

"Jovi, what..." He trailed off as he finally saw what I saw.

Because the waiting room was minimal chic, I was expecting the same from her office.

Instead, there were piles of papers and books everywhere.

I spotted five different coffee mugs on her desk, all with rings of dried coffee around them. This was like an episode of *Hoarders;* I was positive we would find at least a couple of dead cats stuck under a pile of trash.

She flashed a thin-lipped smile. "Come on in." she motioned for us to enter.

I know Scott was horrified by the mess just as much as I was. He swallowed a hard lump. "Ladies first," he said, moving aside to let me pass.

I rolled my eyes, bumping him with my shoulder like a sulky teenager as I passed him.

******

Scott

Did she really just bump me?

I scanned the couch before taking a seat next to Jovi on the loveseat. Dr. Rubenstein sat in a threadbare, lumpy, faded chair across from us. She pointed to the clock that sat beside us.

"This is a forty-five-minute session. This is the first appointment so you guys can tell me a little about you as a couple...let's start with how long you've been married." She waited patiently for one of us to answer.

I felt Jovi's glare. I knew she was bad with dates even if it was our wedding. I didn't answer, knowing full well that she would try to remember just to win this.

"Um...We...I..." Jovi stuttered her way to no response.

I reached out, touching her hand as a show of support. Electricity passed through us; I know she felt it to because she immediately snatched her hand back. Jovi back in the day would revel in the shock. She would even say it's because we have so much chemistry that our bodies need some kind of release. This Jovi now just gave a scowl in return as if I did it on purpose.

"What Jo is trying to say is we've been together for almost fifteen years but married for seven," I answered.

"You get no points for knowing how long we been together," I muttered.

"I should. You don't even know what year we got married unless Facebook reminds you." Anger shot through my veins. I knew she was angry because she didn't want to be here. I didn't want to be here either. We didn't need this! This whole thing was a waste of time; a big misunderstanding. All we needed was some time to talk it over, but Jovi didn't want that. It always has to be her way.

"I do know!"

"So, what year did we get married?" I called her bluff. I knew she didn't know the answer. As her husband, I should be offended that she couldn't remember our wedding date. I'd be lying if I said it didn't hurt that she couldn't remember such a momentous day

When it felt like an eternity and she still didn't answer, I laughed. "Ha!"

"Don't ha me," she said in a low menacing voice, that could give Batman a run for his money.

"It's typical, you don't know what year we got married. Where you even there?"

"Of course, I was there, your creepy uncle drank so much he ended up swimming in one of the fountains because it reminded him of his time as a mermaid!"

She had the nerve to talk about my family? "You know Tío Nuno was part of the circus! He was delusional by the time of the wedding! He couldn't help that he thought—"

"Scott! The man thought he was a mermaid!"

"Why are we arguing about my uncle?!"

"2013!" Jovi yelled, jumping out her seat.

"What?" I was so irritated I forgot what the argument was about in the first place.

"We got married in 2013," she said, revealing the slight dimple on her right cheek as she smirked triumphantly.

Dr. Rubenstein finally decided to intervene. "Okay, settle down." She let out a low whistle. "Wow, you guys are a lively bunch."

We both turned to look at her, Jovi finally realizing where we were, plopped back onto the couch. I smoothed down my shirt as a way to hide the way I was shaking. She began to scratch her palm again. I didn't want to, but I felt myself grin. She was still nervous about this whole deal. Typical.

Her scowl came back in full force as she moved further down the loveseat.

When we were settled, Dr. Rubenstein looked at us from over her glasses. Instead of addressing us, she began to write in her little notebook.

"Dr. Rubenstein, what are you writing?" Jovi asked.

She glanced up with her squinty eyes. "Just a few quick observations."

"Care to share?" Jovi probed.

"Jovi..." I whispered. Why couldn't she just let the therapist work? Jovi's irritation was irritating me and I felt as if I was about to snap.

"I want to ask more than one question before I begin," she

explained, offering a creepy thin-lipped smile instead. “You have been together for fifteen years, that’s a long time. In the phone call, Scott mentioned that you guys have been a little bit out of sorts for the past couple years. Why seek help now?” she asked.

The silence was heavy as we both thought of our answers. My mind flipped through our memories like a scrap book; The good outweighing the bad. I bit the inside of my cheek to keep my smile back of Jovi dancing under the streetlights after a snowy midnight walk. I sighed. "I love Jovi. I know that we could make it work. I *want* to make it work," I said. I turned to take Jovi's hand. "Jo, I want to make this work."

She kept her head down and her hand limp. Tears fell from her eyes. “I found out Scott has been seeing another woman,” Jovi answered, keeping her voice even.

It broke my heart to see Jovi distraught and crying. “Jo, I wasn't seeing her,” Scott said in defense, making sure to keep my voice low. I didn't want to fight and make this worse.

"It was just sex, right?" She wiped her tears away with such force I thought her eyeballs would fall out.

I was getting tired of repeating myself. I closed my eyes to ward off the impending migraine that was threatening to invade my brain. "I didn't have sex with her. We were just friends."

"Friends? Because I send pictures of my tits to my male co-workers just to be friendly."

I felt my gut fill with fire at Jovi's attempt at sarcasm. I didn't think of myself as the jealous type but I didn't want to imagine Jovi sending pictures to anyone. "We were friends. I don't why she sent the picture but she did. I didn't ask for it. Now that we talked about the boob pic, what else is the issue."

“Scott, it’s not about the boobs,” Jovi spat out. I raised a skeptical eyebrow. “Okay, it’s about the boobs, but it’s also about the fact that you thought I was a bad mom—”

Wait...What? "I never said that."

"It's about being tired of sweeping everything under the rug." Jovi focused on a spot of the floor as she spoke, "Okay...so, say that you didn't bang her...we don't talk. You chose to talk to someone else, confide in someone else, laugh with someone else. When you did come to me, it was aggressive and kind of manipulative."

Dr. Rubenstein tilted her head. "Manipulative? Please, elaborate."

I felt my phone buzz in my pocket. I decided to ignore it, I wanted Jovi to know that I was listening.

The fucking phone kept vibrating.

I dug it out of my pocket as discreetly as I could. I peeked down and my heart started racing. I had a bunch of text messages and a missed called from my friend, Aaron. "That's real funny, Scott. Is it more naked pics?" Jovi asked.

My phone began to ring and I picked up a call from Aaron. "A, what's up?"

"Did you read Jovi's new article?" he asked. I could barely hear him over the music that was playing loudly in the background.

"No, why?" I glanced over at Jovi.

"What?" Her eyes widened, waiting for me to relay some terrible news.

"'I'm sending you the link now." Without another word Aaron hung up and no more than a second later, I received the article.

I pulled up the site and scanned quickly. "Are you shitting me?"

"Scott, what is happening?" I could hear the worry in Jovi's voice. "Something happen to Aaron?"

I passed her my phone. Her face paled. "I didn't know they were going to publish it," she whispered.

I took my phone from Jovi and leaned back. "Just to keep you in the loop, doc...Jovi just wrote about our whole marriage for the entire world to see." I needed to escape, I needed to get away. I needed to forget that my wife just told the whole world that she has given up on us. Just by the title alone I knew she agreed to this whole therapy just to humor me.

"*The death of a marriage*? You have no hope."

"I'm sorry." Gone was the emotion. Her apology was forced; robotic.

"Do you write for *New York Life paper?"* Dr. Rubenstein asked. "I think I read that article today."

Jovi nodded and left it at that.

"Why?" I asked.

"I was feeling hurt, as a writer, I wrote it all down as a way to work it through my system; my editor asked for pitches and I pitched our divorce as a story." Jovi shrugged as if that explanation was enough to see my pain. For a second, Jovi dropped her robotic act. "I'm not saying I was possessed when I pitched the idea, but I'm also not saying that maybe a priest or a heavy sage cleanse would've helped." When I didn't react to her attempt at easing the tension, her guard came back up and Robo Jo was back.

The silence was deafening. The only sound was the ticking of the Felix clock behind the messy desk. Between Dr. Rubenstein's pity looks and that incessant ticking, my anger quickly began to spread.

"Scott, Jovi apologized. What are your thoughts?"

"It's a bullshit apology." I turned to Jovi. "That's it? You wrote about us and all you can say is sorry?"

"Just call us even," she spat out.

In that instant my anger faded. "Is this how it's going to be? Hurting each other just to win at this stupid game?" I asked, no longer caring if Jovi saw my hurt. I wanted her to see.

"If I just may add here." We both turned to face Dr. Rubenstein. "Just like most couples, your area of opportunity seems to be communication."

"We know," I growled.

"I think these sessions will help. Together we can create an environment where you guys can be free to say whatever you want; I will be here just to facilitate and bring the conversation back to where it needs to be."

I looked at her skeptically. "I'm sorry, doctor, but you didn't really facilitate anything today."

"I know. I needed to see what I was working with," she answered.

"Okay, we come here to talk, that's it?" Jovi asked, she looked as skeptical as I felt.

Dr. Rubenstein gave a curt nod. "It sounds simple, but it will be hard work. A lot of couples end up holding things inside or bringing up issues with no solutions because they think it makes them a bigger person...but if you're not honest with your life partner then you're begging for trouble. The next couple of weeks we will use some techniques that will help with communication. I will be sending you home with work, are you up for it?"

Jovi sat back with a sigh. "Fine."

"Glad you guys are so enthused...your first assignment—cook a meal together."

"Excuse me?" Jovi asked. I was the chef out of the two of us; she would hate to take any orders from me.

"Cook a meal. Something new, work together as a team. Communicate."

Okay, maybe this skeleton woman knew what she was doing. "But just know that I also want you two to think about what attracted you to each other. Write it down for the next appointment." She grinned as if she were in on some secret that Jovi and I were not privy to.

The rest of the session was a blur. Trying to participate during the appointment was like trying to stay afloat in a pool of quicksand filled with poisonous snakes. All I could think about was Jovi's article.

Jovi really wrote about us! She never thinks! She just lets her emotions rule over her.

Did she even think about the possibility that people at my job would read it?

I'm the gym teacher at one of the top schools in New York, if parents caught wind of any scandal, I could lose my job! It wasn't as if they didn't know who Jovi was. They were always reading her stories no matter how big or small. This seemed huge.

Jovi and I left together, stopping only to make an appointment for the following week.

Without even thinking about it, I walked Jovi to her car. "You didn't have to do that."

I felt major heartburn coming on. "Geez, can't I just do something just because?"

Jovi crinkled her nose. "Fine, Scott. You want to walk me to my car so you can feel—"

"Enough!" I yelled like a crazy person.

It was already dark out; I could feel stares from others walking by but decided to mind their business.

"Don't yell at me!"

We found ourselves close; I felt her breath on my face.

She smelled of mint, which told me that she was concealing the smell of her mid-day coffee.

I wasn't sure if I wanted to shake sense into her or rip her clothes off.

I would never raise a hand to any woman, but she really got my blood boiling. "Why didn't you tell me you wrote about us?" I asked.

She tried to push me back with her hands, although it wasn't enough to move me, I stepped back to give her space.

"Because I needed to let it out. I needed to get it all off my chest. Maybe there's someone out there who would read it and relate to it," she answered.

"You could've said something to me."

"Could I?"

“Jovi.”

“What?”

There was fire burning in her honey eyes. The tension in her jaw was so prominent.

“What attracted you to me?” I asked.

My heart sank as I saw her open her mouth but no words made it out. A squeak sounded as she tried to answer.

"Forget it." I walked away instead.

6

Two weeks later

Scott

The alarm woke me up at 6am and I jumped out of bed with a mission to get Clara ready for school. We were able to get teeth brushed, uniform on, breakfast eaten, lunch and homework packed with little to no hiccups. It was crazy how fast everything has changed in such a short amount of time. Usually, it was Jovi who did all the morning stuff. I was proud to say that this week went pretty damn well.

I was still living with my mother. I could hear the sizzle of salami and fried eggs, as Clara skipped off to the kitchen and I began to dress for the day.

Jovi had long hours at work this week. Apparently, she had been working on a story that was starting to get some buzz and I, still trying to make things right and get out of the doghouse, agreed to take Clara for the week so Jo could get some work done.

I looked at the time. 7:10.

The calls always went one of two ways: either Jovi and I would end up disagreeing about some small thing and end up screaming or she would ignore me completely and just speak to Clara.

If it wasn't about Clara, it felt like it was all business.

That was also the case at our last therapy session. Through the entire thing she only spoke when Dr. Rubenstein prompted. Whenever I tried to speak to her, she couldn't meet my eyes. Her face would flush with anger.

It was a lot of eye rolling and sighing; I always left feeling frustrated. But...I still had hope.

We were supposed to go back this week, but Jovi's been so busy with work, it was hard to nail down a time.

My mind brought me back to last weeks appointment when I walked Jovi to her car only to be caught in an argument that sprouted from a simple goodnight. It ended with her carrying on about the time that she fell down a flight of stairs right after we got married and how I wanted to take her to the emergency room, but she wanted to go to the reception instead; how could I be so insensitive to not want her to celebrate our love?!

The whole thing was ridiculous. I could feel the heartburn radiating through my whole chest.

I glanced at my phone...there was still no call from Jovi.

It was really unlike her.

Should I be worried? Should I call her? No, she would hate that.

I mean it was the end of the week, maybe she finally realized that I wouldn't screw shit up.

Clara bounced into my room. "Daaaad! Did mommy call?" she asked.

I smiled at her mop of curly hair and angelic face, greasy from the salami she ate. "No, boo. You think we should call her?"

Clara nodded, without further thought I dialed.

It rang and rang and rang...and rang.

I was about to hang up, when a frazzled Jovi answered the phone. "Hello good morning, baby." She answered, although it was obvious, she was distracted.

"Good morning to you too, baby." I answered.

That got her attention, she quickly turned to face the phone. "Where's Clara?" she asked.

All business.

With a sigh, I passed the phone over to Clara and went to go put on my shoes.

"Mom, why didn't you call this morning?" she asked.

"I'm sorry, babe. Mommy's friend came over to work on some stuff and I didn't realize the time." My ears perked up.

"What friend?" Clara asked the question that I wanted to.

"My friend Remy, the one that works with me, remember?" Jovi answered.

My heart raced at the sound of another man's name coming from Jovi's mouth. Was it really a friend? A colleague? Or was he a special friend? The kind that'll give her emotional support in this time of need. Or would he try to give her something else?

"Yeah, I remember. Mommy, when can I see you?"

Jovi laughed. "Hopefully tomorrow. I'm trying to get all my work done so we can have a slumber party, Okay?"

Clara nodded at the screen. "Jovi? You ready? We have to get going." A man's voice came through loud and clear.

I lunged for the phone, falling short of the bed and landing on the edge of the frame with a thud. "Shit! Boo, give me the phone, I need to talk to your mom."

"Stop running! What's going on?!" my mother yelled from the kitchen.

Clara handed the phone to me. "Boo, tell daddy I have to go, and I'll talk to him later," Jovi said in a rush.

"Jo, I need to talk to—" I was cut off by the beeping of the phone that indicated she hung up. I let the phone drop to the bed and looked at my daughter. "You know mommy's friend Remy?" I asked.

I hated that I had to resort to asking my four-year-old about my wife's friend, but Jovi wasn't going to tell me anything...I had no other choice.

Clara nodded. "Yeah, remember when we went to mommy's job? He got me icy."

Oh, I remember Remy. I stared at my daughter, waiting for further explanation but when she tilted her head and said nothing else, I waved her to the bathroom. "Let's brush your hair and wash your face, we got to get going."

She ran off, and I was there, with a swelling knee, wondering if my wife had a boyfriend.

******

Jovi

I didn't think Scott was listening in on my conversation with Clara until Remy spoke up and Scott came flying onto the screen, demanding to talk to me. I owed him no explanation since we weren't together.

It was only a matter of time until Scott asked about my dating life. Remy was cute but in a puppy dog kind of way. He was younger than me by a couple years. His curly hair, brown eyes and chiseled jaw made him the office heartthrob, but he wasn't my type. There was something kind of fuckboyish about him. Like...he wore glasses but were they prescribed? I wasn't sure but on the fuck boy scale that would set him very high just on that alone.

Maybe I should take it easy on Scott. Guilt started to set in.

If I started to see someone and it got serious then I would let him in on what was going on, we shared a daughter; whoever was in my life was going to be in her life and no matter what, Scott would always be a part of my life.

At least that's what the maturing side of me thought. But, Remy was nobody. So, why did I feel the need to explain myself? Force of habit?

Scott would get jealous, emotional, territorial for no reason. I was trying to avoid confrontation every time we were together. I would remain quiet and distant during therapy because it seemed that was the only way we didn't argue.

And Scott would walk me to my car and...everything he said would irk me to my core. I was on edge sexually, that could be the issue. It was as if all of a sudden I scream divorce and that's when my body decides to wake up.

This was too much too early and I had a full day of work ahead of me. I grabbed my bag and made my way out the office to the elevator where Remy was waiting. His wide smile made me smile in return.

"What are you smiling at?" I asked.

He shrugged his shoulders. "Nothing, slick." Slick was a nickname he gave me when I wormed my way out of an assignment at the paper, which he ended up doing. He was the only one who could tell I was bullshitting, and he became one of my best pals at work.

"So, what panels are we sitting in today?" I asked.

We were assigned to interview attendees and presenters at the biggest comic book convention of the year. It was a great assignment; people in cosplay, paying homage to their favorite characters. Along with all the theatrics, came announcements of upcoming comics, film and T.V. adaptations, books, panels with authors and creators...it was hard not to get mixed up in all the excitement.

I was reporting on it, Remy was my photographer.

All the excitement of the convention dimmed a tiny bit because I kept replaying the stuff that happened last night.

Remy and I met up with some other reporters for a night out.

The night itself was great; it was rare to be out with adults, talking about something else besides what shenanigans *Vampirina* got into.

Remy drove me back home. He walked me to my front door where we shared a kiss that I hoped we could chalk up to one too many drinks.

It wasn't a bad kiss...it was perfectly fine.

Just...no zing.

I remember zing.

Zing is the thing you feel when you kiss and you feel the butterflies in your stomach that makes your heart race, then you feel nervous for a second before wanting to rip the other persons clothes off. With zing, you want to get so close to the other person even though it's physically impossible without private parts touching.

There was no zing with Remy.

The kiss wasn't the worst part; the worst part of it all was that I cried. Poor guy didn't know what to do as I stood there sobbing. An apology, an awkward pat on the back and he was gone. When I entered my apartment, the sobbing turned into loud obnoxious crying because of the guilt I felt for kissing another man. Eventually, I passed out on the couch; just me, guilt and exhaustion.

It was probably my top cringeworthy moment, pushing down that time that I tripped over a shopping cart in the Ikea parking lot to a really close second.

Before the whole kiss fiasco, we decided to carpool; If I knew that we were going to kiss, I wouldn't had made that commitment. Remy's knock on my front door early confirmed that I overslept.

Ugh! I didn't want to be a grown-up today! To be an adult means I'd have to deal with an awful ride in a car with someone who most likely has feelings for me, that I do not want.

It's going to be dreadful.

And an hour later, I was right.

The ride was filled with an uncomfortable silence that we tried to fill with conversation about the weather and other trivial nonsense.

After an hour commute in the awkward mobile, we finally made it to the convention center. We had a quick video conference call with our editor which, without coffee, felt like it took an hour too long.

This assignment was important for so many reasons; First, I've been at the paper for almost five years covering weddings, obituaries, neighborhood crimes...stuff that others didn't want to write about.

A month ago, I submitted a piece on my impending divorce...it was beginning to get a lot of buzz. So, I took a leap— I submitted another story for our online content about the hardships of being female in the workplace and then a week later I was given this assignment; cover the biggest comic book and pop culture convention but do it from the female perspective.

This was a three-day event. I've interviewed what seemed like millions of women from all walks of life who came together for this one event.

Second, I wanted to write a book of short stories using my life as inspiration. The piece I wrote about my divorce was one of the stories in my book that I decided to release for the paper. Upon querying this book to a lot of agents, with nothing but rejection letters to show for it, I was starting to see that the writing and publishing industry was a tough nut to crack.

I thought that maybe taking this assignment would put me in the right circle...you never knew.

Thirdly, I never took an assignment like this when I was with Scott. It felt like I had to put my career on hold because we had a kid. Scott was more traditional in that sense. Although he never truly came out and said it, I knew he'd prefer that I be the one to stay home and take care of Clara. With this assignment, I'm hoping to prove to myself that I can be successful at work and at home.

An hour later, Remy and I waited for the elevator, as I finger combed my hair for the millionth time, trying to get it to calm down.

Remy began to rattle off the panels we were going to sit in on as we made our way down to the lobby.

The lobby of the convention center was a fantasy world of superheroes, pop culture icons, anime characters and everything in between.

It was such a crazy place to be; I loved it.

After an hour of just walking and observing, Remy and I walked out of the convention center and right to the nearest coffee cart.

I know it's so cliché to say but...I loved New York in the fall; the chill in the air, the leaves that had begun to turn brilliant colors of orange and red, everyone wore their favorite cozy sweater...and today there was an electricity in the air that I've come to love.

Every other place dimmed in comparison to New York City.

"So..." Remy began.

My stomach began to turn; Just that simple word held so much weight; I needed caffeine in my veins ASAP.

I played it cool, raising an eyebrow. "So?"

He gave a nervous laugh. "That was your daughter and your husband on the phone?"

I felt my cheeks flush, why was this question making me nervous? "Yeah..." Before I could stop myself, I blurted, "Scott and I are separated."

I thought that by releasing those words I would feel more comfortable with what happened last night. I didn't stop the kiss from happening, I wanted to kiss him back just to feel desirable...that didn't happen.

Instead, I cried myself to sleep.

Now explaining my marital status just sounded weird coming out my mouth. Who would have thought that my marriage would become another sad statistic?

Remy immediately let out a chuckle. "Oh, thank god!"

I narrowed my eyes at him. "Excuse me?"

He cleared his throat. "Oh no! not good that you're separated...well it is good...but only because we kissed last night, and I was—"

"Remy, it's okay. Just lower your voice." I looked around but no one was paying attention to our conversation...maybe I was just being paranoid.

He looked around as well. "I'm sorry, Jovi."

We walked up to the window and placed our orders. I began to dig in my purse for my wallet, only to feel Remy's hand still me. "It's okay, Jovi. I got this."

Oh, this was new.

We've been in working together all week and not once had he paid for my coffee. Did the kiss change that? Or the fact that I confirmed my separation do the trick? Either way I didn't know how to respond so I gave a quick nod.

Why was I being so suspicious? Maybe he was just trying to be nice.

I tried to sneak a peek at him while we walked to a bench in front of the convention center.

He was looking right at me! "You okay, Jovi?" he asked.

I shrugged. "Yeah. Thank you for the coffee."

We sat in amicable silence as we watched hobbits, spacemen, superheroes and the like enter the building to join the festivities.

I felt as if I were being watched and turned to see Remy smiling at me with a loopy grin. "What?"

"Nothing, just looking at you."

I felt embarrassment creep from my neck to my cheeks; the cheese factor made me nauseous. Plus, I didn't like being the center of attention and it was obvious that that kiss meant more to him than it did to me.

"What about me?" I asked, making sure to focus on the tip of his nose because I couldn't focus on his eyes.

"You're looking at everything like you've been deprived all your life," He said.

I sipped my coffee, pondering what Remy had just said.

He looked like he slept through his alarm clock too. He was usually clean cut but today is brown wavy hair had no gel, his plaid button down and slacks look like they haven't seen an iron in years...even his glasses were a little crooked, even with all that his observation skills were pretty on point.

"You're kind of right."

He chuckled as he gulped his coffee. "How am I kind of right?" he asked.

"I graduated college with every intention of becoming a writer...so this is pretty much heaven," I explained.

"But you've always been a writer," he pointed out.

"I know, but I've been stuck doing crappy stories and lately I've been knocking it out the park. I'm hoping this assignment will push me further."

"The last piece...the divorce story for the website...is true, based on you."

I nodded.

"It's been getting a lot of buzz, I heard they wanted to turn it into a weekly update thing," he said.

What he said was true. We had gotten a huge response from the story that my editors wanted to turn it into a series. My only concern was that Scott would say no to the series.

This was a huge opportunity, and I didn't want to ruin it but I also didn't want to make things worse with Scott.

Remy and I sat in silence once again; I didn't mind it.

It gave me some time to think...a lot of my dreams faded away when I met Scott. It wasn't his fault, I thought that once we committed to each other, our separate dreams were supposed to fuse and become one. That idea was stupid. His dreams were his dreams, and my dreams were my dreams and that was okay.

I thought we would work to buy the house we want and fill it up with kids...but realistically is that what I really wanted?

When I had a good day, yes, that image with a house full of kids was a good one. But then I think about how difficult it was when Clara was born; it was no joke! Sleep deprivation, not eating, not really going out, I had a very hard time. I would lock myself in the bathroom when she started crying because I couldn't handle it; I didn't want to touch her, kiss her...I was overwhelmed.

I went to the doctor and she said that was normal to feel the way I felt, it was most likely lack of sleep.

At the time I tried to explain my feelings to Scott—it would go in one ear and out the other. What the doctor said was good as gold and that was it. That's when he had his talk with me, he didn't think I was helping with Clara.

"Earth to Jovi." Remy's voice brought me back to the real world.

"What's up?"

He had a look of worry. "I thought I lost you there for a second," He answered before asking, "What made you pump the brakes on a writing career?"

"I fell in love and wanted to start a family," I answered.

Remy had a look of confusion. "You could have a career and a family...millions of people do it. Your dream didn't have to end because you met someone."

I looked down at my cup of coffee. "Remy, this is a really deep conversation that I don't want to have right now, if that's okay."

He gave me a reassuring smile. "I'm good. You ready to head in?" I nodded and he reached out his hand to help me up. "You ready for fun?" he asked.

I laughed as we made our way in to see what the *Women of Comics* panel had to say.

7

Scott

I was dropping Clara off with Jovi later tonight. I kept telling myself Jovi had some explaining to do.

How could she move on so fast? We've been to two therapy sessions! Was I really that horrible to be with?

I sat in the teachers' lounge, exhausted from teaching third graders today and thinking too much about Jovi seeing someone else.

Then our first date played in my head on a loop. Sitting in a cozy booth of a chain restaurant that was cheap enough for me to afford but expensive enough to impress her.

"So, what did you think when Millie gave you my number and told you to call me?" this beautiful raven haired creature asked. Her big brown eyes had me mesmerized.

I tried to play it cool but a smile slipped out. "I was just happy that it was you and not one of the other girls."

When I agreed to pick up one of my friends from a birthday dinner, she asked if I can drop of her friend, Jovi, home. There were two other girls in the car; one who looked like Jovi, probably related. And another one who...wasn't a looker, but probably had a great personality.

When Millie gave me Jovi's number the next day, I prayed it wasn't the short, obnoxious one. Jovi laughed at my confession. "You agreed to meet me without knowing who asked you out?" her large eyes practically popped out of her head, her full eyebrows rising up.

Laughter came easily. "I had a feeling! I was just hoping I was right."

She bit her full lips as her cheeks turned pink. "You probably think I'm crazy for being forward enough to ask you out."

"It's a first, but I don't think you're crazy."

The rest of the night went great; conversation never died. We made it to the movie theater to watch the latest comedy. We didn't see a damn thing. Sexual awareness was present, we spent the entire movie making out, her hands grazing over my zipper. When the lights came on, we were both so worked up that we hightailed it to her apartment.

The sound of a chair scraping across the floor brought me back to the present.

"Hey man, what's going on?" My best friend and colleague, Aaron, made himself comfortable on one of the chairs. Aaron was one of the history teachers at this school and the one who helped me get this job when Jovi and I first moved in together. It wasn't my dream job, but it helped Jovi and I save for the house we didn't end up buying. I worked through the school year and had the summer off with pay. It sounded great when Jovi and I were working towards our future; it was stable.

"I think Jovi's seeing someone," I admitted, there was no point in lying to him when I was going to tell him eventually.

His jaw dropped in surprise. "No way man, sorry about that."

"It's cool, we're not together," I said with a shrug, trying to make it sound like I haven't been thinking about it for the past couple of hours.

"Damn, that would hurt me. Her moving on so fast probably means she had someone else all along and might be the reason she asked for a divorce in the first place," Aaron said matter-of-factly.

I was upset that Jovi moved on so fast, but I didn't think that that was the reason for the divorce.

"You really think she cheated on me?" I asked.

Aaron, noticing that he hit a nerve, quickly began to back track. "Well...you know...Jovi is one of the good ones...I don't think she would've done that." he coughed uncomfortably.

"Clara knows him and I met him before at one of her work things," I explained.

"Oh, shit. Jovi's a gangster."

I felt my jaw tighten up. "No, she's not. She's crazy, impulsive, irritating and emotionally unsound right now."

"And what are you?" Aaron pointed towards me. "Because this whole mountain man look you've got going isn't really screaming emotionally sound."

I touched my beard that I started to grow a month ago and was unruly now. "You don't like it?" I asked.

"It looks like a mix between a bird's nest and pubs...it looks like you're auditioning for a *Lifetime* movie about the Unabomber," He answered. "It doesn't help that you haven't gotten a shape up in forever...that mini-afro on you just looks sad." He added.

I caught my reflection in the window, and I had to admit, I did look like a mess. "You know what you need?" Aaron interrupted my pity party.

I was afraid of what he was going to say because ever since kindergarten, Aaron was the one always toying on the line of danger and foolery. At five years old, he was looking up girls' skirts, in middle school, he was setting off fire alarms. In college he barely graduated because girls were a big distraction. All these years later there were things he was doing that were border line illegal, but he was my soul brother, so I let him live his life and made sure that I had bail money for whenever he needed it.

"What?" I asked.

"I think we need to go out, get you drunk and laid," Aaron said.

I laughed it off. "No, thank you." I looked down at the curriculum I was trying to prep for the next couple of weeks.

"Why? I know you were with Jovi for forever but it's like riding a bike."

Truth be told, I was nervous. I didn't know what women wanted. Jovi was the one who made the first move all those years ago. If it was left to me, she would've remained a drunken stranger that I drove home.

I wasn't a lady's man; it wasn't in my nature.

"You think they're fucking?" Aaron asked.

I looked around the lounge, making sure the other teachers weren't listening. "Shhh! Come on man, that's the mother of my kid." If he wasn't my friend, I would've punched him right in the mouth.

He held up his hands in surrender. "Sorry, dude. But you either have to suffer in the fact that she's getting some dick and do nothing about it, or you can take that news and go out and get yours too."

One of the other teachers in the lounge looked up.

"Can you keep your voice down, A?" I begged him.

One part of my brain told me that the man had a point; then there was the other side of my brain that couldn't really grasp the concept of being with someone else besides Jovi.

Aaron was still trying to convince me to have a night out when Kim walked into the lounge. "Hey, Scott," she waved before taking a seat at the adjacent table.

"Hey."

Kim. The source of most of my problems. She was the one who had sent me the sext—the person I've been texting for the past six months. Kim was very attractive; But she was no Jovi.

Kim had been a friend, listening to my problems when I didn't think I could talk to Jovi or when Aaron would get uncomfortable and crack a joke every other second.

I haven't spoken to Kim since the whole separation. If it wasn't about work, I didn't want to hear about it. It just felt like all eyes were on us and if we said more than two words to each other, word would somehow get to Jovi and it would not fair in my favor.

Aaron leaned over trying to get her attention. "Hey, Kim. Scott and I are going out tonight, you want to invite some of your friends and come along?"

I felt the heartburn coming on as I swallowed my annoyance. I wanted to kill Aaron.

"No, Kim. It's fine, we are just having a guy's night," I interjected.

Aaron dismissed me with a wave of his hand. "Don't be stupid, Scott. Kim, you're in?"

Was he serious? This felt like a bad idea. Actually, it felt like a bad idea because it was a bad idea. I could feel Kim's stare burning my forehead, but I pretended to work while imaging ways to kill Aaron.

"Is Jovi coming too?" she asked sweetly.

Before I could answer, Aaron stepped up to the plate. "They're in the middle of a divorce, so this is a single man you are looking at."

Along with everyone in the office who had read Jovi's article, Aaron knew what happened, but he was the only person who knew all the parties involved.

He knew Kim was *the other woman*, as Jovi put it.

Kim's full lips turned into a beautiful smile, showcasing straight white teeth. "Okay, I'll text some friends and we'll meet you guys. Just let me know when and where."

Kim turned around in her seat with phone in hand most likely sending out a mass text to all her friends.

"I can't believe you did that," I whispered.

"What? Invite a beautiful woman out?"

"Don't play dumb," I sighed, collecting all my papers and leaving Aaron in the lounge to think about what he just did.

I just wanted to be alone. I couldn't stop thinking of Jovi and Remy...ugh!

What kind of name is Remy anyway?

The thought of Jovi and Remy took up every corner of my mind, until it was time for me to pick Clara up from my mother's place.

I wasted a day of work thinking of my wife and her boyfriend. When I was supposed to be coming up with new activities to get the kids moving, I was preoccupied with whether Jovi and Remy were doing any physical activities of their own. Did he know her sweet spot on her neck? Did he know that she liked...*don't think about it!* I felt myself get hard thinking about the ways I found out about Jovi's sweet spots. Thank God I was heading home for the day because walking around with a boner at school wasn't a great look.

I know I should stop thinking of Jovi as my wife, since we were already separated, but it was hard to think of her as anything else. In the car, I thought back to when things were at its worst.

"Scott! Leave me alone!"

"Jo, I'm just tired of finding the baby crying. Have you even showered?"

"No, I haven't. I've been working on my book."

I raked a hand down my face. Not again with her book, every time I confronted her about what was happening, she would blame it on working on her book. I was always one for supporting your partner, but this was just ridiculous.

The house looked like a sty, Clara was crying in her crib and Jovi looked like...a different person; wearing my t-shirt and sweats, the same that she's worn all week.

"Jovi!"

"What?" she growled. It scared me just how different this Jovi was.

I took a deep breath to steady myself. "I need you to pull yourself together. The house needs to get cleaned. The baby needs to be taken care of."

"She is!"

"YOU need to be taken care of. You haven't showered. Have you eaten? Has the baby eaten?"

"Of course, she's eaten, I have milk leaking out of me at all times."

I looked around the kitchen. I was exhausted from work, but someone had to get this place back into shape. It wouldn't be the first or the last. I looked at my wife who's hair laid in a greasy lump, all color gone from her face. In the last couple of months, she hadn't been eating enough, she lost some weight which made her bug eyes seem more sunken.

"Go take a shower. I'm going to get dinner started and clean up a bit."

Jovi just stood there like a ghost. "I'm sorry, Scott." I heard the tremble in her voice.

I nodded. "It's alright, Jo. I know it's been tough. Just shower."

She walked up to me, slowly wrapping her arms around my neck, laying her head on my chest. "I'm sorry. I just have all these things running through my mind. I..." She sniffled before continuing. "I don't know how to slow down the thoughts long enough to function. Then the baby cries, time passes by and before I know it...I haven't really done anything."

I kissed the top of her head. "It's okay. Go shower."

"I should be a better wife. You deserve someone better," she whispered. I felt her warm tears wet my shirt.

"I just want you, Jovi." I held her in my arms a little longer because that's the most normal we've been in a while.

I shook out the memories as I pulled up to my mom's apartment building. Looking back...maybe I should've done more. I barely made it through dinner with my mom and Clara; I was so distracted that she was able to talk me into hosting bingo night at the church.

After the last time, I promise I would never host again. The elderly take bingo very seriously and when I said the wrong number, a riot broke out. Thank god I was able to escape with only five stitches.

When dinner finally ended, Clara skipped away to get her things, giving my mom time to corner me. "You're dropping Clara off with Jovi?"

"Yes, Ma."

"And you guys are still getting a divorce?"

I closed my eyes, answering the same question she's been asking me since I moved back in. "Yes, Ma."

She began clearing off the table. "I don't know how I raised such a stupid man!" she scoffed at me.

I shook my head in utter shock. I was her one and only precious baby...she always did her best to spoil me. Her hair was set in rollers, her nails freshly painted as she stood in front of me, hands on her hips.

"What?!"

"I can't believe you're just going to let her walk away."

I felt my anger bubbling to the surface. "What do you want me to do?" I kept my voice even because I knew that my mom would smack me upside the head if necessary.

"When your dad was on my shit list, he would come home with flowers, candy...whatever to make me feel better."

I knew that at this point in my marriage, small gestures would not salvage anything, but I didn't have the heart to let my mom in on that. "Did it work?" I asked instead.

"You're here in this world." She added with a wink, making me cringe at the thought of my parents getting busy.

She laughed at my reaction as she continued to clear the table.

Clara came running out. "I'm ready!"

"Thank God."

"Maybe today you can stay home," Clara said, her little angelic face waiting for me to say yes.

"Mmmhmm, look what you guys are doing to Clara." I could feel my mother's smug look boring into my back.

I turned to my mom. "If Jovi doesn't want me then I'm not going to force her to be with me," I whispered.

"I didn't think I raised a coward." Her disappointment was evident.

My eyes widened with shock at my mothers' brazen statement. I was frozen in place; *Did Jovi think I was a coward?*

I willed my mind to shut the hell up.

Clara began to pull my hand. "Come, daddy, let's see mommy."

I gave my mom one final glare before I walked out. She obviously thought this was my fault.

How did this whole thing turn into my fault? I didn't ask for the nudes, I didn't want them.

Jovi said that I emotionally cheated. I thought back to all those text messages back and forth. Then it hit me...was it really my fault? Was I opening the door to someone else while closing the door on my wife?

I shook my head.

Jovi should've stayed to fight.

I refuse to fight a losing battle; I'm not going to fight for someone who doesn't want to be with me.

Maybe she was waiting for me to fight for us.

I shook my head at my inner voice.

I buckled Clara into her seat and took my place in the driver's seat.

I sat and stewed at the confusion happening in my head until I began to laugh like a crazy person at my mother's words. I was not a coward; I was a realist.

Let's be real...it sounds like you're scared to have it out with Jovi.

"Daddy?" I turned around to give my daughter a reassuring wink and I started the car.

As we drove away, I kept telling myself that this whole situation was not my fucking fault!

Flowers wouldn't hurt.

I really wanted to kill the little voice inside my head.

8

Jovi

We finally left the convention. I was thankful to almost be home and out of a confined car away from Remy.

This was uncharted territory; this was a place that I did not want to be. I said a quick goodbye before practically jumping out.

"Jovi?" Remy called out before I could grab my purse.

I bent down to look into the car. "Yes?"

"Can I come up to use your bathroom?" he asked.

I swallowed my sigh that wanted to come out because I wanted to be polite. I really wanted to be alone for a few minutes before Clara came home.

Why couldn't a grown man hold his pee? I know he used the bathroom before we left the convention center.

I forced a smile. "Sure. Come on up."

We walked up in silence. *He'll use the bathroom and be gone*, I told myself.

"Welcome to my place," I said as I opened my apartment door and dropped my bag. "Bathroom is down the hall, to the left."

"Thank you so much, I'll be right back." He walked down the hall until he was out of sight and I went to my kitchen to get some water.

I felt a little panicky; It was weird to have another guy who wasn't Scott, my brother or Aaron in my apartment.

I refilled my cup and still no Remy. *What? Did he drown in the toilet?*

I walked into the living room where I found Remy staring at a picture on my bookshelf.

"What you got there?" *Put it down!* People looking through family photos usually had every intention of staying.

He looked up and pointed at the picture. "That's you with the purple hair?" he asked.

"Yeah, my hair has been ever color under the rainbow. Once Clara was born, I stopped dyeing it crazy colors."

"Why?" he asked, placing the picture back on the shelf.

I shrugged. "I don't know. I thought, I'm married, we have a kid...I needed to look like a grown up." I sighed. "Plus, the moms at school were fake nice; they loved my hair but gave me the shittiest jobs at the fundraisers."

Remy dipped his head low, eyeing me from under his lashes. "How'd that work out for you?"

Is he going to kiss me again? "I'm a woman in my thirties who is getting a divorce...how you think it worked out?"

Remy's brown curls were illuminated by light, causing a halo effect; but I knew his thoughts weren't so pure. He had that look on his face. You know the same one that Richard Gere gives Julia Roberts in *Pretty Woman*, when she finds him in the dining room, and they end up having sex on the piano.

I was definitely not going to have sex with him, and I hope he didn't—

Oh no...tucking a stray strand behind my ear, he moved closer.

"What are you doing?" I asked as I stepped back.

He reached out his arm, pulling me into his embrace. *Oh god, I'm going to have to kick this guy in the nuts.*

"Finishing what we started the other night," he laughed.

Before I could reply, his lips touched mine.

I didn't feel any excitement. I stood there motionless; trying to think of a good way to let this idiot down while at the same time resisting the urge to kick him square in the balls.

Then I heard a cough behind me, which caused my hair to stand on end.

I jumped, pulling away from Remy, pretty sure of who was in the apartment.

And I was right. It was Scott fuming in the entry way with our daughter sound asleep in his arms. Was he holding a bouquet of flowers?

"Sorry to interrupt but I thought you were taking her tonight," Scott said, his eyes narrowed in our direction. He gestured towards Remy. "You got a little lipstick right on the bottom of your lip, I don't think it's your color."

"You were supposed to call me," I said, not sure whether I was annoyed at the fact he just barged in or that he walked in on another guy kissing me.

Scott waved the flowers at me. "These are for you," I stood there in surprise. "Clara wanted to bring you flowers," he added, before turning back to glare at Remy.

I took the flowers. "Thank you," I muttered before turning to check on Remy. He looked as if he were wondering how he could magically disappear.

"I have to get going. See you tomorrow, Jo," Remy said quickly before making his exit, leaving me in a glaring match with Scott.

When he heard the door slam shut, Scott shook his head and walked towards Clara's room.

"How long have you been seeing him?" he asked as I quickened my steps behind him.

"We're not seeing each other," I answered.

"Well, it looked like you were seeing each other with the way you had your tongue down his throat."

I sucked my teeth, fighting the urge to bash him over the head with the flowers. "I did no such thing. I was just standing there—"

"Oh, poor guy can't get the engine going, huh?"

"I don't even know why you're mad, you need to calm down."

He laid our daughter down on her bed, stood straight, seeming taller than his six foot, five inches.

"Oh, I'm calm." He sneered, before crossing his arms and asking, "Were you seeing him when we were together?"

I felt every hair on my body stand on end from the rage I felt burning in my soul. "No, Scott. I wasn't seeing anyone when you and I were together...I'm not you," I said.

I felt the tension in my shoulders, forcing me to wiggle until they loosened up.

Scott pursed his lips, raising an eyebrow in question.

I walked out of Clara's room, straight to the front door; I just wanted him to leave.

I opened the door without hesitation and waited. "It was lovely seeing you, Scott."

His eyebrows dropped as he squinted at me. "Are you really kicking me out? Is it because I walked in on you and your little boyfriend?"

I took a deep breath to steady myself. I knew that he was trying to irk me—it was working.

"He's not my boyfriend," I growled.

"Then why you so defensive?"

"Scott!" I barked. His eyebrows scrunched together making me lower my voice. "Remy is my co-worker...whom you met."

He shrugged. "I didn't like him then and I don't like him now."

I rolled my eyes. "I never understood why you never liked him."

"Because he liked you then and you were mine," He said as if this was something I should've known.

The weight of his words settled around us.

...and you were mine.

"It's kind of a douchey thing to do...preying on a vulnerable divorcée like yourself," Scott said with that stupid smirk on his face.

Stood up straighter, shoulders back to show how much his words didn't affect me. "Well, we're not dating," I said, my voice higher than I wanted.

Scott shrugged. "I went and set a therapy appointment for Wednesday." he looked directly at me. "We didn't accomplish anything in the last session...I want us to try again."

At my lack of reply he continued, "I just wanted to say...that if either one of us starts dating and it's serious, we need to meet that person before Clara meets them."

"I agree." I had to fight the ball of emotion that began to crawl up.

The rules that we just set-in place for dating other people stirred up a giant wave of sadness that I didn't want Scott to see. It all felt...wrong?

Isn't that what you wanted?

"Good, have a good night...enjoy the flowers." He stepped out the front door into the hallway. "I'll leave you alone so you can go write in your diary on how *Reeeemy* is so dreamy, with his Zach Morris pretty boy looks." Sarcasm was oozing out of his pores.

I shook my head. "Stop saying his name like that," I chastised.

Scott turned to face me. "Like what?"

"Like his name is code for some infectious disease."

"Speaking of infectious diseases—"

"Shut up." I tried to interrupt him, but he kept going.

"—he has those hipster glasses, which he probably got just for the look, and you know with a name like Remy...he's bound to have something oozing."

I clutched the flowers that I still held in my hands, doing my best not to hurl them at his head. "You know, jealousy is not a good look for you," I said as he began to walk down the steps before coming back up, sauntering back over to me, and lowering his face down to mine so that we were nose to nose

"Me? Jealous of him? I know what gets your pussy wet. I know what makes you scream a mans name as you cum." My heart raced a million miles a minute as heat rose in my belly and began to spread like wild fire. Suddenly, he stood straight, smirking like an asshole. "Besides, his jeans were tighter than yours...he looks like a reject from the Backstreet Boys." Scott spun, strolled down the steps and was out of sight before I could throw back something clever.

"See you Wednesday!" he yelled from somewhere below, probably the depths of hell.

I really wanted to choke him...but maybe after he fucked me hard. *No! Jovi. You can't have sex with someone you're in the middle of divorcing! That just makes things more complicated!*

I winced as a thorn stabbed me. I forgot I was holding on to these flowers. Of course, there was a random thorn in the roses he got me.

It was a sign, a warning, that Scott was a problem and I had to let him go.

All that from a thorn?

I ignored that little voice inside me.

I closed the door, threw the flowers on the couch and went to check on Clara.

Scott was so irritating; our whole interaction made my blood boil. He walked in with roses and our child. *Which you found sexy?*

I walked to around the apartment with no real purpose but to walk off the horniness. Scott really knew how to talk to me.

All of a sudden, I stopped in my tracks; for some odd reason Scott's words bounced around in my head. "Backstreet Boys? It's 2022, come up with a better topical reference," I whispered to the quiet room like someone who lost her mind.

A cold shower would set me straight.

******

Scott

I sat in my car for what seemed like forever because I didn't know what to do. I walked in on Jovi kissing someone else.

I had called when I was parking; she didn't answer.

I assumed that she wasn't home from work yet, so I took the initiative to go upstairs to put Clara to bed, just to show that we could be friendly.

Remy and Jovi flashed in my mind and I couldn't do anything about it. I sat with a silent rage burning inside of me.

If I wasn't holding Clara, I think that I would've pounded him to the floor.

A thought I hated even more than that? Jovi kissing other men. I didn't expect to see someone else's mouth on her mouth.

The scary thing is that I've never been a violent person; this whole situation had my mind going bananas.

Then I had to go and dirty talk to her? Who was I?!

I was a man on a mission to get his wife back. I know that I got her worked up by the way her eyelids fell and her lips parted. Maybe Jovi was feeling the withdrawals as much as I was? *I could fuck her until she forgot all about Remy.*

Great, now I sat in the car with a hard on.

Next time I'll just keep calling until she answers her phone.

I rather do that than walk in on her making out with someone else...okay, maybe they weren't making out as passionately as I was making it seem, but their lips were definitely touching.

I had to relax my hands that had balled up; I was having cave man mentality that I had to suppress to keep what little sanity I had left.

But if Jovi was really moving on? Should I?

I wasn't sure.

She already thinks I cheated. We're not together anymore and she's seeing someone else, did I need any other reason? I'm not going to sit around like some asshole, waiting for his almost ex-wife to come back.

I took my phone out my pocket and dialed Aarons number.

"I'm coming out tonight," I said before he even uttered a word.

"Thank god! I thought you were bailing."

"Nope. I think I just need to go out...just relax for a minute," I said it more for myself than for him.

If Jovi was going to have fun with other people, so was I.

An hour later, I was sitting at this table wishing I was home in bed.

Why did I think it was a good idea to come out?!

"You don't dance?"

I shook my head. "I could think of other things we could do," I whispered in her ear.

"I promise, you'll have fun."

Jovi looked at me with those puppy dog eyes. "Fine, Jo." I rolled my eyes at her as if I was annoyed. The truth was she always brought me out of my shell. She enthusiastically grabbed my hand, dragging me to the dance floor. She wrapped her arms around my neck, I instinctively grabbed her waist, wanting our bodies to touch.

"You see, aren't you having fun?" Jovi yelled over the loud music.

I smiled wide. We bounced around, sweat dripping between our bodies with no care in the world. After an hour of this, we decided to call it a night.

The cool night air greeting us. "That was so fun!"

"I've never danced like that before," I admitted.

"What else you want to do?" she asked, her lids dropping down.

"Let's take a walk." I wrapped an arm around her shoulders. "You happy?" I asked.

She closed her eyes. "Very."

"What else would make you happy?"

"A bacon cheeseburger," she answered with a giggle.

"Jovi..."

"What would make you happy?" she countered.

"Being with you."

"You're already with me," she opened one eye to peer at me.

"Okay," I laughed. "Then I want...to get you home so I can have my way with you," I nuzzled her neck making her giggle.

"That's a given. But tell me something real, what do you want? What'll make you happy?"

I looked around the bar at these twenty somethings trying to hook up with each other. I felt like their dad crashing the party. This didn't make me happy. This made me sad.

Everything was loud, everything was dark; something inside me told me this is not where I needed to be.

It was midnight; all I wanted to do was be in my bed watching *Sports Center* with Jovi's warm, curvy body next to me. Instead, I was here watching what felt like mating rituals on *National Geographic.*

This wasn't my scene at all.

Not even when I met Jovi. We would hang out in a club for an hour at most before we decided to find a spot to rip each other's clothes off.

I took another swig of my beer, wondering when it would be an appropriate time to leave.

"Scott!" I heard someone squeal over the too loud hip hop music blasting through the speakers.

The lights began to go into a psychedelic dance in time with the music, making Kim and her friends look distorted.

Kim strutted her stuff with a posse of overly made-up women, wearing short skirts and dresses and the highest heels I have ever seen.

Kim leaned down and lightly kissed my cheek. I was immediately engulfed in her perfume. I felt as if every part of my senses were under attack.

"I didn't think you were going to make it!" she yelled over the music.

I smiled politely. "I made it. You guys just getting here?" I asked.

She nodded. "Yeah, we pre-gamed at my place, so I'm a little tipsy." She giggled, giving me a wink.

Was this what it was like to be on the dating scene?

"These are my girls! Lisa, Brandi and Nicole." Her arm swept over her friends who all gave nods as they sat down at our table.

"Is Aaron here?" Kim asked, looking around.

She sat right next to me. If she were any closer, she'd be on my lap.

"Yeah, he's just getting us another round," I answered.

We fell into an awkward silence. I looked at the other girls who immediately began filming themselves, seductively dancing in their seats for whatever online followers they had.

I looked around the room again, hoping to find something to talk about.

"Are you shitting me?!" I heard a familiar shrill voice yell.

I heard my sister-in-laws voice loud and clear over the music. The hatred and distain for me was evident in the way she spoke and in her body language; Curly hair all over the place, hands on her hips, tapping her foot, lasers shooting out of her eyes.

Liz was the one person in Jovi's family that hated me, and I never knew why. She even went so far as to lie right before my wedding and say that I had cheated on Jovi with a stripper.

Hate was such a strong word. But when it came to Liz, I couldn't think of any other word.

I felt Kim and her friends looking at us. I refused to give them a show.

"Hey Liz, how's it going?" I asked, hoping that my politeness would change fifteen years of mutual hatred.

"My sister left your sorry ass so...it's safe to say I'm good." Liz eyed

Kim slowly and turned back to me, "Looks like you're doing well. Does she read?"

"Excuse me?!" Kim cried out.

"Oh, I'm sorry did I talk too fast for you?" Liz was looking for trouble and I needed to squash this.

"Alright, enough. Are you leaving now?" I asked.

I needed her to leave. Jovi and Liz were wild, but the years of domesticity calmed Jovi down. In those same years Liz just turned up the dial on crazy.

"Yes, my fiancée is waiting for me outside."

Fiancée?

"Oh shit! You found someone insane enough to fucking marry you?" I couldn't help but throw a jab.

"Nice to see you moved on so quickly. Make sure you have her home before her curfew." Liz spat out.

"Me? Move on quickly? Talk to your sister, I dropped Clara off and walked in on Jovi making out with her boyfriend." I explained with a little more anger than I wanted to let on.

"Boyfriend? You must be high! Jovi would never in a million years—"

"Well, she did!" I snapped, the anger that I thought had dissipated came back in full force.

On the upside, it was nice to see the look of shock on Liz's face.

I was getting tired; I just wanted this interaction to end. Liz was an exhausting person, my patience was wearing thin.

Kim and her friends were staring at the drama unfolding between us. I got up slowly. "Aarons here too, I'm going to find him." I tried to extract myself from Liz's murder gaze.

"Oh, shit! Hey, Liz," Aaron said from behind me.

My excuse out of the situation came up with a couple of beers in hand.

She gave him a once over. "Hey A, I see you're still dating Scott," She said sarcastically.

"I see you still have a cheery disposition. Tell me, did you break out of prison or did you make parole this time?" he retorted.

"Kiss my ass, Aaron."

"Again? I thought you said last time was never going to happen again."

"I swear to God—" she stopped short and looked at her phone.

"Are you going to finish that threat?" Aaron asked as he took a swig of his beer.

"No, you can finish that when you fantasize about me tonight. I'll see you two around."

Just as quickly as she came to harass me, she left without a backwards glance.

"Damn, I'm not gonna lie...she still turns me on," Aaron said as he watched Liz leave.

I cringed at the thought of my best friend and sister-in-law engaging in sexual activities that might be considered illegal in most countries.

They had a one-night stand the night before my wedding. I know this because that's the drama that Liz brought the next day right before Jovi and I flew out for our honeymoon.

It was a whole day of hostility because right after *the act*, Liz confessed everything to Aaron's girlfriend at that time, yelled at me for hooking up with a stripper, which did not happen, bought a ticket to California and stayed away for a whole year leaving him to handle the mess alone.

Although it's been years since then, it's safe to say that there was still animosity between the two.

"She's getting married," I said as we took our seats with the girls at the table.

"No shit," Was all Aaron said on the matter.

"Who was that psycho?" Kim asked.

"That psycho is my sister-in-law."

Her eyes widened in shock. "What's her problem?"

I looked at Kim's full lips, almond shaped eyes, sleek hair and cleavage baring dress. "Her problem is that I'm out with a beautiful woman."

Kim's smile widened and she leaned closer to me. "Want to go and get some air?"

I looked over at Aaron, who was too busy chatting up Kim's friends.

"Yeah, sure," I answered.

We got up and left our friends in the club.

What's the harm with a little walk when Jovi was already kissing other men?

9

Jovi

I was enjoying a night in.

Clara slept in her room. She's been sound asleep since Scott dropped her off earlier.

I cringe when I remember the look on Scott's face when he walked in on Remy kissing me.

God! Remy was an idiot!

I know how to make your pussy wet. Scott's words echoed in my head.

He really did. Just his words alone was enough material for me to satisfy myself in the shower but I still craved him.

It was hard to break a fifteen year habit.

I began to think about the divorce; I questioned my decision every day. I kept telling myself that what Scott and I had wasn't working and then I remind myself that he fucked another woman.

I couldn't fight for a love that I didn't trust.

As desperate as Scott was to fix this marriage, he wasn't innocent in all of this.

The thing that hurt me the most was that I knew the woman. Tits McGee was no other than his secretary, Kim Pacheco.

I bought this woman a birthday gift, a Christmas gift as a way of saying, *hey, I know you work with my husband, let's be friends.*

All this time she was thinking about banging him.

No one thought about me when they were flirting with each other; when Scott disclosed his dreams, ambitions and fears...I was a joke to them.

Kim: Is she screaming again?

Scott: No, she's asleep already

Just one of the many messages I've read throughout the course of a year. But I wasn't asleep. The light of his phone let me know that he was texting while I laid, faking sleep because I didn't know how to talk to my husband anymore. Now Scott had the audacity to get mad at Remy?! Poor little Remy who didn't even say anything flirty to me when I was with Scott.

How dare he! Scott can kiss my ass.

Well maybe not kiss, because I think I might enjoy that too much...

I shook my head as I tried to not think of the sexy times. Scott had always been good when it came to sex. He'd been more than good, he was amazing— mind blowing.

I took a sip of my wine. God, I missed the sexy times. *I know what makes you scream a mans name as you cum.*

I jumped out my skin when I felt my phone begin to vibrate.

It was Liz.

I loved my sister, God knows I do, but I didn't want to deal with her issues right now. I let the call go to voicemail.

My joy was short lived because the phone began to vibrate again. Without looking I answered. "Hello, baby sister."

"Hey, I'm in the car with Eddie."

"Who's Eddie?"

"My fiancée."

"Hello, Jovi." I heard the baritone of a man's voice greet me.

"Hi?" I answered.

This is the first time I heard her fiancées name, let alone, heard his voice. The family knew that Liz was engaged but we knew nothing else. My parents didn't press her either because deep down they knew it wouldn't last.

"What's up, Liz?"

"I just heard that you were making out with someone and wanted to make sure that you were okay. It doesn't seem like you to be kissing men two months after you just left a fifteen-year relationship...but what do I know? I've never seen you in a breakup."

"Liz, what are you talking about?"

She sighed. "I ran into Scott at *the Red Light* and he told me you were kissing some guy."

"What was Scott doing at *the Red Light*?" I asked.

Scott wasn't one to go hang out at a club. He was more the sports bar kind of guy; beer, wings and home by eleven.

"I don't know, Jovi. Rebounding? He was out with Aaron and a bunch of girls who—"

"Girls?" Now that really got my attention; he was hanging out with other women.

Liz fell silent, I could hear the car radio playing in the background.

My heart sank and it felt as if someone was kicking me right in the stomach...I felt sick and it was all my doing. I asked for the divorce.

I knew it was coming but I couldn't stop the image of a Kim's boobs from entering my brain.

Hers were the kind that still had a bounce to them and were still sitting nicely above her belly button.

My breast fed another human being for two months until there was no more skin left on my nipples.

"Hello!" Liz yelled through the phone. I was so startled that I almost dropped my phone.

"Yeah, I'm here. Did you recognize any of the girls?" I asked.

I honestly didn't know what kind of answer I was expecting to hear, I didn't tell Liz about Kim. She didn't know who to look out for.

"He was there with a group of girls and Aaron."

Okay, no one specific. They were probably sitting with girls they just met.

"There was this one girl he was sitting with. Curvy, brunette, tits that'll stop the pope in his tracks."

I sat as still as a statue. There was this feeling of dread that I knew the girl he was sitting with.

I felt the hot tears burn my eyes as they began to form.

"Jovi?" Liz's voice was soft, I couldn't help the sniffle that came out."Jovi, if you don't talk to me now, we're coming over."

"We?"

"Me and Eddie," She answered.

"No, don't come. I'm just a little emotional."

"You see! I knew he was wrong," Liz said.

"Who Eddie?" I sniffled.

"No, Scott! He said that you had already moved on. That he caught you making out with some guy."

Anger took over and I wiped the tears from my eyes. "I was not making out with some guy. Remy needed to use the bathroom and he came up. Then before I knew it, he kissed me."

It was Liz's turn to go radio silent. All I heard was the station playing and then a heavy sigh. "Jovi, I'm calling Tommy and we're coming over. I feel like you're leaving out a big, juicy detail."

"I'm not leaving out any detail."

"Jovi, stop bullshitting a bullshitter!" My sister yelled.

I sighed. "Scott cheated on me."

"I'm going to kill that motherfucker," Was the last thing that Liz said before she hung up the phone.

I prayed there were no witnesses if Liz couldn't control herself. I didn't have time to deal with a murder.

I laid back, letting the wine work its magic. Before I knew it, I fell asleep on the couch waiting for Liz. I thought sleep would bring me peace but I had weird ass dreams about Scott whispering sexy things to Kim while I stood back. I couldn't move, I couldn't yell...I couldn't stop it. When Scott started kissing her neck, that's when I forced myself to wake up.

I opened my eyes and jumped from being scared shitless by my four-year-old daughter who was staring at me from the entryway like some kid in a scary movie who's possessed and is about to make me levitate or something.

I put my hand to my chest. "Shit, Clara!" I exclaimed.

"Don't say that word," She said with her voice still raspy from sleep.

"Sorry, baby. You scared me." I stared at her; she looked like me except that she had a mess of curly hair. Although she had my looks, Clara had Scotts disposition—she was a quiet kid but very smart.

"Where's daddy?"

"He had to go back to grandmas," I answered.

"Why?"

"Because..." My mind was too loopy to think of a good excuse. "...Grandma is afraid of the dark."

I opened my arms, and she ran straight into them. I missed the feel of having her in my arms. I placed a kiss on her head. "You hungry, boo? Want some pancakes?"

She snuggled deeper into my embrace. "Titi Liz is cooking," she said.

That's when I came back to my senses and heard noise coming from my kitchen. I gave Clara another quick kiss. "Go brush your teeth, stinky. I'm going to talk to Titi."

"I already brushed it," she whined.

"No, you didn't. It still smells like hot garbage. Go."

She giggled as she ran to the bathroom; I went to go check what my baby sister was doing.

I groaned as I got up from the couch. My entire body felt so stiff. I stopped in my tracks in the entryway of the kitchen.

"Liz?"

My sister turned and gave me a brilliant smile. "Hey! I started breakfast, Clara got up and I didn't want her to wake you."

I rubbed my eyes and walked over to see what she was cooking. "You're making breakfast?" I couldn't believe it.

She gave a wry smile in return. "I'm domesticated now."

My eyebrows shot up in surprise. "Really? Because of Eddie?"

I picked up a piece of bacon. "He's part of the reason," She answered.

I raised an eyebrow in question. "Are you pregnant?"

"God, no! Could you imagine?!"

I stood there staring at my sister, flipping a pancake. "You do look happy."

She gave me a side eye.

Before I could probe, I heard someone opening my front door, and as a result I had a mini panic attack thinking it was Scott.

I started to make my way to the door, but then I stopped. I began to give myself a pep talk before starting again, only to stop mid-stride.

"What is happening? Are you malfunctioning?" I heard Liz mutter under her breath.

A wave of relief washed over me at the sight of Tommy.

"Sisters!" he yelled with a smile on his face.

"What are you doing here?" I asked, giving him a hug.

"Liz woke me up last night explaining that Scott cheated on you and that we needed to comfort you."

I looked to Liz. "Really?"

She nodded. “Told you. I’m domesticated now. Cooking, cleaning, caring...it’s the new me,” she said nonchalantly.

“We’ll get back to the new Liz after you tell us all about Scott cheating on you,” Tommy interjected.

Liz was flipping another pancake when she added, “I knew he banged someone else. Didn't I tell you?” she pointed her spatula at Tommy, who shrugged in return.

I poked my head out the kitchen to make sure Clara was still in the bathroom. “I don't know if he did. I thought he did and now...I'm not sure.”

Tommy tilted his head. “But...Liz said that you told her he cheated on you.”

I let out a sigh. “Emotionally? Yes. Physically? I don't know.”

Liz and Tommy shared a look.

“Guys! It’s a serious thing. He was messaging someone else, about everything. There were flirty messages there. The intent to get physical was there.”

“But his penis didn’t enter her mouth or vagina?” Tommy asked.

I closed my eyes to steady my anger. “He says no, but if those were the text messages imagine how they were at work. Imagine when they hung out.” I tried to get them to see it my way.

“Wait a minute. They work together?!” Tommy asked.

“You sure it wasn’t Aaron?” Liz jokingly asked.

“It was the school secretary, Kim, and she thought they’re relationship was romantic because she sent him a picture of her boobs. Why would she do that if there was nothing going on outside of those messages?”

Clara came running into the kitchen. “All done!” her eyes landed on Tommy. “Tío! Where’s Daniella?” she asked, scanning the room for her cousin.

“She had karate, I’m picking her up later and I’ll bring her by if you want.”

"Okay. Can I eat now?" she asked as her mind bounced from one subject to another with the ease of a seasoned acrobat.

Without hesitation, Liz fixed a plate and set Clara at the dining table. She came back into the kitchen. "So, you saw boobs? Did he respond?" she asked, picking up as if we weren't briefly interrupted by a hungry four-year-old.

"I didn't give him the time. I saw the boobs and immediately went into action. I yelled that I wanted a divorce, that we were over."

Liz turned the stove off, leaning against the counter, while Tommy folded his arms.

I felt my anger begin to take hold...were they about to take his side? "What? Why are you guys so quiet?" I spat out.

Tommy cleared his throat before answering. "It sounds to me like you jumped too soon. Maybe this could've been fixed if—"

"Are you being serious right now?" I asked. I kept my voice low hoping it warned my siblings to choose their words wisely.

"Jovi, I hate to say it but maybe Tommy is right."

My eyes widen at the shock of my baby sister agreeing with Tommy. "Are YOU serious? Out of all people, I really thought that you would be on my side."

She reached out to me. "Jovi—"

"No!" I stepped away from her touch. "You guys don't know. You don't know how hard it was when Clara was born, and my emotions were too hard and overwhelming to handle. I cried every day...I went back to work as fast as I could, so I didn't have to deal with my thoughts."

"Jo?" Tommy looked worried by my outburst; I didn't care.

"All Scott saw was that I was doing the bare minimum with my kid." I wiped the tears that began to fall. "He imagined what life would be with other people. And then I accidentally saw a message when I went to use his phone and for a year I kept tabs on him. I said nothing. I lost him. Seeing those pictures was a chance to just let it go."

My siblings remained silent, probably trying to swallow the fact that I wasn't as put together as I seemed.

"Did you tell him any of this?" Tommy asked.

"I tried. When he told me that I was a bad mother," I said.

"What an asshole." Liz's fiery temper was finally coming through.

"Yes! I know!" I looked around the room, trying to find the words. "I wanted to make this marriage work, so I sucked it up and cried when no one was around and made it seem like I was okay, but I wasn't." My tears started spilling forward with full force.

"It just hurts that I really was trying my best to be a great mom and wife and I don't think he made the effort to see that. He had it in his mind already that he wanted to be with other people. And even if he didn't physically cheat, if I didn't catch it...I feel like he would've."

Tommy and Liz both wrapped their arms around me. "You know we always have your back," Liz said.

"Are you okay now?" Tommy asked. "With all those thoughts you had?"

I looked up at them. "Yeah, I got a therapist when my mood swings went to extreme highs and lows, and that helped a lot. It's been years, I'm good."

"Next time tell us what's going on. We can't help if we don't know," Tommy added.

"As much as I don't like your husband, I think you need to talk to him," Liz said.

I stepped out of her arms in shock. "What? Why?"

"Because! You love him. And he loves you!" she yelled. "You wouldn't be crying if you didn't still love him."

"I do love him. But...it's not enough."

"I think if he's willing to try, you should try...for real," Tommy added.

"We have therapy later in the week."

Liz shook her head. "Don't wait to talk to him."

I sighed; it was too early, and I had no caffeine in my system.

Maybe they were right. Maybe I needed to talk to Scott.

Would we get back together? Did I want us to get back together? To be honest? I didn't know.

I'm starting to realize that I need to let him into my thoughts; really let him know where I was coming from.

"Jovi?" Liz said my name quietly. I just looked at her and she continued, "He was out last night because he thinks you were with someone else. Only a man who is still attached to the relationship would go out to try and settle the score. He went out to get some ass because he thought you was getting it from someone else," She explained.

I shook my head in disbelief. "I don't know who you are anymore." Liz looked offended but what I was saying was true. "Don't be mad, Lizzie, but it's true. Now you're this woman who cooks, cleans and you're empathetic and sensitive...it's a lot to take in," I joked.

She shrugged her shoulders. "I'm evolving. But seriously, Jo. Go talk to your husband. As much as I hate to admit it...I think you guys can work this out."

Tommy, who was taking in the whole scene, finally chimed in, "We'll watch Clara. You should go see Scott."

I nodded and began to walk away.

"But brush your teeth first. And take a bath, comb your hair," Tommy added.

I raised an eyebrow. "Anything else?"

"Put a little make-up on, if you're going to make up with him, you need to look better than the girls from last night."

I laughed as I ran to go get dolled up to go and speak to my husband.

10

Scott

I now understood why I never really liked to go clubbing; this headache was unbearable. I remember crawling into bed and passing out.

I looked at the clock...fuck!

Almost noon and I didn't want to get up. All I needed was something greasy, some form of painkillers and I'd be alright.

I blindly patted the nightstand for my phone...every bone in my body hurt! What the hell did I do last night?

I see that I have a couple of miss calls from Jovi and a single text message.

We need to talk.

Now that was puzzling. Why would she want to talk to me? Is it about her boyfriend? Is she going to fess up?

That thought alone made my stomach queasy.

Or maybe Liz told her that she saw me out and now Jovi's coming to rip me a new one.

I set my phone back down; refusing to answer her text. I sat up, the throbbing in my head intensified.

I rolled over; all the blood in my veins turned to ice.

Lying next to me was Kim.

I closed my eyes and cursed the day that I was born. I can't believe I let this happen. We definitely didn't sleep together, so that was a relief.

But the fact remained...she was in my bed!

I reached out to wake her.

She opened her eyes and instantly smiled. "Hey, good morning." Kim stretched her curvy body against me.

I rolled out of bed, not wanting our bodies to touch in any way, shape or form. I threw on a t-shirt and shorts because I felt her eyes scanning every inch of me. *Every* inch of me.

I wanted none of it.

I can't believe she slept over.

I gave a quick nod of acknowledgement.

This could get messy.

Who am I kidding? The way my luck has been going, it will get messy and that will show everyone how unprofessional I am, and I'll get fired.

I needed to keep this job. When Jovi and I get back together I want to have my stable job with good pay, insurance...I want us to get on track, buy a house...just be happy.

I turned back around and finally noticed what she was wearing. This woman was wearing one of my t-shirts, one that I wore to one of Jovi's writing conferences. It said, "I'm with the writer."

It was one of our jokes. I told Jovi she was like a rockstar and everyone was going to see her perform and she said, "and you can be my groupie."

So, I had the shirt made.

And now this woman was wearing it to sleep in.

God, I need this woman out my apartment. It's not that I don't like Kim.

Kim is a perfectly fine...secretary.

I just don't want her in my mother's apartment, in my bed...I needed to be alone and think.

She gave me a kittenish smile, she probably thought I was checking her out. "Why'd you get dressed?" she asked.

Okay, here it goes. "Kim, I don't want to sound like a jerk but...I need you out of my apartment."

It slowly came back to me; We were hanging out at a bar, not really talking. Just watching a game on the T.V. while the drinks kept on coming. There was no kiss, no big sexual crescendo. Just two people who were tired and drunk. She suggested sleeping over; I was too drunk to say no.

She raised a perfectly shaped eyebrow. "What?" She asked, her smile faltering.

I let out a nervous laugh. "I—" I clear my throat once more. "I am living with my mom; I honestly don't want any problems. You and I? We work together...plus, I'm trying to work things out with Jo."

Her smile was replaced with a pout. "I thought you were getting divorced."

I shook my head. "I'm sorry, Jo and I are trying to make it work."

Before she could say anything else, a knock sounded on my door.

Kim walked up to me, wrapping her arms around my neck. "We have something, Scott."

Before I knew it, she planted her full lips on mine and tried to shove her tongue in; I kept my mouth shut and just stood there.

That is until another, firmer, knock sounded.

I wanted any excuse to get away from this woman, so I yanked myself out of her arms.

"Hold on, Ma!" I turned back to Kim. "I have to go answer that...I'm...uh...expecting a package."

God! I needed a minute to figure out how to kick this woman out without it causing problems at work.

I opened the door and practically shit myself.

I slammed the door shut on my wife.

Jovi knocked again.

I reluctantly opened. "Jovi!" I say with faux enthusiasm, making sure to not open the door past a crack.

I looked behind Jovi to see my mother with a smirk on her face, letting me know she knew Kim was in here.

Jovi's smile turned to a scowl. "That was a warm welcoming. You throw the door in everyone's face or am I just that special?" she quipped.

I ran a hand over my face. "I'm sorry. What's up?"

I could see Jovi getting upset with every second that passed by. "Are you going to let me in or are we going to talk out in the hallway for your mom to hear?"

I stood there weighing my options; I can let Jovi in and have her kill me, kill Kim and go to jail for our murders or I can slam the door in her face again.

Both options didn't sound all that promising, and I just stood there staring.

"Hello! God, Scott. Can I come in?"

"Is Clara okay?" I looked back at Kim who looked terrified, her eyes kept darting around the room as if looking for a place to hide.

Jovi stomped her foot to get my attention. "Scott, I don't know what is going on but either invite me in or I'm going to push my way in," she threatened.

Great this is all I needed, a riled-up Jovi.

I looked to my mom who did nothing but shrug.

When I didn't move, she pushed her way into the room, stopping dead in her tracks when she saw Kim.

Kim stood stunned, dressed in just my t-shirt.

After a long silence, Kim spoke first. "Hi, Jovi." She tried to re-adjust the shirt she had on, trying to pull the hem down further.

To say Jovi was in pissed was keeping it light; she was about to go ballistic.

Her head turned slowly to look at me and then turned back to Kim. "I think you need to put some clothes on and go," She said with her voice menacingly low.

"Jovi—" Kim stepped forward.

"*Cochina*!" my mother yelled, charging to the room with a ladle.

"Ma!" I yelled to bring her back to her senses.

She stopped mid-charge.

I didn't want to, but I slammed the door to keep my mother out.

"Unless you want me to knock you out, I suggest you don't come near me," Jovi threatened.

Although Kim had a couple more inches on her, she was smart enough to go and grab her clothes from last night.

"Where's the bathroom?" Kim asked barely above a whisper.

"Out the door, to the right," I answered.

"Your mom isn't going to attack me, is she?"

I shook my head. "I doubt it."

Kim left the room, stopping short when she saw my mother down the hall.

"Ma, she's gonna get dressed and go."

My mom walked back to the kitchen, while Kim dressed in the bathroom.

Jovi and I stared at each other for what felt like a million years.

Her eyes were bloodshot red, her fists balled up at her sides.

Kim dressed in record time, hurried through the room, picking up her purse and coat; leaving without a backwards glance.

I thought once Kim left that Jovi would go into a hate fueled monologue but instead, she just stayed in place. Not moving...which I found more unsettling.

I raised my eyebrows, thinking that the slight movement would be enough to get her going.

But again, I was wrong.

"What are you doing here, Jovi?"

"I don't know," she whispered.

"What do you mean you don't know? You had a reason. You came to my mother's place."

"Okay."

This woman was infuriating.

"Okay?" I asked. When she didn't respond, I began to lose my patience. "So, you mean to tell me that you had a reason for coming by unannounced and you suddenly don't because Kim was here?"

She ran a hand through her hair. "Yeah."

"Yeah?"

"God! What do you want me to say?!" she yelled.

The sudden outburst fueled my anger. "I honestly don't understand why you're the one that's mad?!" Great. Now I was yelling.

She turned, trying to escape the tension filled room. "I don't know what I was thinking coming here."

I laughed sarcastically, knowing that that would get a reaction out of her. "Okay. Alright, Jovi. Walk away. Thank you for coming, next time I prefer that you call before stopping by."

Jovi stopped in her tracks. "Why?! So, you can kick her out before I come over!"

"Yeah, that's exactly why!"

"Ugh! God, Scott! You're disgusting!" I could see the rise and fall of her chest, the anger flushing her face, stirring something in me.

Images of how spontaneous and passionate she was in the bedroom began to replay in my mind. The way I spoke to her the night before.

But I forced them back down. "What? What is your problem? You left me, Jo! Remember?"

"I know! But—"

"But what?"

"But you're seeing her! I was right! You said you weren't having sex with her. But then I come here and she's here! Naked! In our t-shirt!"

"You are killing me! I think I can actually feel my blood pressure rising!" I yelled.

"Don't blame that on me! If you die of a heart attack it's not because of me!"

"It's most definitely your fault!" I found myself yelling an illogical accusation at her.

"Excuse me?!"

I shook my head in aggravation. "Why are we still yelling over something so—" she began to open the door and I panicked. My arms shot out with a mind of their own and slammed the door back.

She stood with her back towards me.

"Why did you come over, Jovi?" I asked.

I lowered my voice, partly because I was fucking exhausted and partly because I knew I couldn't get the truth out of her if we were screaming at each other.

She turned towards me, but our eyes didn't quite meet.

I couldn't help my hands; they tangled in her hair, lightly tilting her head back. I wanted her to look at me. I wanted her to see how broken, how lost, how angry I was without her. My lips crushed down against hers. I pressed my dick against her, she moaned into me, pressing herself against me. My hand ran up her ribcage, taking hold of her full breast and squeezing lightly.

I wanted her.

I wanted all of her. Every single ounce of pleasure, every single moan, every part of her heart...I wanted nothing more than to make this woman happy.

I felt her body begin to melt into mine for a brief second before pulling away from me. "Scott, no!" She pushed at my chest and wiped her lips aggressively.

“Liz told me she saw you last night.” Her voice was low, Jovi’s eyes finally landed on me. “I don’t want Clara around her. I just wanted to say that to your face.”

“Jovi—”

She began to shake her head. “We’re not together. But I am the mother of your kid," her voice shook with rage. "So, have a little respect. I don’t want Clara around her, and I’ll call before I stop by.”

All I wanted to do was kiss her, touch her—wishing that that would be enough to fix our problems. But I knew that sex would cause more damage than good.

My hand reached out to stop her before she left. “Jovi.”

She looked at my hand around her arm and then at me in question.

“Jovi, I didn’t sleep with her last night. I know it doesn’t look that way. But believe me, nothing happened.”

She looked down as tears began to well up in her eyes. “Okay.”

Jovi pulled her arm free and closed the door softly behind her.

11

Jovi

What a fucking liar!!!!

They totally slept together!

I can't believe I came over with the idea that we can make this work.

I was so freaking stupid to believe that he wasn't sleeping with Kim. I was angrier with myself for almost caving in.

Not only was Kim sleeping with Scott, but she was also sleeping in the t-shirt that Scott had made!

I don't think I have ever been this angry in my life; I was hurt. When Scott came over the other night, I thought that his kisses were genuine. I honestly thought that I had been wrong about the affair. I thought I was ready to finally talk it out and fix it.

I came to a red light and punched my sisters name on my phone.

I put the phone on speaker, becoming angrier with each ring.

She finally picked up.

"Jovi! How'd it go? Did you have the best sex?"

"How'd it go? She wants to know how it went," I scoffed.

"Uh-oh," Liz's voice grew grim and I grew more agitated.

"What?" I barked.

"You're alone in your car." She pointed out.

"Yeah, so?"

"Every time you repeat a question to an invisible person, that means you're super pissed. So, take a deep breath and tell your baby sister what happened."

I took a minute to get my thoughts together.

I didn't know what information to disclose to Liz and not have her murder Scott.

Maybe I'll keep the information simple and vague, but something deep in my gut warned me that *he moved on* wouldn't suffice.

I said it anyways. "He moved on and I should too."

I could hear the heavy, silent judgment through the phone.

If I had called Tommy, he would have talked me off the ledge. The only reason I dialed Liz was because I needed someone who hated him to fuel my anger and jump on my band wagon.

Her silence stumped me; I didn't know why she was so hesitant to spew her hateful rhetoric. Her lack of hate was really putting a damper on my anger.

The light changed to green and the blood in my veins began to simmer down. "Liz, I'm going to call mom and dad and have them watch Clara because you and I are going to pick up men."

Liz let out a heavy sigh. "I have a fiancée."

"Again, you mention this fiancée that we have never met."

"I will go with you because you are emotional, and I think you need someone to be your eyes and keep you safe."

I thought about that for a minute. "Okay, so we'll bring Tommy too."

"I'm going to ignore the fact that you think I can't be your eyes and keep this conversation going. Why do you want to pick up men all of a sudden?"

"I think it's time."

"I think you're moving too fast. You and Scott have been together for fifteen years. You have a kid together. You guys are in therapy! Maybe just take your time."

I snapped. "I'm going to say this but don't get mad—"

"I already feel myself getting angry."

I ignored her. "This new guy, new you...it's really a bummer and I'm not into it."

"Thanks, I definitely feel the love right now."

"This relationship couldn't have come around at a worse time," I said.

"You're just a teddy bear today, aren't you?"

"I need you to be the Liz that got arrested because you kissed the girlfriend of a biker and started a bar fight." I stopped at another red light. At this rate I was never getting home. The traffic gods and the love gods were conspiring against me.

"I picked the wrong night to be a lesbian."

"I need you, Liz."

"Fine!" She huffed. "Tommy!"

Liz yelled and a car honked behind me. "The light just changed!" I yelled back; my anger resurfacing.

I heard Tommy's voice. "What's up?"

Liz voice came through muffled. "Jo is going through some kind of weird angry meltdown and we're going out tonight."

"Hey!" My yell falling on deaf ears.

"Why?" Tommy asked.

"I think she's been rejected by her husband and she wants to sleep with someone so she can numb the pain." Liz explained, sounding like an expert in break-up sex.

"Fine. But I can only be out for an hour because last time I left the baby with mom and dad and she came back home singing the theme song to moms novella."

I smiled at that memory. My niece sang that song all day, every day. It was amusing until she taught it to Clara, and I had to hear it nonstop.

"Okay, guys. I'm going to hang up on you and call mom," I said.

"Okay, fine. Hurry home, so Tommy and I can go home and get ready to get you laid."

I hung up in a better mood. I had a plan to get over Scott and that alone was calming to my nerves.

Before I met my husband, I was no angel. I can count the number of lovers I had on all my fingers and a few toes. But it's been Scott's penis that I've been sexing for fifteen years...until earlier this year when he closed the tap.

I saw the traffic light turn yellow and sped up a little bit and made it before the light turned red. Making it past the light made me feel as if the tide was turning in my favor.

When the sun had long gone down, I was dressed in my version of a sexy outfit; granted in my thirty-three years of existence, my definition of sexy has evolved.

"I can't believe you're wearing that band tee!" Tommy yelled over the sound of EDM vibrating off the walls of this club.

I looked down at my choice of top. "The rolling stones is like one of the biggest bands of all time."

"It's not the band that's the problem, it's the whole outfit choice," Tommy explained.

"I don't get it. I paired it with a leather mini and stilettos. My feet being this uncomfortable is a great indication that I'm dressed provocatively," I said.

"The fact that you said the word 'provocatively' makes me question how seriously you are about getting laid."

As Tommy continued pointing out the lack of sexiness of my outfit as we sat in a section guarded by a velvet rope, Liz hit me on my side with her elbow.

"How about him?" she asked.

She gestured towards a guy that was dressed in jeans so tight everyone could see that God gifted him something big, even in this dim lighting.

"Go over and see if he wants to dance," Liz prodded.

I took a sip of my cocktail and shook my head.

"Why not?! You've said no to every guy I pointed out."

"Well, first of all, do you see his package?" I asked.

"The aliens in outer space can see that he's packing," Tommy interjected.

"I want to have sex, but I want to still be able to walk in the morning," I explained.

I caught the eye rolls that passed between Tommy and Liz.

I was reevaluating my decision when Liz startled me out of my thoughts as she choked on her cocktail.

"What?" I asked as I began to pound her back.

Tommy was the first to locate the problem. "Aww, shit."

I followed his gaze. "Are you shitting me?" was all I could say as my eyes landed on Scott, Aaron and the girls they were talking to at the bar.

Our eyes connected from across the room and the smile he had plastered on for his date turned into a scowl.

He excused himself and began to walk over to me. I turned to Liz quickly. "Tell me if I have something in my teeth."

"What?"

"Liz! I don't want to give him ammunition, do I have something in my teeth?"

She did a quick scan and shook her head. "You're good. So, are we going to verbally attack him or are we getting physical?"

God bless my sister.

I looked towards Tommy for guidance, but he only shrugged his shoulders. He was trying his best to stay out of it, but I knew deep down that he was always team Jovi.

I looked back towards Liz. "We'll wait to see his hostility level first."

Scott was fast approaching; he was looking more put together than when I saw him earlier in the day. He clearly saw a barber, the shapeless mini afro he been sporting for a month was nowhere in sight. His outfit was way sexier than mine— Dark slacks, fitted short sleeve button down that hugged his biceps and showed the tattoos that he got throughout our years together.

Most of them he got with me and I could give a detailed story about each and every one of them; and here I sat with a graphic tee and mini skirt and these stupid heels that were killing me. I was genuinely afraid that I would lose a toe today.

I felt middle aged.

Men had it so easy. They all were born with the Clooney gene; they got better looking with age.

I hated to admit it; Scott looked good. I want to lick him...*No! Jovi! Get a vibrator.*

"Why are you here?" he asked in lieu of greeting.

"Kim knows you're out with another girl?" I said, ignoring his question.

I felt Liz and Tommy by my side sit up a little straighter; Protection mode was activated.

"I told you, I'm not seeing Kim."

I shrugged. "I know. You're just fucking her."

Tommy spit up his drink at the profanity that I used.

Scott closed his eyes, probably counting to ten. "I told you we did nothing."

"Scott, what you do is not my business anymore. And frankly it hasn't been for months."

"Fine, Jo. If this is how you want it to be, that's how it'll be," he huffed, his hostility making him shuffle from one foot to the other as if he had ants in his pants.

"What the hell does that mean?"

His eyes started from my toes and travelled to the top of my head. When his eyes finally settled on my eyes, I could see the heat there.

My body began to betray me, and I felt heat in my belly from the thought of his hands on me.

People were dancing and trying to hook up and here I was fantasizing about my soon to be ex-husband.

That was until Liz shook my arm. "Jovi! I need your phone, mine just died and I have to text Eddie."

I shook my head, angry with myself.

"Who?" I asked.

"We're not playing this game again," she answered.

I absent-mindedly handed over my phone to Liz and turned back to Scott. "I'm not going to bother you, so you have nothing to worry about."

His full lips formed a grim line. "I'll keep to one side of the club and you stay on this side."

I gave a curt nod in agreement. "Fine."

Scott leaned in, his lips almost touching my ear and said, "Great legs."

I felt the heat all over my body but acted indifferent. "Shut up."

With the quirk of his lips, he gave a sly wink and walked away.

Shut up?!

I'm a writer; a goddamn wordsmith! And the best comeback I could come up with was shut up?

I cringed inside, as I sat back down between Tommy and Liz.

Liz handed back my phone and Tommy nudge me on the side.

I felt overwhelmed by how loud the music was.

"You look like you're having a hot flash," Tommy pointed out.

I felt my eyebrows narrow in disgust. "I despise that man."

Tommy sat up straighter. "Are you going to finally tell us what happened this morning?"

I felt Liz move in closer. "What's happening?" she asked.

"Jovi is upset that Scott can still get her panties wet and now she's going to tell us what happened this morning."

"Are you serious? You wanna bang him?!" Liz shouted in dismay.

I quickly began to deny all accusations. "No! I don't!"

"Good!" she yelled back.

"So, what happened this morning?" Tommy nudged.

I sighed. "I went to talk to him and when I got there..." I don't know why it was hard for me to say. But I rolled my eyes and finally let it out. "...Kim was there."

"NO WAY!" they shouted in unison.

"Kim was there with no pants on, wearing his t-shirt," I added.

"That fucking asshole!" Liz jumped up ready to fight. She made it two steps before I pulled her back.

"I'm so sorry, Jovi." Tommy rubbed my back.

I told them what I had eventually rationalized in my head. "It's fine. I'm fine. I think it was just a way of the universe telling me that it needs to be over. He's moved on. I should move on." I reached out and pulled Liz back onto the seat. "We are not starting trouble," I told her.

Liz huffed her disappointment and Tommy continued comforting me. "I'm so sorry, Jo. He's moved on and now you want to get your freak on."

What I really wanted to do was cry. Cry because I thought that maybe I could sit with Scott and figure out a way to fix us. But the universe told me it's too late. I should've sat down and spoke to him about the way I felt before I filed for divorce. I should have told him when I saw that first text message.

Now I was in this stupid club with shitty music in my mid-thirties wearing my version of sexy outfit that was so outdated that I felt like a fool.

I felt the hot tears burn the back of my eyes. I didn't want my siblings to see how hurt I really was, so I quickly jumped up. "I'm going to get another drink," I said as I left the comfort of the VIP section and made my way to the bar.

I tried to flag down the bartender who didn't even glance at me.

"You know maybe if you ripped the front of your shirt and showed some cleavage you can probably get a drink."

I tried to ignore Scotts silky smooth voice as he stood beside me.

I turned quickly, almost knocking him over. "What's your problem?" I couldn't stop myself from lashing out.

He put his hands up in surrender. "Sorry, but I thought you were going to stay behind the velvet ropes of the VIP section."

"I needed a drink, and the bottle girl was taking...why am I explaining this to you!" I snapped.

When no snide reply came from him, I tried to peek from the corner of my eye. Yup, he looked hot. His shape up and shave, made his chin and jaw look more chiseled.

And he was looking at me too! "Why are you looking at me? Do I have something on my face?" I asked.

"I just haven't seen you with make-up and a short skirt in a long time, I don't know how to feel about it."

The anger I felt ignited in me. "Well, I wore make-up and short skirts for date nights, but you would always cancel, and I'd take it all off before you got home," I admitted.

I hated that he didn't really grasp the effort I put in when we were together.

"Well, hell, Jovi I—"

"Jovi!" Scott and I both turned at the sound of my name being shouted out by...Remy?!

Scott looked like a bull seeing red.

"Oh, I didn't know you invited your boyfriend."

"Scott, he's not my boyfriend. He's my colleague and I didn't invite him."

Remy finally made his way to me. "Hey! I made it." He leaned down to give me a kiss on the cheek, completely ignoring Scott, who stood took a step back drinking his beer.

"Hey, Remy! What are you doing here?" I asked, I didn't know what else to say without sounding rude.

His face fell into a frown of confusion. "What do you mean? I got your text and now here I am."

"My text?"

I could see Scott nodding his head before walking away.

Then I finally caught on. I turned to where I left my brother and sister, locking eyes with Liz, who tried to look innocent; I knew it was her who sent the text.

I wanted to kill her.

Remy leaned in, smelling like an *Axe body spray* ad. "You look great!"

I felt myself blush at the compliment. "Thank you, come with me." I pointed to where my siblings were sitting.

"VIP?" He asked in surprise.

"Liz's fiancée managed to get us in."

Remy grabbed my hand and together we made it back.

Tommy took in Remy, his eyes roaming slowly, sipping his drink.

Liz was smiling and nodding, obviously pleased with her meddling. She was the first to stand up.

"Hi! I'm Liz, Jovi's sister."

He smiled and gave a polite response. Remy looked at Tommy.

"This is my brother Tommy," I introduced.

They both shook hands and I guided Remy to the plush seats. I prayed that Liz and Tommy would be nice and...normal.

I leaned close to Liz. "I know you text him," I whispered.

She ignored me, leaning forward to get closer to Remy. "So, Remy! Are you the one who was kissing my sister the other day?"

******

Scott

The music kept pounding, people kept dancing, trying to not leave alone and Jovi was on the other side of the club with Remy.

The strobe lights of the dance floor mixed with the effects of drinks and thoughts of Jovi's short skirt made me want to ripped Remy's face off.

No matter how hard I tried, I could not tear my eyes away from the VIP section.

"Who's that guy Jovi's with?" Aaron asked.

"Remy."

"Who the fuck is Remy?"

I ignored Aaron. I tried not to think about Jovi and Remy; but then he placed a hand on her leg while he leaned forward to talk to Liz.

"Are we going over there to punch his lights out or what?" Aaron asked.

I finally looked away and took in the spectacle in front of us. Aaron had pulled enough girls over to us to start a harem and they were all dancing seductively with each other. Other men would be turned on by this, but I was more turned on by a raven haired nymph wearing a concert tee and short leather skirt who was getting cozy with someone else.

"I say we just go over and fuck with his mind," Aaron yelled over the girl who was trying to get his attention.

"No, I told her I won't cause any trouble."

"Why'd you say that?" Aaron asked genuinely perplexed.

"What do you mean? She is obviously on a date."

I casually rolled my head to the side, trying to catch a glimpse of Jovi. She really did look good tonight. She always had great legs.

I knew what was under that skirt.

I shifted in my seat. My hard-on was getting uncomfortable.

Why was I sexually attracted to this woman who was able to drive me psychologically insane?

"I think if you don't want anything to do with Jo, you should talk to one of these girls."

I looked back at the girls; skintight dresses and twenty pounds of makeup...it's not what I wanted.

I looked to where Jo was sitting just in time to see that snake Remy putting his arm around her. Jovi huddled closer as they continued their conversation.

"I don't think it would hurt if we went over to say hello," I tried to rationalize.

"So, let's go over and say hello."

We made our way to the velvet ropes and we were stopped by security.

"What do you guys want?" Liz was the first one to pipe up.

"Hey, Liz can we mooch off your VIP booth?" Aaron asked.

"Only if you kiss my ass."

"I don't think your fiancée would approve."

Her eyes came to a squinty angle and I was sure fire was going to shoot out of her eyes. I looked to Jovi who was in the corner of the booth taking in the whole scene. Remy's hand was on her knee and I saw red.

"Hey asshole, get your hand off of her."

Everyone looked around stunned.

I knew why.

In the years that Jo and I were together, I had never raised my voice at anyone; I never showed an ounce of jealousy. There was one time that we went to a club and a random guy approached her. I reacted by giving her a high-five. Jealousy had no place in my body because I knew that she was going home with me.

But this time it was different; there were no guarantees.

If I couldn't have her, no one could have her. As irrational as that sounds; it made perfect sense to me.

"Scott, I don't want any trouble. I think—" Remy began.

"Remy, no offense but this isn't your business," I said.

I knew the guy was pissed when I saw him push his glasses back and his face flush red.

I've always heard that you should never hit a man with glasses but the way I was feeling right now, I would knock him out in two seconds flat.

Jovi jumped up. "I need to talk to you alone," She said to me.

"Hey Jovi, you look great. I don't mind if you talk to him alone." Aaron gave his consent like it mattered.

He passed by us and plopped down next to Liz. "I'll just catch up with Liz, see whose life she's messing up now."

Before I could hear Liz's comeback, Jovi grabbed my arm, dragging me towards the back of the club where the bathrooms were located.

As soon as we made it, she let go of me, taking her warmth with her, and proceeded to yell, "What the hell is wrong with you, Scott?! I thought this is what you wanted?"

"What I wanted?!" My voice rose to an octave. "Jovi, I asked for none of this!"

Our yelling was drawing stares from the ladies who were waiting in line.

Jovi noticed and huffed right before pulling me into the empty men's room and locking it.

"You asked for all of it, Scott."

"When?!"

"When you started fucking another woman and talking to her

about your inner most thoughts and secrets!" I saw the tears welling up in her eyes, when I reached out, she pulled away, her face distorting with anger. "You told her things that I begged you to talk about!"

"Jovi, when did we ever have the time to talk?"

"Exactly!"

"Now you're really starting to piss me off," I spat out.

"You had time to text her! We're in the year 2022, we may not have flying cars like *the Jetsons,* but we have fucking cellphones that send messages. A quick call or a text, something to let me know what's going on with your life!"

"I don't want to sound like an asshole—"

"Too late," she quipped.

"—But you didn't make it easy, Jo."

"What the hell are you talking about?"

"With your mood swings! One minute you were up and the next you were down and then you were up! I didn't know what I was coming home to!" I had to put my hands on my hips to keep from strangling her. I never felt this angry before and I didn't know what else to do!

"Get a fucking clue, Scott! I was going through postpartum! I couldn't control how I was feeling!"

"We went to the doctor and she said—"

"She said what she thought I wanted to hear. But anyone could see it! I couldn't handle being a new mom. Anytime that baby cried I wanted to lock myself in the bathroom and not have to deal with her!"

I slowly began to shake my head. "How can you say that?"

"Because that's how I felt! I was drowning and you come home and told me how you imagine being with other people and I needed to get my act together! Like, who says that?!" Her breathing came faster, her voice rose with each word.

"Because I was taking care of EVERYTHING!" My voice boomed in the empty bathroom.

“BULLSHIT!” she yelled back.

I was growing desperate for her to stay quiet. I wanted her to make life easier and stay quiet and not make this messy. I wanted us to go back to normal.

I couldn’t keep my hands to myself anymore, it was either choke her or kiss her...I kissed her.

I grabbed her by the shoulders and kissed her lips. I felt her melt into me, I took the opportunity to move my hands to her waist. She moaned into my mouth, and I instantly hardened.

I moved my hands to her round, firm ass and squeezed. Rubbing my hardness against her warm pussy.

My lips moved down her neck to that sweet spot I discovered almost fifteen years ago.

I lifted her onto the sink, and she opened her legs for me.

I pushed her skirt up to around her waist and almost came in my pants at the sight of her barely-there lace thong.

My finger traced her silky slit through her panties. “Mmmm, you’re wet for me, baby?” I didn’t even recognize my voice. "Is this what you wanted? Me to touch your pussy like this?"

She had her eyes closed, answering with a sigh as her tongue flickered out. I continued rubbing her, feeling her saturate her panties. I wanted to taste her. "Fuck me, Scott." I removed my finger, passing it over her lips before tasting it for myself.

She widened her legs, rubbing her tits, squeezing her nipples through the thin fabric of her t-shirt. "God, I want you to fuck me." I crushed my lips against hers, unbuckling my belt.

Suddenly, I saw her desire fade into panic.

“What’s wrong?” I asked through the haze.

“Someone’s knocking.” Jovi pushed me away and jumped off the sink, pulling her skirt down.

“Jovi...” I reached out for her, but she moved away.

“Scott, this didn’t happen,” she said sternly. "It can't happen."

The knock came louder. "Jovi? Are you in there?" Tommy's voice rang out.

Jovi yanked the door open, letting the bass of the music envelope us.

Replacing her frown with a smile that didn't quite reach her eyes. "Yes, I'm here."

Tommy looked into the bathroom. "Am I interrupting something? Your face is a little red," He said.

Jovi quickly shook her head and began to walk past. "Nope, you interrupted nothing. Is Remy still here?"

She walked out the bathroom without looking back; I felt this stab in my chest that I couldn't name.

Was I hurt?

Maybe.

Was I confused?

One thousand percent.

One minute we were arguing about some heavy shit and the next minute I was about to fuck her brains out on a dirty sink in this random club.

Tommy looked at Jovi as she walked away and then back at me. "There's some guys waiting to use the bathroom. You might want to buckle up." He gestured towards my belt.

I nodded and fixed myself.

"You good man?" he asked me.

I didn't know how to answer that question and Tommy sensed it. He held up his hand. "You don't have to answer that, but I think you need to let her be for a little bit. It was my fault to invite you, I'm sorry."

I nodded again; my mouth unable to articulate a single thought.

Tommy gave me one final nod as he solemnly made his way out the bathroom.

"You're good?" A voice I didn't recognize asked.

I looked up to see an audience of men who wanted to use the bathroom.

I said nothing and walked out.

I looked over to where Jovi sat with everyone; she, Liz and Remy were having an animated conversation. I could hear her burst of laughter over the pounding sounds of music.

As if she sensed my stare, our eyes locked for a second and her laughter faded. In that one second, I witnessed a range of emotions; sadness, frustration, confusion and anger.

We kept eye contact until Remy leaned in, whispering something in her ear.

She smiled shyly.

I couldn't bear to see anymore.

I left the club.

I didn't even look for Aaron, God knows what he was up to.

I walked to my car and drove home on autopilot.

I felt a numbness that I hadn't felt before.

I knew about Jovi's postpartum depression. The signs were there but I didn't know how to help. I suggested a doctor but I couldn't make her go.

Regret weighed heavy in my heart. When I began my friendship with Kim, I needed to be heard. There was no inkling she had a crush on me, but I always inserted Jovi into all conversations hoping she wouldn't get any ideas. I never in my wildest dreams thought that she would send me a nude.

I haven't even brought it up at work. I didn't want to.

I didn't want any more problems than the ones I already have to deal with. I didn't want anything with Kim.

Then why did I talk to her about things that I didn't even speak to my wife about?

These are things that I should've asked myself months ago.

Seeing Jovi with some other dude's arm wrapped around her like she belonged to him was triggering something in me.

I looked up at my mom's building, surprised that I drove here in record time.

Did I want to go up?

Even though my mom was on a trip with her girlfriends, I didn't want to go up.

I missed the sounds and smells that was around when I was living with my family. I missed the sound of Jovi calling out to Clara as I made my way into the house after a long day at work. I missed holding my kid every day.

I missed us.

Reluctantly, I made it upstairs, I didn't even bother to turn on the light. I sat in darkness of the living room. Until someone knocked.

"Coming!" I yelled when the knocking became more persistent.

I yanked the door open, ready to yell at Aaron.

"You're not Aaron," I said with surprise.

"Shut up," Jovi walked in.

I shut the door and followed her into the living room.

I stood at the entrance of the living room and observed her as she took in the place. Jovi slowly turned around to face me.

"Is your mom home?" she asked.

"No."

Jovi walked up to me, pulling me in for a kiss.

I didn't know what we were doing or what any of this meant; all I knew was that this is something I needed and apparently, so did she.

I lifted her up from the ground, she instantly wrapped her legs around me.

I carried her to my bedroom, bumping into furniture and walls as we went. I laid her down, eagerly taking off that t-shirt and tiny skirt.

12

Jovi

What the hell are you doing?!

My mind yelled at me between Scotts's lips tracing kisses down my neck and the sensations it sent throughout my body.

I needed the relief of friction.

I don't know what we started in the bathroom back at the club, I just couldn't stop thinking about the heat that had passed between us. I was sleek and wet with desire.

Even after I returned to VIP, my mind went back to Scott. I stayed an hour and instead of going straight home, I ordered an Uber to take me to Scotts place.

Now here I am, naked and ready to have sex with my soon-to-be ex-husband.

He lifted me onto the bed with an eagerness that I had long forgotten. His lips grazed my body as he worked his way up and down; sucking and nipping as he went—moans escaping in small breaths from my lips.

My eyes could not stay open as I succumbed to the pleasure. My body needed a release and Scott was the only person who knew how to give me what I really needed.

His lips landed on the sweet spot of my neck and I was in heaven.

"Is that what you like?" his husky voice was low, reaching the solar plexus of my soul. That alone was enough to send me over the edge.

"Yes," I replied meekly.

He rubbed his manhood on my wet slit; I arched my back making it easy for him to take my nipples in his mouth.

"You want it?"

I cried out with need.

"I need to hear it, Jovi. Tell me that you want this dick."

I refused to answer. I felt his breath as he chuckled. "I'll make you tell me," he threatened. Scott kissed his way down my body, spreading my legs wide. "What a pretty pussy you have, Jovi."

First, I felt his fingers spread my juices up and down. I couldn't stop my hips from rubbing against him. He bit the inside of my thighs before spreading my pussy apart, licking my center lightly. My legs closed around his head. "Uh, uh. Leave them open. I want to eat it all."

He pushed them back apart, this time sucking my swollen clit. I cried out, holding his head in place. His moans intensified the warmth building up in my body.

"You taste so good," he moaned. I felt it. The beginnings of my orgasm.

He licked me until I arched in ecstasy. Scott had no mercy, he kept licking me until I laid as limp as a wet rag.

Before I could come back down to earth, Scott flipped me over, slapping my ass. I gave a little shake, hoping he would just slip it in already.

Scott grabbed my arms, forcing me on my knees, my back flushed with his chest.

He nipped me in the neck. "I'll give it to you, just tell me what you want."

He wrapped his arms around me, his giant hands cupping my breast and squeezing.

My head fell back. "You're playing hard to get?" his voice was low.

My eyes fell shut; I felt his hand roam down my belly to my center. Spreading my juices and slipping one finger in, then two.

I moaned, feeling his dick jerk against my ass.

I kept trying to rub faster against his fingers, but he stopped!

"Say it, Jovi."

"No."

His fingers slipped out of me, I couldn't stop the whimper that came out. He began to trace my lips with his soaked fingers. "Suck them," he demanded. I did as he asked. Sucking them, I reached behind me to jerk him off. He was so hard, the sound of his groans as my hands pumped him up and down was my breaking point; I couldn't resist any longer. "Give it to me, Scott. I want your dick inside of me. Please fuck me," I begged.

Scott unwrapped his arms, pushing me down onto the mattress.

I didn't have time to process; all I could do was feel.

Scott grabbed my waist, his fingers digging into me. There was pleasure in the pain.

With one hard thrust he entered me and filled me perfectly.

I let him take it.

He fucked me hard, pulling my hair in his fists so I could take all of him in. "Your pussy feels so good."

"Yes, yes, yes," I chanted. The sweat dripped from his body onto mine. I pushed back against him, wanting him to lose control.

He squeezed my ass. "God, I don't think I can last. I'm going to cum."

"Cum for me." I squeezed the walls of my pussy around his hard cock. He held onto my waist, gripping it tighter. His groans grew louder and his breathing erratic. I knew he was close.

"Fuck!"

I felt the heat of his cum inside of me. I collapsed against the mattress in a satisfied stupor.

For this one night only, I belonged to him...again.

******

I could barely move when Clara jumped in the bed with me. "Mami! Wake up! I'm hungry."

I rolled over, trying to make out the time on the clock but all I could see was a red blur.

"Baby, what time is it?" I asked.

"Time to get your ass out of bed and make breakfast for your kid," Liz snapped as she walked into my room.

I managed to get into the house undetected while Liz slept in Clara's room, which was why she was so grumpy. Her grumpiness could also stem from the fact that she woke up early because my parents dropped Clara off at the crack of dawn to go to church and she had to deal with it because I couldn't get myself up.

I stretch to relieve the soreness.

Last night was a whirlwind of emotions. I cried for a little bit in the dark when I finally crawled into bed. I don't know why I went to Scott's place...I mean, I knew why I went but I didn't want to admit to the lack of will power I had.

"Mami, what's that? And that? And that?" Clara asked stabbing something on my neck.

"What?!" I sat up straight in bed, a prickling sensation wracking my body. This was not going to be good.

"Do you have chicken pox?" She asked innocently.

Liz's gasp is what finally made me get out of bed and check. "Chicken pox are not blue," Liz pointed out.

"So, what is it?" Clara asked.

I finally looked into the mirror; I could not believe what I saw. "What a fucking asshole!" I shouted.

"Mami, you can't say that," Clara chastised.

"Sorry, baby," I said, examining the marks.

"Clara why don't you go play on your tablet and I'll have a quick talk with your mother about how stupid boys can be," Liz shooed Clara out the bedroom and stalked towards me.

Without warning she lifted my shirt. "Oh my god, Jovi! you have hickies all over your body!"

I looked down and she was right! I looked like a leopard! But there was one right on my neck that just looked ridiculous.

"Did you bang Remy? I thought he put you in an *Uber*."

Liz sat patiently on my bed, legs crossed, bringing me back to when we were teenagers talking about boys and the things that they did to us.

"No, it wasn't Remy," I groaned.

Her eyes widened with realization. "Jovi...you did not!" her hand came to her mouth in shock.

"What?" I asked, unable to tell her the truth.

"Is Scott the one that made you look like you have an incurable disease?" she whispered harshly, trying to keep her voice down so Clara wouldn't hear us.

I covered my face and answered, even though I didn't want to, "Yes." She began to shake her head. "Stop shaking your head, Liz."

"I just can't believe what you did! I thought you guys were over, I thought you didn't want him."

"We *are* over," I answered quickly.

She began to nod as sorted all this information out in her head. "So, you guys made out. You let him get to third base. No big deal, right?" she shrugged her shoulders nonchalantly.

"No, Liz...I...we..."

I didn't think her eyes could get any bigger. "No, Jovi!"

Clara came in, with her tablet. "Why are you guys yelling?" she asked, her big eyes looking between me and her aunt.

"Because your mom is being stupid," Liz said.

"Titi, you can't say that word," she chastised again and walked back out.

Liz jumped out of bed, looking down the hall to make sure Clara was out of ear shot. "You slept with Scott?"

I gave a curt nod.

"And this means nothing?"

I nodded because I didn't want to have an in-depth conversation with my baby sister about how hot and thrilling the sex was. Did I want him back?

I needed to get my thoughts together and every time I talk to Liz about it, my thoughts seemed to be more jumbled.

"How was it?" Liz whispered.

I looked at the door and listened to the sound of Clara's footsteps running down the hall. "Okay, I'm hungry, is someone going to feed me?" she asked.

I looked at her curly mop of hair and big eyes.

"I am!" I feigned excitement.

With a turn, Clara ran down to the kitchen and I proceeded to follow when Liz caught my arm. "Come on, tell me how was it? I'm living vicariously through you," she begged for details just like when we were in high school and I was caught in the janitors closet with John Varios. After the janitor caught us, I was a legend at that school. Ever girl wanted to get with him, but I had been the lucky one. Liz begged for details, but I never confessed because we didn't do anything. He was too shy and nervous to make a move…I never told a soul.

Something she said sparked my interest. "Why are you living vicariously through me?" I asked.

I knew my sister and I knew that no matter who she was with, sex was a vital part of her relationships.

she looked everywhere but at me. "Fine, Jovi if you don't want to tell me how it was then don't," she huffed.

"Are you guys not having sex?" I needed to know because this was something completely new for her and I don't know...maybe it was a good thing.

She began to walk towards the kitchen, I followed behind her waiting for an answer.

"If you must know...we are not," she said, before stomping her foot. "I'm dying inside. I think I'm developing carpel tunnel just from going solo."

I laughed. "Shut up, maybe this a good thing. Sex always clouds your judgement."

She sighed. "I guess..."

"I like it, when can we meet him?" I asked.

She shrugged. "Maybe soon."

I began to take out eggs and bacon from the fridge. "Hey, kid!"

"Yeah?!" Clara yelled back from the living room.

"You want to help me make breakfast?" I asked.

"No!" she shut me down hard.

I looked towards my sister who was smiling. "Don't look at me, that's your daughter."

"Fine!" I yelled back.

I always felt mom guilt every time I came back from a business trip, so I tried to make it up by spending quality time with Clara, even if it was just something as simple as making breakfast.

Liz noticed my disappointment and pulled me in for a hug. "I'll make breakfast with you."

I smiled. "Okay."

"And you can tell me how sex was last night." She wiggled her eyebrows at me.

"What the hell are you doing?" I laughed.

"Come one, Jovi!"

"It was beyond great," I sighed.

She eyed me up and down. "Well, don't sound too excited." She crossed her arms and looked at me, likely waiting for me to confess some deep dark secret.

"It's just..." my brains scrambled again. There was no way to put my words into a coherent thought and it was frustrating to say the least.

Her eyes narrowed in worry. "What's wrong?" she placed a hand on top of mine.

"It's just...I know that this doesn't change anything. Sex was always good," I confessed.

She nodded her understanding. "So, did you want more?"

"I don't know what I wanted. I just missed us."

She squeezed my hand. "I have to tell you something," Liz said.

"What?" She was so serious, I prepared myself for the worse.

"Mom wants us all over for dinner tonight, I told her okay."

I would've have choked my sister but because I was working like crazy, I hadn't seen them in a couple of weeks, as crazy as they made me, I still miss them.

"Fine," I sighed.

"But Jo, you need to cover up your bite marks. Mom and dad would never let you live it down."

My anger resurfaced as I remembered the hickeys. I know why he did it, he was staking his claim.

But I wasn't his.

Liz bumped me, bringing me out of my thoughts. "What?" I asked.

"What did Scott say when you left?"

I shrugged. "He didn't say anything, I left when he was sleeping."

Liz laughed. "Whoa, look at you! Take what you want and leave."

I laughed along with my sister just to keep from crying.

Was that really who I was now? Is that who I wanted to be?

I heard the door unlock and Tommy yell, "Hello! Where you guys at?"

I heard Clara's squeal of delight.

"Kitchen!" Liz yelled.

He walked in carrying Clara and holding on to his daughters' hand, stopping at the sight of me. "What the hell happened to you? You look like a freaking mess," He said as his eyes travelled all over. "Is that...is that what I think it is?"

"Tio, Mami has blue chicken pox," Clara explained.

Tommy's eyes shot up. "Chicken pox? I think your dad had chicken pox," he said mischievously as he put my daughter on the ground.

He set Clara down and the girls ran away. I turned pointing a spatula at him. "Don't. Start."

He held his hands up in surrender. "Scott really did a number on you didn't he?" he let out a low whistle.

"He got her on her stomach and god knows where else," Liz added with a smirk.

"How do you know it was Scott?" I asked.

He rolled his eyes. "After what I interrupted and the way you guys kept eye fucking each other, I'd be surprise if it wasn't him," he laughed. "You going to moms for dinner?" he asked, picking up a piece of bacon.

"Yup."

"Then you need to cover that up."

I rolled my eyes and continued to make breakfast.

******

Scott

The morning sun peeking in through the blinds woke me from a sexually satisfied coma.

I rolled over to pull Jovi closer to me.

She was gone.

I got up, searching the apartment; she was nowhere in sight. I just had a one-night stand with my wife.

God!

This woman drives me insane!

Today was Sunday, Clara was with Jovi and they were the only two people that I cared about.

I heard my phone ringing in the pants that I wore last night.

As I got up to answer it, I saw that Jovi left something behind—her lace thong.

She went home with...no underwear?

That thought sent chills down my spine; I began to feel primal again.

I answered the phone. "Hello?"

"Where did you go?" Aaron asked.

"I couldn't stay and see Jovi with another guy."

"She didn't leave with him," he assured.

I know because she was with me last night, is what I wanted to say. But, I felt played. I felt like a fool. Last night obviously didn't mean anything to Jovi. I just scratched her itch and that was that.

Instead of sounding cocky, I asked, "Who?"

"You know, the gorgeous short woman with really shoulder length black hair who happens to be the mother of your child."

"I'm going to ignore the fact that you called Jovi gorgeous."

"Well, she is, isn't she?" he asked.

"She is but not to you." I heard him laugh. I should've known better than to fall for the bait. "How's Liz?" I asked knowing it would get him.

Aaron gave a heavy sigh. "She's a pain in the ass but what else is new?"

"Is there something going on there?"

Aaron laughed as if that was such a far-fetched idea. "Been there, done that. She has a fiancée."

"Do you think it's going to last?" *If I kept asking these questions he would probably leave me alone.*

"I don't know but she seems like she's in it for the long haul."

Aaron and Liz had some history, and a lot went down when Jovi and I got married. It was fairly obvious to everyone that Aaron pined for her even though he acted indifferent.

"I don't know how this conversation turned to me and Liz," he scoffed.

"I just don't want to talk about Jovi," I confessed.

"I don't want to talk about Liz...I thought you were going to punch the guy." Aaron pressed.

"I wasn't going to punch him, I just wanted to scare him a little."

"Because you love Jovi."

Of course I was still in love with Jovi.

"What do I do?" I asked.

"I don't know, man. I can't tell you anything that's going to satisfy you, I can only help you when you need."

I sat down abruptly on my couch, deciding finally to confide in Aaron. "I need to tell you something."

"I'm listening."

"I slept with Jovi last night," I said. I don't know what I was expecting to hear but it surely wasn't silence. "I left after we had a thing in the bathroom, and she ended up coming over."

"Wanna go for a run?" Aaron asked.

"Yes."

13

Jovi

We were driving to my parents and I glanced over at my daughter; she was admiring her light pink manicure that she had gotten earlier in the day. Today was a self-care day and we took full advantage. Not only was it great quality time, it was a way to stop thinking about Scott for a brief second. Even with the distraction, forgetting about Scott was proving to be a hard task.

I caught Clara in the rearview mirror and blew her a kiss. "You happy, kid?" I asked.

"Yes, Mami," She replied while blowing me a kiss back.

"Good."

Red and orange leaves fell from the trees scattering on lawns, making the neighborhood look like a golden fairy land. We made it to my parents' house, I could already hear the noise filtering onto the quiet street.

I hadn't parked the car for more than a second when my mother opened the front door. Draped in a shawl to ward off the cold, she stood with arms folded, worry furrowed her brow.

"My babies, hurry in, your brother is about to tell us something," She said.

We ran to get away from the autumn chill that was starting to settle in.

I walked in and the smell of my childhood hit me; fried pork chops, rice, plantains and whatever she decided to make for dessert.

"Guys! The girls are here!" she shouted to the others.

She planted kisses on our cheeks, took our coats and took the wine I brought.

"Let's go see what he's going to tell us. It better not be a divorce because I don't think the family can take another one so soon after the last one," She said as she walked into the living room.

I took a deep breath and counted to three.

God forbid that we have something so scandalous as two divorces within the same year. The cousins would have a field day with all that bonchinché.

I said my hellos to my family, giving everyone a kiss and took my place on the floral couch that's been in this house longer than I've been alive.

"What's new, daddy?" I asked.

He squinted at me. "Jovi, *y que eso*? On your neck, what's that?"

I felt my face flush. "It's an allergic reaction to some make-up," I quickly said.

"Mom has chicken pox," Clara explained.

That caught my mother's attention. "But you already had chicken pox, it doesn't look like chicken pox...it looks like a bruise..."

She reached out to examine it and I swatted her hands away. She pulled back, her glare warning me to keep my hands to myself. "Sorry, Mami." I pointed towards my brother who was sitting with his husband. "Didn't Tommy have something to say?"

"Actually, WE have something to tell you guys," he began. Tommy stood up, holding onto Franks hand. "We are adopting another baby. It's a boy and his name is Jaxon!"

My brother and his husband shared a kiss.

I looked around; Liz and mom were in tears. My dad sat in shock while I jumped and congratulated them.

One by one, everyone came to embraced them; there was a lot of hugging and kisses being shared and I thought *this* is what family is about.

I envied Tommy and Frank. They loved each other; they are partners and not just spouse.

Where Scott and I ever partners?

I looked towards Liz who began to text feverishly, presumably to her invisible fiancée. She gave me one quick glance before she walked out the room.

I wonder what that was about.

Before I could question Liz, the doorbell rang. "Jovi, can you go answer it?" my mother asked.

I nodded.

When I opened that door, my eyes widened in horror, I quickly shut the door.

"Jovi, please open up," Scotts muffled voice came through the thick mahogany door.

I took a deep breath to steady myself and opened up, still not letting him through. "What the hell are you doing here?"

"Hi, Jo," Aaron said from behind him.

"Hello," I sighed.

"Is Liz here?" he asked.

"In there," I pointed behind me and that's where he headed.

Scott began to follow behind him, I grabbed his arm. "Not so fast. Where do you think you're going?" I asked.

"To say hello to everyone," he answered.

His hand reached out, his finger passing over the bruise that he left on me last night.

I swatted his hand away. "I can't believe you left hickeys all over," I whispered angrily.

He shrugged. “Did I? I don’t recall.”

“They are all over my body. I don’t know what game you’re playing but I’m not into it.”

“I’m the one playing games?” he looked offended. “I’m not the one coming in and seducing my ex and then leaving in the dead of night as if nothing happened,” He pointed out.

I ran a hand through my hair. “Because nothing happened! It was nothing,” I spat out.

"So, you admitted you used me for a booty call? Your boyfriend not enough for you? Does he know about the spot on your neck? That when I kiss—"

"Enough," I whispered. I didn't want the others inside to hear what was going on.

"Was it enough? As I recall, round two is where you really turned it up a notch. The way you were on your knees..." he trailed off, checking my reaction.

I hated how turned on I was. I closed the door, keeping us outside. "I need you to leave."

"Why? Mad that you want another round?"

"No!"

He took one step closer, my chest heaved from the blood pumping. He hand reached out, placing a loose strand behind my ear. He lowered his lips so that they were a breath away from mine. "Come on, Jovi. Admit that you want more."

Before I could admit that he was maybe kinda sorta right, my mother ripped the door open and poked her head out. “Scott? How nice! I was wondering why Aaron was here.”

“I just came to talk to Jovi,” he explained, taking two steps back, letting the chill cool me down. She came out to give a quick hug and kiss on the cheek and I came back to my senses.

“Well, you have to stay for dinner, then” she pulled him into the living room.

Clara caught sight of her dad and ran to him in excitement. “Daddy!”

He caught her small body and held tight.

Am I messing up my family for no reason? No! he slept with someone else!

“So, what’s going on?” he asked, looking around the room at everyone embracing each other.

“Tío Tommy and Tío Frank are having another baby,” Clara said.

“No shit! Congrats!” Scott went to hug them.

“Thanks,” Tommy said.

My mother clapped her hands. “Okay, everyone let’s go eat and drink to the happy news,” she clucked, herding everyone to the dining room.

Scott stopped me before I had a chance to leave the room.

“Jovi, for real, we need to talk.”

I nodded. “Fine. After dinner.”

“Jo! Go see if you can find your sister,” My mother yelled.

I ran without hesitation up the stairs to my childhood bedroom; anything to put some space between Scott and I.

Without a second thought, I pushed the door open. “Liz, mom wants—” I stopped dead in my tracks, horrified at the scene I walked into; Liz was tongue deep with Aaron on top of her bed.

They jumped apart and I felt angry. Liz's fiancé didn't deserve this. “You’re engaged, Elizabeth,” I said as I quickly shut the door.

I ran downstairs and took my seat quietly at the dinner table. "She’s showing Aaron...something. She’s coming down now,” I informed everyone.

What the hell is happening to this family?

******

Scott

When Tommy called and invited me over, I decided to take the chance to see Jovi. I wanted answers; I *needed* answers.

When she opened the door, I didn't expect so much hostility right off the bat. I kind of figured she would be mad about the whole hickies thing, but I wasn't really sure.

When we were together last night, I felt possessive. Something came over me and I needed to mark my territory. If there was a chance that Remy would see her naked, I wanted him to see that I had her first.

I knew how completely wrong I was in that thought.

I came to apologize but then her irritability pushed me to goad her. I didn't expect to get dirty but I'd be lying if I said I didn't revel in her reaction to my words. If her mother didn't open the door, I think we would've fucked in the car.

Now, sitting across the table from her, I wanted nothing more than to apologize, but an apology was getting harder to form. She refused to look at me. *Why was she being so difficult with everything?*

I wish she could see things my way.

Just as she was struggling as a mom, I was struggling as a dad.

When Clara was small, I knew that Jovi was going through something, I didn't know how severe it was, I didn't know how to help her. That did a number on me.

I struggled with trying to keep the house together while she tried to sort out her mental space. I thought that that would be the safest and best thing for all of us.

Until it all started weighing too much. I resorted to using a scare tactic when I shouldn't have. When I confronted her, thinking that if I was harsh or aggressive with my approach that she would snap out of whatever zombie mode she was in. I was beginning to realize that it had the opposite effect—what I said really stuck with her, closing her off to me.

I thought tough love would help; it completely backfired and now we found ourselves in this situation.

I looked across the table again, Jovi made no effort to even breath in my direction.

I looked around at everyone else; there was a weird, strange vibe around, and I couldn't figure out what was happening.

The only ones oblivious to everything was Jovi's parents.

Something was clearly going on between Liz and Aaron, I wasn't sure what...they still hadn't come back downstairs.

Tommy and Frank, although they were on cloud nine with all the baby news, were looking at me and Jovi, trying to make sure we didn't snap.

The table was eerily quiet. "The food is amazing," I said.

Liz and Aaron entered the room; looking...*damn, did they just fuck?*

I could feel the drama about to erupt like a volcano.

Jovi's mom spoke up. "I wanted to cook because all the kids are here and when Tommy said he invited you, I thought let me just make it a feast."

I looked at Tommy, whose fork stopped mid-way to its destination. Our eyes connected, trying to pass over a message with his eyes that I couldn't quite read.

"You invited him?" Jovi asked.

I heard her dad sigh at the head of the table. "If you guys are going to argue, I suggest you go to the room." He gestured towards the kids, who were oblivious to the drama between the grown-ups.

Jovi pushed away from the chair. "Fine. We'll be right back."

"I guess we're going to the room," I said.

We made it to her bedroom, the one we moved into after Clara was born to save for a house...until she got irritated with her parents and we ended up back at the apartment.

I shut the door and immediately she turned on me. "Tommy invited you?!"

"I didn't ask to come. I wasn't going to come but..." I stopped myself.

"But what, Scott?" she asked with so much venom in her voice, it made me angry.

"We had sex!" I snapped.

"That didn't mean anything!"

"Fuck it did, Jovi."

We locked eyes. "No, it didn't," she said through her clenched teeth.

"It meant something to me!" I yelled.

The truth silenced her; the truth was so overwhelming that she looked away.

I decided to keep going. "Jovi, do you think it was great watching you laugh with someone else? Watching while his hand rubbed your leg? I wanted to kill him, and I probably would have if you hadn't stopped me."

I saw the silent rise and fall of her chest as she just stood there, taking in everything I was saying.

"I hate going home to an empty apartment. I miss my daughter. I miss you."

She looked up; I could see her eyes turn red from restraint.

I couldn't keep my hands to myself; I took any opportunity to touch her. My hand reached out to caress her face.

"Did you hear me?" I asked.

Jovi was always the one to yell and scream, so the fact that she was standing still as a statue had me on edge.

"I—" she began but was interrupted by the ring of her cell phone.

She shook her head as if trying to snap herself out of something. "It's work, I have to get this."

I wanted to throw the fucking thing out the window.

"Hey, Mar—" she stopped and listened to the other end, "Really? Okay, I'll check the email out...I'll talk to you Monday." She hung up.

"What happened?" I asked.

"They liked my story...about us...they want me to expand on it."

"Expand on it?"

"Yeah," she said quietly. "Apparently, they sent me an email." She shrugged it off as if it were no big deal.

I wanted to hug and congratulate her, but the look on Jovi's face warned me against it.

"What's wrong with your face?"

Her eyes narrowed in my direction. "What's wrong with my face? It's my face."

"It's a great face, would be better if you weren't frowning."

"I'm not frowning, I'm thinking," she said.

"So, your sad face and thinking face is the same? And women wonder why we think they're confusing." When I got no reaction from her, I decided to venture on despite the fact that I wanted to talk about other things. "You got great news and you look like it's not so great."

She finally focused on me. "You're not going to let me write about us."

I didn't answer.

"It's fine. Are we done talking?" she crossed her arms.

"No! we didn't even talk."

"We have nothing to talk about, Scott."

"Yes, we do. Why are you making this so hard? I miss you."

She sucked her teeth. "You don't miss me, you miss the sex."

I wanted to shake some sense into her. Instead, I pinched the bridge of my nose to keep the migraine away.

"Jovi, I'm not gonna lie, I missed the sex because the sex we have is bomb but I'm being honest, I miss you...all of you." I tried to decipher her reaction, but she made it really difficult.

"We have problems," she pointed out.

"I know—"

In an instant, her demeanor changed; it went from angry to sad before morphing into...sultry?

She sauntered over to me, tracing a finger over my chest. "I'd be lying if I said I didn't want more," she said.

"What is happening, Jovi?" I was so confused. One minute we were yelling at each other and in a second she was trying to seduce me.

She stood on her tip toes, pressing her full breasts against my chest. Her lashes came down, wetting her lips with her tongue she whispered, "Take off your pants."

I hardened instantly.

She licked my lips, assisting me with the unbuttoning of my jeans.

We were interrupted again by her phone. I just wanted to chuck the thing out the window, stomp on it, whatever, just to keep Jovi's hands on me.

She looked as if she wasn't sure if she should pick up the phone. I nodded towards her as it continued to ring. "Pick it up, Jo."

With a perfectly manicured finger, she pointed at my pants. "Take them off. When I hang up, I need you ready."

Shit! She didn't have to tell me twice. I practically ripped my jeans and underwear off before she even picked up the call.

Jovi answered the phone without taking her eyes off me. "Hello?"

Her face immediately paled, and she turned her back towards me. I could hear the male voice on the other end. "I just heard!" He yelled. His voice was muffled but I could hear him loud and clear. Remy.

It took everything in my power to keep from reaching into the phone and strangling Remy until his glasses fell off.

Her voice dropped. "Really?" she asked. Jovi looked back at me and said into the phone, "Listen, Remy, I'm going to have to call you back. I'm at my parent's house. Yeah, okay. Bye."

Jovi hung up and began to say something, and I stopped her. "Don't say anything that would ruin this moment."

I kissed her, hoping that would erase Remy from her mind.

I pulled away slightly. "I want you back, I want you with every fiber of my soul."

There was a knock on the door, we froze.

"Are you guys okay?" Tommy's voice came through.

"Yeah!" Jovi yelled. "Give us a sec."

Give us a sec?

Then again, she wasn't that far off. With the way I was feeling, I could cum in a sec; I could make her cum in a sec too.

She frantically began to pick up my pants and I knew sex was off the table. I held out my hands to take them from her, her seductive gaze turned into an evil grin. "Jovi...give me back my pants."

"Um...how about no," she said before walking over to the window.

"Jovi! don't!" I lunged to get my pants back.

She scooted out the way, bumping into the nightstand, sending a lamp crashing to the floor. "Scott, don't you dare come any closer!"

"Why, Jovi?!"

The bedroom door began to rattle. "Hey, guys, let us in!" Tommy yelled.

"Why? Because I have blue spots all over my body! You made me look like a freaking cheetah!"

"Does your boyfriend have a problem?"

I immediately regretted my words. The blood drained from her face. Jovi let out a war cry as she yanked the window open. I jumped to catch my pants, but out the window they went.

At that moment, the door was kicked open.

"Oh my god!" I heard Liz squeal with delight.

"Great ass, Scott. You do squats?" Tommy commented from the door.

Although my back was to everyone, my hands instinctively went to cover my junk.

“Aye, Dios.” I could hear Jovi’s mom.

“Where are your pants?" Jovi's dad asked. With my back still turned, I pointed towards the window. "Okay, Everyone out!” Jovi’s dad yelled. “Tommy grab his pants from outside. Liz, I left Aaron with the girls, make sure they don’t set the house on fire,” he ordered.

One by one, they all began to walk out.

My father-in-law looked back at us with disappointment. “I’m going to need you guys to pay for that lamp...and that door...Tommy broke it because of you,” he said, shaking his head as he finally closed the door as best as he could.

“You still want to be with me?” Jovi asked.

I sighed, dropping my head. “Yes.”

“Why? We’re a fucking mess.”

“Because...” I thought frantically for the right words. “Because I didn’t realize what I had until it was gone,” I blurted out.

She nodded slowly, which in the past told me that wasn’t a good sign. That nod told me that she was getting her argument together.

“I don’t think this needs to go any further than last night.”

“Jovi...” I reached out, forgetting I had no pants...or underwear.

“No, Scott. I’m serious. It was great but...we’re a mess!” she threw her hands up in the air in defeat.

“Therapy Wednesday?” I was trying to hold my composure.

“There’s no point, we’re over.”

She began to walk away.

“It’s your fault to that we’re over, Jo.” I laughed cynically. “This marriage took two of us to break—”

“Three if you count Kim.”

“Fuck Kim!” I roared; I couldn’t hold back anymore.

“Don’t yell at me, Scott, you have no pants!”

“No, Jovi! I’ve had enough! Don’t blame us failing on just me!

You didn't tell me what was going on with you! I had to figure that shit out for myself!"

"You didn't even try to figure me out!"

I balled my fists, not because I thought I was going to hit her but because I wanted to kiss her and tell her that everything would be better. But I needed us to start talking because we sure weren't talking in therapy.

"I am not supposed to figure you out! But if we're putting it all out there, I'll tell you this...you're supposed to have yourself figured out and I'm supposed to be there to help you through it all. I'm not supposed to be the one to help you find yourself."

"That's such an easy cop out for you! I'm the one that's fucked up while you were the one taking care of our kid, you had it so bad, right?" she fired back. "So bad that you went and fucked someone else," she scoffed.

"Goddamn it, Jovi! I had no problems with us until you started pushing me away. YOU pushed me away! YOU did that."

"Are you bananas?! How did I do that?"

"You were going through all this mental stuff, right? I didn't know what it was until you told me in the bathroom last night! Clara is four years old and it took you this long to tell me what was happening with you!"

"You knew!"

"How could I know? The doctor said it was nothing major."

"I was crying myself to sleep every night..." her voice cracked as I saw the tears begin to well up in her eyes. "You didn't see it? It killed me that every time that baby cried, I wanted to disappear. And how could I say that? Because it's the truth and I—" she paused suddenly and cleared her throat. "I feel guilty about that every day because she's so beautiful and amazing and how could I hate our kid for being born?" she shrugged as the tears finally fell.

"But you came home and told me that you were overwhelmed with everything going on, and you thought about how life would be with someone else and I just cried because the person that should've known something was wrong wanted to see other people. I felt overwhelmed. All of my senses were overwhelmed. Then you fucked her."

I felt a ball of emotion in my throat. "Jovi, I didn't have sex with her. I was texting Kim because I was frustrated and needed someone to talk to." I whispered; my voice was too hoarse to continue.

"Why? Out of all people? I saw the messages, Scott. You wanted to travel, you wanted to see shows and concerts and eat at these amazing restaurants...well, I wanted to do those things to. You told her things about me, your wife! You guys joked about me. laughed about me!"

"I'm sorry. Jovi, I'm so sorry. That was a line I shouldn't have crossed." My heart felt as if someone was squeezing tight. I made my wife feel as if she were nothing, that is far from the truth. Jovi is everything. "Jovi, I didn't want Kim romantically." I sighed, tired of having this same conversation about Kim.

"Bullshit, Scott. Read those messages over because you were definitely leading her on. No wonder she sent you those pics."

"Jovi, I really didn't ask for any of that."

"Scott, you asked for it all."

We both stood there defeated; nothing resolved.

A timid knock sounded.

When we turned to look, an arm appeared, holding my pants. "I thought you might want this back. I had to fight a squirrel for your underwear."

I took them and began getting dressed.

"I started therapy that day after you told me how you felt," Jovi said.

"You did?"

"I did. I didn't tell you because I didn't want that to be another strike against me. I tried, Scott...I really did. I tried to make date night a thing but then those plans would change. You'd have a school function, a deadline, parent teacher conference or you were just tired. How many tickets I gave away to my family because you made plans with Aaron instead of just chilling with me. How many little negligées I stuffed in my drawers after you'd go straight to bed without a glance?"

I couldn't answer her.

"You may be right, I did my part to break us...but that should be a reason to let last night just be," she said.

I needed time to think. This was all too much. How could I let this get so far?

I rubbed my eyes because I was tired of the bullshit. What we were going through was bullshit.

"I'm showing up to therapy, I hope you come. I still want us to try," I told her.

I opened the door and the whole family scattered...except for Aaron. "Ready to go?" He asked.

I nodded.

"Then let's go."

I said goodnight to my solemn daughter, who with eyes like her mom's asked me why I couldn't stay.

"Mommy and daddy need some alone time. But I promise I'll call you later," I reassured her. I embraced her little body, kissed the top of her head and made my exit.

The golden trees were just a blur as we drove out of the suburbs back into the loud city.

"Want to talk about what happened with Jovi?" Aaron asked from the passenger side.

I glanced over at him before turning back to the road. "Want to talk about Liz?"

"No."

"Alright then."

"But she's not my wife who I just slept with again."

I pulled over to the side of the road because I was too distracted to drive. "I need to get her back."

"But she said no," Aaron pointed out.

"I know what she said but I want to show her that we can make it, we're worth it."

Aaron eyed me. "You want my advice?"

I turned to him quickly. "You really asking me if I want your advice?"

"Yeah."

"Advice from a guy who is in some kind of weird masochistic relationship with Liz, who happens to be engaged?" I know I was being a dick, but I had to put it out there.

"First off, there's nothing between Liz and I; Second, do you want my advice or not?"

"Go ahead," I prompted. His advice was better than nothing.

"You need to woo her," he replied with so much seriousness that I busted out laughing. He shrugged. "You laugh, but everyone in that house heard all about the dates you guys didn't go on."

He had a point.

Was he right? I would come home tired and barely made an effort. I did tell Jovi that it took both of us to break us, now maybe if I tried courting her all over again, she'll give us a try.

She was it for me.

I needed her to see that.

"I'll woo her, but I can't say 'woo'...let's call it something else."

"Dude, whatever you call it, it's the same shit."

I started the car up and merged back onto the road. "Fine. Now that we figured out what I'm going to do, want to talk about Liz? What's happening with all that?" I asked.

"Nothing is happening," Aaron answered without looking up from his phone.

"You want my advice?"

"Absolutely not."

"Alright, here it goes..." he let out a heavy sigh, but I went on, "You should woo her to—"

"She is engaged. And to be honest, what works for Jovi wouldn't work on Liz...they're not the same kind of crazy."

I shrugged. "Maybe her relationship isn't stable," I said.

"She's not stable. That women ruined my last real relationship. She's a fucking mess." I could hear the hysteria settling in his voice.

Aaron and Liz always had chemistry but at my wedding, whatever they had going on was thrown out the window. Liz confessed to everyone, while making her maid of honor speech, that she and Aaron slept together. Aaron was the best man and attended my wedding with his girlfriend.

Liz left on the next flight to wherever and left Aaron to pick up the pieces.

Since then, it's made him a little bit jaded in his relationships; they never passed the one-month mark.

"She's a fucking mess? So, no wooing?" I tried one more time to crack his façade. No matter how much he played it cool, I know Liz had a hold on him.

"There's no wooing that woman; she would laugh in my face while kicking my puppy."

"Good thing you don't have a puppy."

14

Jovi

In the last couple of days, I've been so tangled up in work that I barely had time for anything else. I tried to keep myself occupied but every time I had a spare minute my mind wondered to Scott and the explosive argument we had at my parents' house.

It was the first time we were both completely honest with each other.

He made some valid points.

But it wasn't strong enough for me to forget it all and go back.

So, why was I back in the therapist's office?

Because when I calmed myself down enough to think rationally, there was this small feeling eating at me.

This stupid feeling kept whispering *maybe,* I just wanted to shut the feeling up.

The clock on the wall told me that Scott was late...again.

I hated sitting here alone; I quickly got up, grabbing my jacket and purse.

I can't believe I came here.

"You're really here." Scotts astonished voice stopped me in my tracks.

I abruptly sat back down. "I'm just as surprised as you," I admitted.

He sat down next to me and I felt...nervous.

Not like, *I'm fearing for my life nervous*; it was more of a, *I hope I didn't have anything in my teeth,* or *I hope I didn't smell like a dirty sock*.

"Garcia's?" Dr. Rubenstein called.

"I honestly didn't think you guys were coming back," Dr. Rubenstein admitted as we took our spots on the loveseat.

Before I could answer with something witty, Scott raised his hand.

"Scott, you don't have to raise your hand," Dr. Rubenstein assured.

He looked at me, looking unsure. "I just have something to say."

I shifted in my seat, deciding the straighter I sat up the better I can absorb his words.

"Remember the first assignment you gave? What attracted me to Jo? I want to answer it."

Dr. Rubenstein nodded.

"Jovi was carefree, in your face...she went after whatever she wanted, she brought me out of myself, out of my mind," Scott began.

I sat there motionless because I had this overwhelming feeling of embarrassment.

Why did we have to do this now?

"I'm not that person. I'm not outgoing, I'm not a go-getter. I think before I jump, but Jovi isn't afraid of anything, she just jumps. Her aggressiveness is what attracted me in the beginning...she was different...she is different," Scott finished.

"What attracts you now?"

"The love she has for me and Clara, I know she gives it her best everyday...it's taking me a long time to see."

"Great. Good start, Scott. Thank You," Dr. Rubenstein said before her eyes fell on me.

Her squinty bird eyes were looking at me, waiting for me to participate.

I opened up; nothing but a squeak came out.

I needed to escape.

I jumped up. "I'm sorry but I have to go."

It's a lame excuse, I know.

I just didn't want to look like this cold-hearted bitch to everyone. I didn't want to hurt Scott.

"What?!" Scott asked, his whole body became rigid, as his voice shot up an octave. He reached for my hand. "Jovi, come on," he pleaded.

"You don't have to share if you don't want to," Dr. Rubenstein assured.

"He left hickies all over my body!" I couldn't take it anymore.

There was all this bottled anger that I had to let out. I was angry at all the confusion in my head. "The things he did to it was magical! And I hate that it was so good!" there was no stopping me.

Scott sucked his teeth; letting go of my hand, he dropped his head down.

Dr. Rubenstein sat looking like the crypt keeper.

"I don't know why I'm shouting! But it's kind of making me feel better!"

"Okay, Jovi, elaborate on your anger." Dr. Rubenstein encouraged.

"I..." I remained standing, hands on my hips. "I...Sex was good, that's never been the problem...I just..." I shook my head in an attempt to shake the words out. I pointed a finger a Scott. "He doesn't like to argue! He hates confrontation! I feel like I'm the bad guy...we had sex...I thought about us reconciling but..."

Scott looked up. "But what, Jo?"

"I don't trust you! I'm angry with you!"

"She means nothing to me," Scotts voice was low. "I love you, Jo! I want you!"

"You're just saying that because you're scared of the future."

"I am scared of the future...I'm scared you won't be a part of it.

Remember our first date? You slammed the door in my face because I turned down a night cap. That's when I knew that you were mine for life. That fire is what I craved. Five minutes later, I ended up in your bed and never left."

"Memories are part of the past. I can't help what I feel right now, in the present."

I could see the twitch in his jaw, the way his hands were clasped tightly on his lap...it drove me nuts!

Being in a relationship with someone for fifteen years, you learn all the subtleties of your partners personality; he was about to blow a gasket.

"Let's go out this weekend."

I did not expect that.

"What?! Are you out of your mind?!"

I just said I didn't trust him, and he wanted to go on a date? I was so confused.

"You don't trust people you don't know. Go out with me, let's get to know each other again...like it's our first date."

There were a million reasons why I wanted to say no; Scott was really trying.

Maybe I should try to.

"Okay," I sighed.

"Okay?" His eyes widened.

I nodded. "Yeah, but...I need to tell you something."

He clasped his hands, waiting for me to drop my bomb.

"I'll be working with Remy for a follow up to one of my stories," I confessed. "He and I will be in PA interviewing a couple of women from the comic convention."

Scott let his head fall back. "Remy," he groaned.

"We're going this weekend."

"You're going with Remy to Pennsylvania? Staying in the same hotel?"

"Yes."

I sat back down on the couch.

It felt as if the tick-tick-tick of the clock was louder than usual as the silence stretched between us.

"You guys are making major steps, even though it may not seem like it," Dr. Rubenstein began. She was so quiet through our whole exchange I forgot that she was there. "Trust is an opportunity for a lot of couples."

"So, what do we do?" I asked.

"Trust takes time, take baby steps. One of the things I tell other couples is not to live in the past. Let's live in the present. This date is a good step in the right direction."

I turned to Scott. "Do you trust me?"

"I trust you; I don't trust Remy."

"Well, Scott, trust goes both ways. If you want Jovi to trust you, trust that she will handle situations respectfully," Dr. Rubenstein chimed in.

Scott used to be my best friend. He knew everything about me. As much as I didn't trust him, I decided to go along with it. If we really wanted to make things better, then we had to start somewhere. And as much I thought we were over, Scott kept fighting for us. "Scott, I'll go on this date," I said.

"Really?!"

"Baby steps, right?"

The corner of his full lips came up slowly. "Let's set it for next weekend?"

I nodded in agreement.

The rest of the session went smoother than the first two. No crazy outbursts, no name calling.

For the first time I let myself believe that reconciliation was a possibility.

Scott walked me to my car, like always.

But instead of being in the comfortable hostility we've been in, we found ourselves in an awkward space.

He went in for a hug; I just stood there like a frozen tin man, only to kiss his ear at the last second.

I didn't mean to; I was aiming for is cheek and...I'm officially a dork.

"I'll see you later this week," he said.

"Yeah," I jammed myself into the car with my ears burning, trying to escape my husband and this scene right out of a high school romcom.

During the week, I had a lot of things going on at work, prepping for my next story.

My editor kept insisting I write a part two to my divorce story even though I had no intention of writing it. Scott and I were trying to make things work and I didn't want to screw it up.

"Hey, Jovi?" I was so startled by Remy's voice, I jumped, spilling my coffee everywhere.

"Shit."

"I'm sorry, I didn't mean to scare you," he said.

Remy grabbed a handful of paper towels and began wiping the counter down. He handed me some so I could clean myself up.

"Yeah, I was just thinking too hard," I muttered.

"About the interviews?" he asked.

"Yeah," I lied.

"Want to take a break and grab a slice?" he asked.

With his wire rim glasses and curly hair he looked like such a good guy.

I swallowed a sigh, knowing full well what I had to do. "Listen, Remy—"

"Jovi, I asked you to get pizza with me. It's not a date, so relax."

Thank God.

"Well...Good, I'm glad you said that."

Remy reminded me of a puppy with his tail tucked between his legs. Only instead of a tail tucked, he had his hands tucked into his jeans. Looking at me with soft brown eyes.

"Yeah, I know you're going through a lot and I don't want to pressure you or make you feel uncomfortable. You're my friend."

I smiled. "Okay, let's get pizza. You're paying."

"Of course, I didn't think any different," he laughed.

We made it to the small pizzeria around the corner. The tables were crowded, I barely snagged one while he placed our order.

It took both of us to break us.

Those words crept out of the shadows in my mind.

Scott was right.

Fear paralyzed me. I closed myself off thinking he didn't want to hear about my issues and problems. I didn't give him a chance. Now with the sex and the unexpected honesty that came out of our arguments, I wanted to give us a chance.

Remy placed the tray on the table. "Every time you're alone you look like you're trying to solve the world's toughest math question," he said.

"I have a lot going on, haven't had time to process it."

He took a bite of his pizza. "Want to talk about it? I'm all ears."

"It's about Scott."

Remy began to shake his head; his eyes lost all its warmth; his lips formed a grim line. "I'm not touching that but if you want, I'll just sit in listen. I won't give any advice."

"Oh, not so eager now," I laughed.

"That's your husband and there's history there that I know nothing about, I don't want to overstep," He said around bites of his pizza.

I took a bite of my slice. "It's just...I thought I knew what I wanted and now things are changing," I said around my bite.

Remy continued eating but didn't answer. I knew he was listening, so I continued on, "We—"

He raised his hand to stop. "No specifics."

I nodded. "I just don't know if I should believe what he's saying. I was hurt by everything, I felt hurt, I felt betrayed. But then screaming at each other the other day..." I sighed. "He said that I can't blame him...I am partly to blame and so now..." I shrugged my shoulders for lack of a better thing to say.

Remy cleared his throat and wiped his hands on a napkin. "I forgot to get us drinks, I'll be back. Don't wander too far, okay?" he said with a wink, the corners of his mouth tilted in a loopy grin.

It felt good to vent to someone...

Is this what Scott felt like with Kim?

No, Jo! Don't make excuses for him. She sent him a naked picture of herself, what he did was worse.

Ugh! I couldn't shut my mind.

My phone began to vibrate on the table—it was Scott's number.

Should I pick it up? I sent the call to voicemail.

It immediately began vibrating again. I picked up. "Scott, I'm on lunch. What do you need?"

"Hey, I got a call from Clara's school. There was an accident and she's in the hospital now. I'm on my way, should I pick you up?" he was spoke fast.

My heart began to race. Ice-cold fear ran through my veins as I waited to hear the news. "What kind of accident?"

"She fell off the monkey bars, I think she hurt her arm," he answered.

"Hey, I didn't know what to get so I brought you a coke just to be safe," Remy said as he placed our drinks on the table. He glanced at me and immediately asked, "What's wrong?"

"Is that Remy?" Scott asked.

"Scott, what hospital are they taking her to?"

I heard the chime of another call coming through. It was Clara's school.

"Scott, that's the school—"

Before I could finish the sentence, he disconnected the call, and I answered the other line. The school explained the same thing that Scott said, along with which hospital she was in.

I glanced at Remy who was staring at me with concern.

"There was an emergency with Clara. Scott and the school called me. I need to go to the hospital." I began gathering my jacket and bag.

"I'll drive you," Remy offered.

I immediately shook my head. "No, that's not necess—"

I felt Remy's hand on my shoulder. "I know that's not necessary, but you look frantic. You're trying to be brave, but you can't hide it well," he said.

"Okay, drive me and I'll ride back with Scott."

It just made sense that Remy drive me to the hospital...I tried to rationalize in my head. I knew deep down that if Scott saw him, he would blow his shit.

We hightailed it out the pizzeria and made our way to the hospital, making it in record time. I was thankful that we weren't pulled over. It was like a scene out of *The Fast and the Furious*...but we were riding in a Geo Metro.

Remy and I raced to the emergency room where a pacing Scott was waiting.

He began to smile slowly when he saw me. His face immediately turned to stone when he saw Remy.

"Really, Jovi?" Scott asked as I approached.

I had a feeling that he would be upset that Remy was with me, but I also thought that being in a hospital would tame him a little bit.

"How is she?" I asked, ignoring his comment.

He eyed Remy up and down, sneering at him, practically foaming at the mouth. "She had a break in her arm."

"She broke her arm!" my voice shot up.

Remy immediately began to rub my back. I tensed up knowing that Scott was standing right in front of us.

"Remy, you can go now. This has nothing to do with you," Scott growled.

"Scott!"

"No, it's okay, Jo. I'll see you at the office." Remy played it cool as he gave me a quick hug. "Call me if you need anything," he said.

"She doesn't need anything, Remy. She's fine!" Scott barked.

Remy shook his head and left.

"What the hell is the matter with you?" I whispered, hoping that others in the ER wouldn't turn to look at us.

"With me? What's the matter with you?" Scotts voice was booming, and I felt the sting from the stares around us. "What are you doing, Jo?" he crossed his arms.

"I'm being a parent. I'm here because my daughter needs me," I said.

My voice was shaking with anger.

"No, I'm being a parent. While you're hanging out with your boyfriend, I've been trying to comfort her."

"You want a fucking medal?" I began to sarcastically give him a round of applause, knowing that it would make him angrier.

"No! I want you to be a mother!"

My body went cold.

Scotts eyes went wide; immediately regretting his choice of words.

"Jo, I'm sorry." His voice was softer.

I felt the tears burn the back of my eyeballs. "Fuck you, Scott."

"Jo, I—"

"Where is she?" I asked through clenched teeth.

I didn't wait for an answer, I pushed passed him and asked the front desk for my daughter. I found her room; my heart immediately dropped when I caught a glimpse of her cast.

"Oh no, baby, are you okay?" I asked.

I went immediately to her, trying to gently hug her without touching the cast. I couldn't stop kissing her head, the smell of her baby scented shampoo comforting me.

"I'm fine, mom. Daddy gave me a popsicle and he brought my tablet." Her small voice was muffled against my shirt. I kissed the top of her head. I kept her there until my heart settled.

"Yeah, I had it all taken care of."

I looked towards the door where Scott was leaning against, arms crossed.

"I didn't say you didn't have it taken care of," I growled.

"Are you guys going to fight again?" Clara's voice trembled above our anger.

We both answered, "No."

We looked at each other sheepishly. "I don't want to argue. I just want to be with my kid," I sighed.

"Can I talk to you outside for a minute?" Scott pointed towards the door.

I kissed Clara once more on the head and made my way out.

"What is it now, Scott? I don't know why you are so upset. I did nothing wrong, I thought we were passed all that Remy stuff."

"I'm sorry." He reached out to tuck a random strand behind my ear, but I pulled away.

"No, Scott. You don't get to call me a bad mother and in the same breath apologize."

Scott ran a hand over his face. "I know, I'm just stressed and...that's no excuse. Just let me say something."

"What?" I waited, not really expecting much.

"I'm sorry. You didn't deserve that. I was just worked up because I saw..." he closed his eyes and let out a sigh, "I saw Remy and...I don't like him."

"He's my friend," I said for the millionth time.

"I don't like him."

"We work together," I tried to explain.

"I don't like him."

"I'm not seeing Remy."

"Jovi, you can tell me he's a goddamn eunuch, and I still won't like him."

"Why?" I asked.

Scott laughed cynically. "Don't act stupid, Jo. You know why I don't like him."

"Why?"

"The guys a weasel. He's had this crush on you when we were together and he's now pursuing you."

I sighed. I don't know what I wanted to hear but it wasn't that.

"Scott, let me point something out to you. The way you acted when I came in with Remy was what I feared. How quickly you threw my insecurities back in my face. That's not what people who care about each other do."

"I know."

"Then why'd you say it?" I heard my own voice crack.

"I told you, I was thrown when I saw Remy."

"That's not it."

"What more do you want, Jo? I'm trying to be honest."

I couldn't let it go so easily. "You threw it in my face. I'm a good fucking mom, Scott. that little girl wants for nothing."

"I know," he whispered.

"Then don't make me feel like I'm not doing enough. I work, and when I get home, I'm taking care of her."

"Jovi, I know."

"Just know when I started having my moods, I didn't want to tell you because I was afraid that you would use it against me." His silence encouraged me to keep going, "This is why I kept everything to myself. Do you understand now?"

He ran a hand down his face. "Jo, I really am sorry."

"Mami. Daddy." Clara called from the room.

"Coming baby," I left Scott in the hallway to think about what just happened. How quickly we went from flirty couple to feuding exes.

The doctor came in behind me. "Hello, are you mom?"

"Yes, doctor. How long does she have to wear the cast?"

"I told your husband everything that happened. Clara fell from the monkey bars and suffered a fracture. It should be four to six weeks for recovery."

"Thank you, doctor."

She nodded. "There will be someone coming by to give you informational care packets and to help you discharge. Did you have any other questions?"

All the questions that I had compiled on the way over here, evaporated without a trace and my panic started to kick in. "Honestly, I had a billion of them before you walked in and now, I'm drawing a blank."

She chuckled softly. "It's okay, I'll be around, so if you need anything answered let me know."

"Thank you."

Scott came back into the room. "I assume you need a ride home since you came with Remy."

"Yes, I do. But if you need to go, I can call—"

"She's my daughter too, Jo. I'm driving you guys home."

The ride home was heavy with silence...that was until Clara killed it with her chatter. If her arm was hurting, she didn't show it. Every time she asked a question, either Scott or I would answer but we would never speak to each other directly.

After a very long drive, made longer by the tension, we finally made it upstairs.

I immediately went into mommy mode. "Okay, baby, why don't you relax, I'll whip something up and then we can take a bath—"

"Why don't the both of you relax and I'll make dinner," Scott interjected.

I immediately felt my body tense up; he was probably trying to make nice after the blow up in the hospital. But I wasn't going to give up that easy. For what? So, he can throw it back in my face again? So, he could tell me how I was slacking as a mother?

"No, I'm good. I can make something easy and fast." I sprinted to the kitchen and began putting pasta to cook, leaving Scott and Clara in the living room.

I had just set a pot of water on the stove when Scott came into the kitchen. "Don't you have work tomorrow?" I asked.

"Yeah, but I want to make things right between you and me."

"I'm alright," I quickly said, hoping that he would just leave.

"No, Jovi. I was out of line back at the hospital. I was just frustrated and tired and jealous. I shouldn't have said those things."

I understood the power of frustration and jealousy really well; I shrugged my shoulders. "It was a really shitty thing to say, even if you felt like crap you shouldn't have said it. I didn't deserve it." I kept my voice low but firm. I didn't want to upset Clara, in the hospital she showed how we were really affecting her, I wanted her to be okay.

"I'm sorry, Jo. I really was an asshole." He sighed. "Why don't you go shower and get comfortable. I'll watch Clara and finish dinner." His voice was gentle.

I was reluctant to concede to this, but I did.

"Okay. I won't take long," I said.

I passed our daughter on the way to the bathroom, stopping to kiss the top of her head.

The call from Scott and the school really freaked me out and I questioned a lot of things during the fifteen minutes to the hospital.

As soon as I entered the bathroom and locked myself inside; I let the events of the day finally sink in, a wave of emotion hit me, and I was too tired to stop it.

I cried the ugliest of the ugly cries; Kim Kardashian had nothing on me. If I was completely alone, I would've cried loud with heavy heaves and maybe a paper bag to assist. But I was conscious that I was not alone, and I cried silently.

It was a crazy mix of emotions; fear, anger, relief and guilt. I was never going to be a good enough mom or the wife that Scott needed me to be.

I got into the shower, spending the next fifteen minutes washing the tears way. When I had myself under control, I put on my robe and ventured into the living room.

I stood rooted in the spot; the light was dimmed, and it was quiet.

I looked around the room but no Clara.

The sound of Scotts size thirteen feet stomping down the hall startled me into action, I began to fluff a pillow on the couch although it wasn't necessary.

Scott coughed giving me no choice but to acknowledge him.

"She fell asleep while I was cooking so I put her to bed," he explained with a slight tilt of his lips.

"That's fine."

He slowly eyed the terry robe I wore.

When his eyes finally made it to mine, he nervously ran a hand down his face. "Um, I left your food on the table. I was going to head out."

Okay, maybe it was a good thing that he was leaving. It'll give me a little more time to think.

"Thank you for making dinner, you really didn't have to."

"It's not a big deal, Jo."

He didn't move to leave.

"Yes?" I asked.

"How's your exposé about us going?"

"I'm not writing it."

"Really?"

I shrugged. "When I wrote about us, I just needed to get it out my system. I was sad, frustrated, angry, disappointed...it was all bottled up."

He raised an eyebrow. "And you decided to let millions of people read it?"

I laughed. "Relax, we don't have millions of readers...just a couple of hundred thousand."

His shocked face made me smile.

The shitty confrontation from earlier began to trickle into my mind again, I felt my smile fade.

"Liz is going to watch Clara next weekend because I have to leave for work," I reminded him.

I wanted my mind to relax; it was difficult to.

When I thought we could be better, issues from the past come up.

Dr. Rubenstein says that the past should live in the past; that was easier said than done.

"Remy's going with you?"

"Yeah, Remy's coming with me," I answered.

I could see the clench of his jaw as he took in that information. "I'm not seeing Remy. He's coming along because he's the photographer," I reassured him.

Scott stepped forward and his giant hands reached out, pulling the tie allowing the robe to open, revealing the nothingness I wore underneath.

I should've covered up immediately, instead I was rooted to the spot curious of what he might do next.

His finger traced a spot on my belly, making its way down to another bluish bruise.

I felt the heat of his gaze roam back up to my face, looking for my reaction.

I leaned in, so close to his lips that he didn't need much to ignite. When I heard his groan of desire, I slapped his hand away. "You're worse than a chick," I laughed.

I snatched the tie from the robe, covering myself back up and stomping into the kitchen.

"What?" I could hear him behind me.

He sounded like he was on the verge of hysteria; trying to control his irritation.

"With your manipulation."

"Manipulation?"

"Yes, Scott. You can't be mad at me and then try to make nice and then turn me on."

He raised a thick eyebrow. "I was turning you on?"

I ignored his question. I didn't want to tell him that the way he had branded me, infuriated me and indeed turned me on.

"You marked my entire body with hickies. You revel in how they look."

"I'd be lying if I didn't say I was proud of my handiwork," he shrugged.

"You can't yell at me at a hospital, call me a bad mom and act like everything's back to normal."

"I'm so sorry, Jo. Sex was such a big thing for us, that's...that's the only way I can think to make things right in the moment."

"Scott no more mind games," I said, pointing my finger and hoping my eyes could shoot lasers at him.

His eyes began to travel again.

We both fell quiet; just the sound of our breathing as the electricity of awareness and attraction began to take over my body...but I was strong; I will not give in!

He looked up to the ceiling, just as flabbergasted as I was. "I'm sorry. I honestly don't mean to...it's just this whole situation drives me crazy, Jo. I don't want anyone but me to have you," he said.

“People don’t belong to people.” I began setting my dinner plate up and poured myself a glass of wine.

“You’re wrong, Jo. I’m not ashamed to admit that I belong to you.”

I laughed. “I want to say something slick but I’m too tired to fight.” I drop into my chair, like a noodle. “I know you said you were leaving but do you want a glass? I know I’ve been on edge since your call, I can imagine your nerves are shot too.”

“Sure.” He sprinted to a chair; probably afraid that I would change my mind.

For the next ten minutes, nothing but the sound of me eating like a bear filled the room.

“God, Jovi. When was the last time you ate?”

My eyes automatically narrowed in his direction. “Don’t start.”

“Just relax, no one’s going to eat your food,” he joked.

“You done?”

“Yeah,” he laughed bringing out the dimple in his cheek. “Is Remy really going with you?”

I ignored the question by asking my own. “How’s work going with you?”

He drank some wine, taking his time to answer. “It’s going. I’m trying to fine tune activities that will help with motor skills development.”

“You really love it, don’t you?”

He shrugged. “It has its moment. I also got the green light to develop a baseball team for the school. I’m holding tryouts later this week.”

“Baseball?”

“Don’t start,” his voice was flat.

“No! I’m actually excited for you. You’ve been trying to start a baseball team for a while.”

He squinted at me, unsure of whether to continue. “I just figured since I lost my chance at playing, might as well introduce the next generation to the game."

I smiled. "That's good thinking."

"And it's been proven that sports can complement academics, kids have better brain functions and concentration levels." He shrugged as if it were no big deal. "Even if the kids don't pursue baseball, it'd be nice to know I made some positive difference."

This was the person I hadn't seen in a while. The person who was passionate about a job he didn't know he wanted.

Scott took the job at the school because we had just gotten married and he thought that that's what I wanted from him. I just wanted him to be happy.

"Do you like your job?" I asked.

"I mean it pays the bills."

"Okay, yeah, but if you could do anything in the world what would it be?"

Scott sat back in his chair, crossing his arms, which emphasized his tatted biceps. I wanted to bite and leave marks of my own...maybe wine wasn't such a good idea.

"I would've love to be a baseball player but I'm too old now," He said with a smile.

"Okay, grandpa what would you want to do then?"

His chuckle sent chills down my spine. "I'm content with where I am. Those kids need me." I nodded my understanding. "What about you, Jovi? What would you do?"

"Be a writer. I am a writer. But I wish that it hadn't taken so long to figure out."

I went to college and graduated with a degree in psychology, which was not my passion. Tommy was the overachiever when we were kids. He set the example and I was expected to follow in his footsteps. I wanted to please my parents.

They put it in my head that I should be a social worker; I did one internship before realizing that wasn't for me. By then it was too late. Instead of switching majors I decided to finish my last semester and graduate.

Scott listened to my frustrations back then; I didn't have to explain my answer to him.

Scott looked at his phone. "It's getting late. You'll call me if Clara needs anything?"

"Of course. I wouldn't keep her from you," I assured him.

Scott was still Clara's father; although he and I had problems, our beautiful daughter had nothing to do with it.

I followed Scott to the door.

He hesitated before opening the door; pulling me close, making me aware that I only had a robe.

He reached out to tuck a wayward strand behind my hair like he used to do. My body came to life under his touch.

I wanted his masculinity, but my mind brought me to reality. "Scott, don't."

With a chaste kiss on the top of my head; He let go of me and made his way out.

I closed the door behind him.

As if on cue, my phone began to ring.

I ran to where the phone laid on the kitchen counter. "What's up, Liz?"

"My niece broke her arm and all you can say is what's up Liz?!" her voice rose with each word.

"Relax, we're home. The doctor says it should heal in a couple of weeks."

"Mom and dad are going to be mad that you didn't tell them."

I sat on my couch; a question came to mind. "Liz, if mom and dad don't know, how did you find out?"

She cleared her throat with nervousness. "That's not the point."

"Could it be that you found out from some tall, lean, handsome guy with a beard that I caught you making out with at mom and dad's house?"

"God, take a breath. "

There was something going on between the two, I'd be dumb not to notice. But Aaron was a sore spot for her so getting information was like pulling teeth. "What's going on with you and Aaron? Aren't you engage? To someone the family hasn't even met?"

She sighed. "I'm still engaged and there's nothing going on with Aaron."

"Okay."

"It's just...this primal attraction, nothing to do with his personality," she explained.

"Okay."

"Just like you and Scott, right?"

I should've known she'd find a way to bring it back to me.

"I'm not talking about it, Liz."

"We have too."

"Why?" I felt a migraine coming on, so I went to pour myself another glass of wine.

"Because he marked your body. If that's not a sign of marking one's territory...I don't know what is."

I chugged my wine because my sister was annoying me with questions I didn't want to answer. "Shut up, Liz."

"Dogs usually pee to mark their territory, so let's be happy he didn't do that...unless you're into that."

"That's so gross," I laughed in spite of myself.

"Some people like it."

My sister always knew how to bring me out of my mood. "Hey, can you work from home a couple days?" Liz's job as a make-up artist allowed her to travel and make up her own schedule.

"Maybe, what do you need?"

This was Scotts weekend off from watching Clara, I didn't want to bother him. My family was always helpful babysitters whenever I needed it and I was always grateful for that.

"I have to go away this weekend for work, could you watch your niece?"

"Yes," she answered with no hesitation.

"Thank you."

"You know I have no problem with it but why don't you ask Scott? He's the dad."

"I know this but—"

"He sexed you down and you don't know how to act."

I gave a heavy sigh at her response because it was true. Sex was a mistake. Period. I didn't want to be at his mercy.

"You know what you need?" Liz asked, bringing me out of my thoughts.

"To go to bed?" I groaned as I laid on the couch wondering what the best way was to hang up on Liz.

"You need a dildo."

"Goodnight, Liz."

I was about to hang up when her voice came through, "Jo! Listen to me, hear me out. You get yourself a grade A dildo and sex yourself down and you won't think about Scott."

I know that Liz's reasoning was ridiculous, but it was also a fun way to distract my mind. "Fine. We'll go to the sex shop and pick something up."

She laughed. "Yay! Okay, text me when you're free. Maybe we'll go before you leave on your work trip."

"Okay. Love you, sis."

"Love you more."

I hung up; the weight of what happened today making my body melt onto the couch. What the hell is my life?

15

Jovi

During the rest of the week Scott and I had minimal contact. He came to visit with Clara, and they spoke on the phone as long as her four-year-old attention span would allow her. I was leaving for Allentown, PA tomorrow, staying through the weekend.

I made it my goal to work as much I could from the office, pick Clara up from school and spend as much time as I could with her before I left.

It was the afternoon before I had to leave, and I had some time before I had to pick up Clara. I decided to meet Liz for our sex shop date. Why not bring a little bit of fun with me to my solo trip?

Although it was a gloomy fall day, I wore big heavy sunglasses.

"If you're thinking you're being inconspicuous with those shades, you're actually drawing more attention to yourself," Liz said skeptically.

"I just don't want anyone to see me," I said.

"Don't nobody know you! You write one little story about your divorce and you think you're famous." Liz shook her head.

"I'm just not comfortable being here," I admitted.

"Damn, Jovi."

"What?"

"What happened to you? You used to be so fun," she said grimly.

"I grew up, got married and became a mother."

"That doesn't mean anything, I know a lot of mom's who are freaks. I bet half the moms at school have more than a drawer full of dildos."

I gagged at the thought. If you knew those mom's, you'd gag to.

Walking into the store was overwhelming to say the least. The store was as if Christian Grey himself owned the place; there were overhead T.V. screens playing the latest gangbang, all kinds of whips and chains, inflatable dicks hung from the ceiling in an array of color...like the weirdest rainbow I've ever seen.

I felt the heat rise to my face; I was thankful to have my shades on.

Liz guided me to a giant wall full of dildos of every size, color and texture. I looked up at the giant sign above.

"The wall of love?" I read.

Liz laughed next to me. "Isn't it great?"

"Do you come here often?" I asked.

"Not often enough," she sighed.

"Hello ladies, how can I help you?" we both jumped in surprise.

We were approached by an elderly lady; a mix between Dr. Ruth and Betty White...but with bright pink hair.

"Oh, I'm sorry. I didn't mean to startle you," the little old lady apologized.

I laughed nervously. "Oh, it's fine. You...work here?"

"Work here? This is my store," she declared proudly.

"Yaaas, girl!" Liz gave her approval.

The owner smiled wide with pride. "What are you girls looking for?"

My embarrassment kept me silent while Liz was a chatterbox. "My sister here needs a new companion to get over her ex-husband who she can't stop sleeping with."

"Been there, done that," Betty Ruth said with a conspiratorial wink.

"Good, so you get it. What would you recommend?" Liz asked, genuinely intrigue by this whole situation.

The Betty Ruth eyed the wall of love. "You said the last piece you had was your ex-husband, how was the size?"

"E-excuse me?" I looked at Liz who was moving in closer to hear my answer.

"Well, you clearly enjoy your ex-husband, let's try to get you something that you like," she explained.

I quickly pointed towards my selection, which came in a pretty pink color.

They both looked at me with raised eyebrows with surprise, shock...envy?

"Oh, no wonder you went back," the owner wiggled her eyebrows before giving me another wink.

"And what about you honey?" the owner asked, addressing Liz.

Liz began to shake her head. "I have a whole drawer full of these guys, every shape, size...you name it, I got it."

"Well, if you girls need anything else, let me know. I got a sale going on stimulating gel I know you girls would love. Buy two get one free." She left us to stare after her in amazement.

Liz spoke first. "I hope I'm that bad ass when I'm her age."

I laughed. "Can we go now?"

"Come on, let's browse. I need new restraints anyways."

I closed my eyes. "Please, don't tell me anymore."

Forty-five minutes later, after Liz stocked up on the things that she said she needed and made me cringe and blush, I made it to Clara's school for pick up.

I felt the other mom's stares as I helped my four-year-old with a cast into the car; it's like they knew where I just came from and what I was planning on doing tonight.

I gave them a look that hopefully translated to, *please fuck off. I have a bag full of sex toys and I'm not afraid to use them.*

I pulled into the parking lot of our apartment complex to see Scott leaning against his car.

The way he was dressed automatically had me salivating; now I knew how Pavlov's dogs must've felt.

Scott's polo shirt hugged his tatted biceps in the best way; showcasing how great they looked.

"What are you doing here?" I asked.

"Daddy!" Clara ran up to Scott, hugging him as best she could.

"Hey, baby girl!" he bent to hug her back. When he looked up, he noticed I was pulling grocery bags out the car.

"I can help you with that."

"No, it's okay. I got it."

At that moment, one of the bags ripped, dropping all its contents on the floor. Scott immediately bent down to help me pick everything up, pausing when he began to exam a bright pink box.

Scott held onto the package with his big hands; eyes wide, tilting his head in question.

It would've been hilarious if I wasn't completely mortified. I felt the heat rise to my cheeks.

Clara's voice came from behind him. "What's that daddy?"

I snatched it from his hands, hoping Clara didn't see anything.

"Gimme that," I whispered.

"Having rough nights?"

"My nights aren't your concern."

His flirty grin dissolved into seriousness as we finished picking up everything.

The three of us marched upstairs with Clara filling Scott in on her day. I was aware that Scott had the bag with my new sex goodies. I also knew that he wasn't going to let the subject drop.

"Okay, baby girl. I'll help you take off your uniform and then it's homework time."

"And then dance party?" She asked, her brown eyes as big as saucers.

"Yup, dance party." I nodded.

"Dance Party?" Scott asked while placing the groceries on the table.

"Yeah, me and mommy have dance parties with lights and everything." Clara ran to her room to drop her bookbag off.

I could feel Scotts eyes on me. "It's just to tire her out some more before bed," I replied.

He laughed. "That'll do it."

"Are you staying for dinner?" I asked.

******

Scott

Was I staying for dinner?

After seeing what she had in one of the bags, I wanted to stay for dessert. I wanted to show her there was no need for that sex toy.

I knew that that wasn't the right response.

"Nah, I just wanted to see that you guys were alright. You're leaving tomorrow?" I asked.

"Yeah. Early morning, I'm driving down."

I wanted to ask if Remy was really going but I knew that would cause more problems, so I kept that question to myself. I hated the way I snapped at her at the hospital and how that made her feel. I kept my distance during the week so we could both get our bearings.

I thought I had all my bearings until I began taking out the groceries out the bag. Instead of finding fruits and vegetables, I pulled out bottles of lube, a pocket rocket and handcuffs.

I lifted the cuffs out of the bag with one pinky. "Damn, Jovi. what the hell? Did you buy out the place?" I asked.

I was slightly mortified because...well, why the hell did she buy this stuff? Who was she handcuffing?

I was also slightly aroused, which did me no good.

The last time I handcuffed her, she had a panic attack, kicking the nightstand, spraining her toe and sending the key flying. It took me an hour to find it, while she was crying hysterically.

She snatched the handcuffs from me, hiding it back in the bag. "I didn't buy that. Liz, threw it in the bag to be funny."

"And the dildo?" I asked.

Her eyes didn't quite meet mine. "No...no, that I bought."

I felt myself begin to stiffen with the image of Jovi using the toy.

Stop thinking about your wife sexing herself! My mind screamed.

I cleared my throat for lack of a better transition. "You nervous about the interviews tomorrow?"

Jovi began looking in the kitchen drawers. "No, not really. That's the least of my worries."

She pulled a menu out.

I sat down at the table. "What are you worried about?"

She shrugged. "I'm worried that I won't do these stories justice." At that moment our eyes finally connected.

The electricity that was always there, intensified.

"You're a great writer, Jo. There's no doubt in my mind that this won't be great."

I don't know if I imagined it, but I thought her eyes began to well up. "Thanks, Scott."

"No, problem. I wouldn't say it, if it weren't true."

"Um...you can stay for dinner if you like." She waved the menu. "I'm ordering pizza."

"I'll stay," I quickly answered before she changed her mind.

"How's the tryouts?"

I smiled thinking about the fourth and fifth graders who tried out; some were athletically inclined; most were not as coordinated. "It was interesting. It's hard to tell kids they didn't make the team. I'm trying to come up with ways to have kids involved even if they're not playing."

"You'll figure it out."

It's been a long time since we sat at the dinner table; no TV, no phones. It felt amazing to sit and talk without picking fights or getting into an argument.

Conversation was safe; Jovi made sure of that. It was all about Clara's school, picture day, homework, friends; laughing at Jovi's impression of Clara's principal, who approached Jovi about donating her time or money to the school.

"She likes you more than she likes me!" she laughed.

"What?" I laughed with her.

"Oh, come on, Scott."

"What?"

"Every time she sees you, she has to primp. It's probably the tattoos, that's what got me." She laughed.

"Oh, really?" I was surprised at the admission. Jovi didn't even realize what she said, she just continued to laugh. Her smile was wide, reaching her eyes, cheeks flushed with laughter and amusement. She was beautiful. She was relaxed. And in that moment, I wanted her more than anything.

Clara's little fingers traced the outline of the tombstone tattoo that I had on my arm. "I think they're cool. When I'm old like you, I want one."

That sobered me up. "Who you calling old?"

Jovi continued laughing.

We laughed and ate until we were so stuffed from dinner and it took too much energy to do anything else except sit there.

Jovi wiped the tears from her face. “It’s time to get ready for bed.”

Clara jumped up to change into her P.J.’s, while I got up to clean up the table. “Scott, you don’t have to do that. I know you probably need to go home.”

“I need to be here.”

“Scott...I—” Jovi immediately closed up when Clara came running.

“Mami, I need help putting this on.”

I clapped my hands together to get their attention. “Get her dressed, I’ll clean up. Then it’s dance party time.”

A shadow of a smile appeared on Jovi’s face. “Meet us in the room.”

Minutes later, I walked into Clara’s room which was glowing with multicolor lights.

“Wow, this really is a party.”

“Mom bought a disco ball.” Clara pointed to the center of the room at a glowing ball.

I could see Jovi from the corner of my eye. I turned to see her press the speaker on; the intro to *Let’s Groove Tonight* came on.

“Oh, so this is a funky party,” I said.

I began to do a little two-step; never fully realizing until this moment that I probably looked like one of those middle-aged dads that I always used to make fun of.

Jovi began to shimmy while Clara began to spin around her.

This. Was. Amazing.

I stopped; overwhelmed at the sight of it all.

“You can’t just stand there, you have to dance,” Jovi laughed.

Her eyes sparkled under the glow of the disco lights; her hair bouncing around like a colorful lion’s mane.

“Dance, daddy! Dance, daddy!” Clara yelled.

I pushed back the regrets that began to creep in—the long work-days that made me too exhausted to do things like this with my girls, the boy’s night I preferred instead of hanging with Jo, the arguments

I refused to have with Jo because I thought no conflict meant all was fine.

The realization hit me; I gave Jovi the ultimatum to sink or swim, giving her all the responsibility of being a parent when she needed me the most, and then I bailed. I let her handle Clara, her job and just about everything else. While I tried to indulge in a social life that I thought I had been missing.

Smiling, Jovi reached out for me and we began to dance.

Instinctively, my hands went to Jovi's waist moving her along to the beat. I spun a laughing Jovi around, giving Clara enough time to cut in.

"Oh, no she didn't," Jovi joked.

"Oh, yes she did," I laughed as I took my daughters hand and swung her all over the place, doing my best not to bump her injured arm.

I looked at Jovi who was clapping her hands to the beat. This is what I wanted.

The song was coming to an end.

Although we were having a good time, Jovi looked as if she were lost in space; she was physically here but mentally somewhere else.

I tilted my chin in her direction. "You okay?"

"Yeah, just got lost in thought." She put her hands on her hips to help steady her breathing. Jovi flashed a mega-watt smile at our daughter. "Okay, now it's time for bed."

"Aww, man." Clara began to pout but climbed into bed anyway.

"I love you, kid." Jovi bent down and placed a kiss on our daughter's head.

"Love you, too."

"Say goodnight to daddy."

Clara's big chocolate eyes landed on me. "Love you, daddy. Good night."

"Good night, baby."

I kissed her before making my way out the room, leaving Jovi to tuck our daughter in.

"That was a lot of fun," I said as I heard Jovi's soft footsteps.

"Yeah, it really was," she whispered.

"Can I ask you a question?"

"You can ask it; I don't promise that I'll answer it."

"Why can't we do this every night? Why can't we be a family?" I asked. I felt the emotion rise in my throat; I wanted my family back so bad that it hurt.

"We are a family, Scott." she shrugged. "We're just not together."

"Why?" I asked.

Her eyebrows narrowed. "Why what?" she asked.

"Why aren't we together?"

It took everything in me to not take her into my arms and just hold her.

Her big round eyes and long lashes, wild hair, creamy skin, full lips and a hint of the hickies I left on her neck was what I wanted more than anything.

Jovi stood there playing with a broken nail— silent.

I swallowed the lump in my throat. "I have to go," I said.

"What do you want me to say? You know why we aren't together, having to keep saying it, hurts me more than you know." Her voice cracked and my guilt came back in full force.

As much as I wanted to stay, I hated that I was pushing myself onto Jovi.

There was only so much that I could do.

If she was reluctant to meet me halfway then why should I continue?

I stopped in front of the door and turned around. "I need your contact info, just in case there's any emergencies."

Although Liz was going to watch Clara, I wanted to have a way to reach Jo if something went wrong.

She walked to her desk in front of the living room window and took out a piece of paper. "Thanks for reminding me. I wrote it down earlier."

I clutched the paper tight.

"Night, Jo."

16

Scott

At work, we had early dismissal today to conduct teacher meetings. All departments sat in the cafeteria, going on about the rest of the school year and mid-term progress. It was one of those dull days where concentration was hard to hold on to. On a normal teacher meeting day, I would fight to keep my eyes open. I'd have to be careful or I would drool on my notebook and snoring would commence right after.

But today was different.

It was difficult to focus on anything, let alone sneak in a nap, because I felt Kim's eyes boring into my back which forced me to focus on my notes just a bit harder than usual. My eyes felt sore and tired as I kept reading the same line over and over again.

Aaron, who was seated on the bench next to me, lightly shouldered me in an attempt to get my attention. "You okay?"

"I'm fine."

"You're focusing really hard on that chicken scratch," he persisted.

"I'm just concentrating on baseball practices," I whispered, trying to ignore him. "Aren't you supposed to submit copies of your midterms? Why aren't you focusing on that?"

My mood was foul. I couldn't stop thinking about Jovi. The way we left things last night just felt like the end.

"What's wrong with you? You're not trying to ignore Kim who's been trying to grab your attention?"

"Nope," I pinched the bridge of my nose. Aarons line of questioning pushed me past annoyed.

"Just making sure."

I decided to sneak a peek at Kim to see if she was still looking my way.

Shit! She was.

I shifted my gaze back to my notes. I hope she didn't notice; I prayed that she didn't try to start a conversation with me. We've been keeping our distance and have literally said no words to each other since that damn morning when Jovi showed up to my place.

If I was called to the office I would ask Aaron to scope it out for me in advance just to avoid any interaction with her. So immature of me but my anxiety spiked up a couple notches anytime I was near the woman. It's my own fault.

Making eye contact was a bad idea because now Kim was headed in my direction; the hard set of her jaw told me that it had nothing to do with work.

"Hey, Scott. You got a sec?" her voice was low, Aaron pretended he was playing with his phone, but I knew his ears were opened.

I looked around the cafeteria, checking to see if the other teachers would see that things were different between us. No one on the faculty mentioned Jovi's article, I assumed I was in the clear, but you never knew. "Uh, yeah, sure. What's up?"

"I wanted to see if you wanted to hang out tonight...you know just the two of us." Kim was dressed down today in jeans, but men still noticed her...like Aaron, who was looking over his phone at her.

I cleared my throat and looked her directly in the eye so that there would be no misunderstanding. "Listen, Kim...I don't think that would be a good idea," I said, making sure that I kept my voice low enough so no one could overhear.

Her eyes narrowed as she pouted. "Why? You and Jovi aren't together."

I began to nod in agreement. "Technically, you're right, but I'm trying to work things out with Jovi."

During the time that Kim and I were friends, I never wondered *what if*; I loved Jovi more than anything...despite all the nonsense we were going through.

I found myself in a staring contest with Kim. Images of her going crazy in front of the entire school made me begin to panic.

"I want to work things out with Jovi," I reiterated in hopes that my words would sink in this time.

"We can hang out...just as friends?" she asked.

"If I'm being honest...I don't think that's a good idea either."

"Why?" her perfectly shaped eyebrows gathered together as her annoyance bubbled to the surface.

"Because you sent me a nude selfie," I whispered. "You slept over my mother's house and tried to start something the next morning. I don't want you to think there's something here when there's not."

Before she could answer, my phone began to ring; I've never been so happy for a distraction. I looked down at the number. "I'm sorry but I need to take this."

With her cheeks flaming red, she turned on her heels making sure everyone saw her leave as she click clacked out of the meeting.

I got stares from other teachers; I felt the beads of sweat begin to form at my temples.

"Hey, Tommy what's up?" I answered the call, ignoring the others around me.

"Just wanted to see if you want to hang out tonight."

Hang out? I wanted to scream hell yeah, but I didn't want to come off too desperate. Tommy and I were close before everything went down. One of the downsides to divorce was that not only do you divorce your spouse but it felt like you divorced the family as well. I was an only child and Tommy was like a brother to me. It felt awkward reaching out to him because he was Jovi's brother; that automatically put him on team Jovi.

I honestly missed him.

"Yeah, sure, buddy. I could use a drink."

"Please don't call me buddy. That just sounds awkward and I'm not into it," he said.

I laughed. "So, we'll meet at our spot?"

"God, yes!"

An hour later, I made it to our usual spot called *the Dirty T*, a strip club that we discovered during my bachelor party that we kept coming back to because we loved the wings. With its dim lighting, wood paneling, red vinyl seating, and sticky floors, it wasn't the classiest of places. Its VIP section was nothing more than a curtained off room with a couple of red velvet booths.

The two of us made small chit chat until Tommy dropped a bare chicken bone on his plate.

"So, you and my sister...what's the deal?" he turned to look at me; the same big eyes as Jovi.

I took a swig of beer, hoping to buy time as I tried to think of an answer.

"There's no deal. We didn't work out..." I shrugged.

"Well, I saw the big fucking hickey on her neck, she said it was you."

I took another wing in an attempt to seem unfazed by his line of questioning. "Oh, yeah?"

"Yeah, so are you guys seeing each other or are is it just sex?"

I looked at him out the corner of my eye. "I don't know if I should talk to you about this, Jo is your sister."

"I know but the both of you are being dumb. You obviously

have this attraction." My minutes long silence encouraged Tommy to continue. "She moved in with you two weeks after you met! That was fifteen years ago."

He was right. Jo and I were crazy about each other from day one; we stayed holed up in my apartment having sex, talking about everything and anything under the sun, and back to having more sex. When we hit the two-week mark and she had to start her semester, she began to pack the little belongings she brought over, and I suggested that maybe she just move in.

Jovi jumped for joy and we lived in a studio apartment in the worse neighborhood in New York city... it was some of the best years of my life.

I sighed. "Listen, I love your sister."

"I know."

"But..." How do I explain this? "I don't know what to do."

"You gotta show her you still want her," he said like I didn't already know that.

I threw my hands up in the air. "I have! I tried! But she doesn't want anything to do with me!"

He rolled his eyes. "A couple of hickies and a great time dancing doesn't tell her you want her back, it tells her you want what you think a family should be."

"She told you about the dancing?"

"I'm her brother..." his look of sympathy began to irk me. "You know Jo is not like other girls."

"I know that." My voice came out a little harsher than I intended.

"Okay, you know that. Just...do something that says you miss her as a person."

"I thought going over and cooking—"

He put his hand up to stop my words. "I'm going to stop you right there. Jo doesn't care about that stuff."

"Oookay." I was beginning to wonder if he was going to tell me what she was into because I apparently didn't know what the hell I was doing.

Before he could continue, one of the dancers, dressed in nothing but rhinestone pasties and a thong walked over to us. "You guys looking for a good time?"

Tommy scrunched his face. "Oh, sorry, sweetie but no...just no." He waved his hands, trying to shoo her away.

Ignoring him, she began to move her hips along to the music. "I'm sorry but no." The strippers face fell to a pout. "Oh, no. it's nothing against you!" Tommy reached into his pocket and handed her singles. "Here, for your troubles."

She looked down at the bills in her hands. "Thanks?"

"Have a goodnight." Tommy turned his back on the dancer. "Like I was saying, Jovi wants to feel a connection with you, other than sex. Let's be honest, when the sex wears off...which we know it has..." he stabbed me with his finger and continued to enlighten me, "She wants to know you will be around, loving her for her. What made you guys special before?"

I sat back exhausted with what he was saying. Tommy was right. I know that Jo wanted something on a deeper level. We let each other down in the past; now we need to bring each other up.

I need to make the first move.

The first REAL move.

What that entailed? I had no idea. I just know it had to be that thing that reconnected us.

Tommy and I went back to eating more wings when another dancer approached us. "Hey, boys—"

Tommy gave her no chance. "I'm sorry, sweetie but we're here just for the wings, but..." he went into his pockets again and pulled out more singles. "...here's a little something for your troubles."

The dancer took the money and walked away.

"You know the wings are costing us more here because you're tipping the girls for nothing."

Tommy turned to me appalled. "For nothing? These girls have kids or working their way through college or both...if I want to enjoy these wings, I have to tip them too. I can't just sit here—"

"Okay, I get it."

"They just make the best damn wings," Tommy huffed.

17

Jovi

While Remy was taking photos of the women we were interviewing, I scanned my questions for the millionth time. Although I did this for a living, it didn't stop the nerves from coming.

This was the first time I was asked to do a part two for one of my stories; this was a big opportunity for me.

I was being asked to take on societal norms, sexism, chauvinism, women's rights; there was also the responsibility of presenting the lives of these women in a way that everyone involved would be proud of.

The pressure was on.

There's a certain tattooed man that you know, who you are still married to, that knows how to calm you down. The little voice inside my head was a a fickle bitch who continuously made me think about Scott. The bags under my eyes where my only consolation prize.

I closed the notes app on my phone and fiddled with the idea of calling Scott. My finger hovered over the call button...

"The questions haven't changed," Remy's voice startled me out of my thoughts.

I quickly tucked my phone into my back pocket and busied myself with looking over the printed pages of notes that I had on hand. “Questions?"

"Yeah, you keep looking at your phone," he pointed out.

I shrugged. "I know...I’m just nervous. I’ve never been this nervous before.”

Remy laughed. “You’ll be fine.” He pointed towards the ladies. “I’m done with the group shots if you want to start the next round of interviews.”

“Okay." I smiled, showing that I was happy to be here and not busy thinking about a gentle giant that I was beyond confused about.

It took everything I had to stifle my yawn. It had been a long day. We conducted four interviews so far; I still had two more to go.

Three long hours later we wrapped for the day. I practically ran to my hotel room. To say that I was exhausted was an understatement; I was fucking done.

I had just taken off my jacket when a knock sounded on the door. I exhaled heavy because I had a pretty good idea who it was.

I didn’t want to deal with his unrequited love.

All I wanted was a relaxed night in with...my new vibrator. I knew that would kill the sexual tension I had left over from Scott and it'll also relieve the heavy tension that I felt all over my body. I attempted to use it this morning but was so embarrassed all alone in the room with the buzzing sound I knew the other guests could hear that I threw it on the nightstand in defeat. But I was determined to relax tonight.

I opened the door; my heart catching in my throat.

“Scott, what are you doing here? Is Clara okay?” I looked behind him into the hall, not really knowing what I was looking for.

“If she wasn’t okay you think I’d waste time by driving all the way to the Allentown, PA to tell you?”

I stepped back to let him in. “So, if our kid is okay, what are you doing here?”

I closed the door and crossed my arms, hoping that would show that I was being serious.

With his hands in his pockets, Scott looked around the room. "I...um...I..."

"Just spit it out, Scott." Exhaustion, hunger and desire making me more impatient by the second.

"I want to take you out for dinner tonight," he sheepishly admitted. He rubbed the back of his neck and I bit the inside of my cheek to keep from smiling.

This was unexpected.

"You want to take me to dinner? Why?" I asked back to encourage him to continue. Because in reality, I wanted him to continue. I didn't know what his words would reveal, if they would bandage some wounds, but I was eager to hear.

"What do you mean why? Because I...I didn't like the way we ended things last time. I didn't want to give you a week to flake on me," he answered with a sly grin, bringing my focus to his full lips.

I felt the electricity coarse through my body. I was reluctant to acknowledge it but in the same turn I wanted to dig deeper into it. My chest heaved with just the thought of our lips touching. *I really needed to get a grip.*

"I have to get up super early tomorrow."

"So, you don't want dinner? You gotta eat." He grinned. "What do you say? I saw a Chinese buffet down the road."

He stood rigid, unmoving; his eyes pleading with me to say yes. I wanted to say yes!

But, in the back of my mind, all the lonely nights, the arguments, the tears...slowly clouded my thoughts. "Why are you frowning?" his voice was low.

I shook my head to clear the doubt. *He travelled to see you*. "It's nothing...fine."

"Fine?"

"Fine!" I did my best to sound indignant, but a giggle escaped my lips as I grabbed my jacket again.

Scotts eyebrows were raised so high in surprise, they blended with his hairline. "Was that a laugh?"

"Absolutely not. I don't know what you're talking about," I teased as I walked passed him towards the door.

I dared another glance at Scott; dressed down in jeans and a t-shirt and he still managed to look yummy. I sighed and let the butterflies in the pit of my stomach takeover.

His cocky grin assured me that he caught me checking him out. "Like what you see?" He slowly sauntered over, stopping right in front of me.

I was thirsty. Parched!

I would fuck him here and now if he so much as touched me with one finger and he knew it. "Jo?"

"Hmmm?"

He lowered himself; his lips a breath away from mine. "Let's go eat."

I slowly nodded but didn't move. Scott raised one eyebrow in silent question. I grew angry at myself. I spun on my heel and stomped out the door.

I wanted sex so bad. I wanted sex with Scott so bad. I just didn't want to muddle whatever unspoken truce we came to. Sex would complicate things and it made me angry that I wanted to give him my body but not my trust.

There it was.

The truth was like the cold shower I needed.

We were silent in the elevator. Our eyes connected through the reflection the the metal doors but we didn't say a word. The awareness that filled the elevator was almost unbearable. There was no doubt in my mind that Scott knew I was horny.

"Don't look at me like that," he chastised.

"Like what?"

"Like I should stop the elevator and give you what you want."

"And you're so sure that you know what I want?"

"Babe, I could tell as soon as I walked through the door." He smirked, revealing the dimples on his cheeks. Before I could make the first move, he stopped me. "Don't do it, Jovi. I want us to have a good time tonight. I don't want to confuse you more than what you are," he added.

"How do you know if I'm confused?"

The elevator doors opened. "Because I know you." He held the door open and waited for me to walk through. "You coming?"

We walked out into the quiet lobby to the car, not saying a word. *He doesn't know me,* I thought to myself. *He doesn't know me now.*

The five minute drive to the restaurant was also accompanied by silence. *I wonder what he was thinking about?* I snuck a glance; Scott was relaxed, cool...sexy. His hands on the steering wheel were big...long...*Enough, Jovi!*

I practically jumped out of the small car and power walked to the restaurant. The smell of dumplings greeted us when we walked in, making my stomach growl. I didn't realize how hungry I was.

As the waitress guided us to a table, I took in the restaurant; it was huge, quiet. Red and gold were the main colors for the décor.

The buffet itself showcased everything from dumpling and rice to French fries and pizza.

After placing our drink orders, we headed over to the buffet.

Our eyes met over the steaming fried rice.

"Yes, Jovi?" he asked, his smile was wide as if he knew what I was thinking about.

"Nothing." I continued adding to my plate. "Just hungry."

"I bet." My head shot up, ready to fire back something witty but no words came out. "Good thing we're here then," he added with a wink.

We made it back to our table, where after a few minutes of mutual feasting, a random thought popped into my head.

“Remember that time we went to that couples’ resort and we were the only couple who wasn’t of retirement age?”

He smiled wide, showing his teeth that were corrected by the best dentist in East Harlem.

Scott nodded. “Of course, I remember. You wouldn’t let me live it down.”

“Imagine my surprise—”

“Here we go again,” he sat back, letting me rant.

“—When we pull up to a rundown resort in the Poconos and everyone,” I squinted at him for effect. “Everyone was old enough to be our great grandparents!”

“Your point?”

“This has kind of that same vibe,” I finished.

Scott squinted right back at me. “You had a great time then, right?”

“Of course, I did! No one said I didn’t.” I giggled.

“Alright, then. It was all I could afford back then,” he confessed.

Back then we only cared about spending every free moment together. We did archery, took a pottery class, got massages and when the old folks went to bed, we skinny dipped in the lake that was nearby.

His smile brought the laugh lines in his eyes.

“You wanted my company today, huh?” I asked as I popped another dumpling in my mouth.

I saw a faint blush flush his face. “Yeah, I did.”

"And how's it going?" I asked the question knowing that he was enjoying it. I just needed to hear him say it.

“Better than I expected,” he said with a satisfied nod.

“What do you mean?” I played the scraps of food left on my plate. I felt my insides start to twist with fear of a wrong answer that would change this night for the worse...or it could be heartburn from the Chinese food.

His answer could be a good one. Scott drove hours just to have dinner with me. Maybe I should let down my guard a little bit.

"It's nice talking to you without getting into an argument or having something thrown at my head."

Be nice to hime, Jovi. "I get how not having objects thrown at you can might put you at ease."

"You think?" he asked with a raised eyebrow.

"It's a new year, new me." I took a sip of my cheap wine to hide my amusement. It all reminded me of when we first started dating; the banter, the spark, the love.

Scott laughed. "We're in the middle of October...the year's almost done!"

"It takes some people a little longer to get into that mindset." I took another sip.

"You're right, it does."

His reply settled heavy around us. Was he talking about us? Our marriage? It was tough for me to not read into it. That night at the apartment, in reminding him why we weren't together, I reminded myself. *He cheated.*

His phone buzzed on the table and I couldn't stop myself from thinking, was that Kim?

Scott didn't glance at his phone. The playfulness of the night vanished in an instant and I was ready to go.

"I need to head back. I have to finish the interviews in the afternoon, but I wanted to sleep in, it's been a long day."

He frowned but nodded. "Yeah, of course." He called the waitress and asked for the check. I began to take my wallet out; ready to pay for my portion of the meal.

Scott placed a hand on top of mine. "No, it was my idea for coming out."

"But...I'll pay for half." If he paid for it all he would consider this a date. He would have the upper hand.

"No, Jo, I insist."

I looked at the hard set of his jaw. Scott knew something happened. *He doesn't know me.*

"Okay." I put my wallet away, he paid the bill. The five minute drive back was polar opposite of earlier in the night. No longer was I fantasizing about Scott's hands or the delish things he could do to my body. We drove back to the hotel in silence. A calm before the storm because in all honesty, it felt like something was brewing and...I was to blame.

The elevator ride was devoid of any flirtatious banter. I strode down the corridor with Scott right behind me, if felt as if we were walking to battlefield.

When we got to my door, I turned to ask, "Did you get a room here?"

He shook his head. "No. I'm driving back home tonight." Time stood still for a second as we stood in front of the door. Scott's lips formed a grim line across his face. "What happened?" he asked in a whisper.

"I'm just tired and it just—"

"Don't bullshit me."

I stood as if my spine were made of steel. Scott wanted the truth? He was going to get it. "Who text you during dinner?" I asked.

His head tilted slightly in disbelief. "Are you serious?"

"Answer the question, Scott." I fought the urge to fold my arms and tap my foot. I was ready for an argument that would blow up to a fight, but I didn't want to be accused of being aggressive. Without a word, Scott dug his phone out of his back pocket and handed it to me.

When I didn't reach for it, he shook it in front of me. "You know the passcode, just look."

Guilt washed over me. I began to shake my head as I dug out the keycard from my jacket. "It's fine."

"Jo, take the phone and look. If this helps you trust me again, then look at the phone," his voice shook with aggravation but he kept his voice low.

"Come inside, I don't want to wake anybody."

He sighed and dropped is head down. "Do we really have to argue about this now?"

"Argue? I'm not trying to argue," I insisted.

"Yes, you are Jovi. It may not think that you're not, but this will turn into an argument." The door closed behind us and he tried to hand over his phone again. "Jo, I really don't want to argue."

"I don't want to either."

"Why then, after a pleasant dinner you want to pick an argument?"

"I—"

"Yes, you are. I just wanted tonight to be good—"

"Scott, I wasn't—"

He pointed a finger at me. "Yes, you are."

"Get your finger out my face." I felt my face flush with anger.

"Fine, Jovi. This is the way you want it? Then I'm gone." Scott began to open the door.

That made my uncontrollable anger shoot through the roof. "Scott, why are you walking away? Typical!"

Scotts hand dropped from the doorknob. "Bullshit, Jovi! I didn't walk away from anything! You did!" He stopped, visibly trying to calm his voice.

I shook my head. "You were gone before I even asked for the divorce." I felt the sting of tears.

"Why, Jovi?!" his voice cracked. "Why does it always turn into an argument?" His face softened. "And for the record it was your brother who text me."

I felt the uncontrollable urge to make him stay. It hit me like a wave. I needed him to stay and fight. I walked up to him and took his face in my hands. I placed a soft kiss, but he pulled away from me.

"Stop, Jovi. You can't be mad at me and then try to kiss me. Isn't that what you accused me of doing?" he looked so lost for words. "What do you want? Because I know what I want."

I stood there feeling the sting of rejection, but Scott was right. I couldn't manipulate him as I accused him of doing before.

There were a thousand replies flying through my mind, not one could find its way out.

With a wide-stance, hands on hips, Scott looked like a defeated superhero. "Fine. I'll tell you what I want. I want us. I want us together. I want us to be a team, to be a unit. I want us to be easy," he confessed. The words spilling out of him like a running faucet.

I, on the other hand—a writer, a woman of words—still couldn't say anything. My mind was too busy processing flashbacks; from the day we met up until this point in our lives. Everything in between felt like a dream losing its magical qualities.

I felt the emotion in my throat and the tears well up, burning the back of my eyeballs, but I refused to let them fall. I willed them to stay back; will they listen? That was a whole different story.

"Scott..." My voice cracked and I cleared my throat. "I want us to be easy too. You think asking for a divorce was an easy decision for me? I was thinking about it from the moment you called me a bad mom—"

"I didn't call you a bad mom."

"We can agree to disagree. With everything that came out of your mouth that night, that's what I heard. It echoes every time I stay later at work or if I miss a PTA meeting. If I want five minutes alone, the guilt I feel is unbearable. I'm a bad mom. Then at the hospital...it hurt me." I stopped to steady my voice that had begun to shake. "Tonight, the whole phone thing...it triggered me."

Scott ran a hand down his frustrated face; fifteen years taught me that this was what he did when he wanted to be done with the conversation. "Jovi, I love you. You are my wife. I did nothing to her," he said. His tan skin flushed red. I wanted to believe his words but...it was hard.

"I was a good wife. I am a good mom. I'm more than those things. I want...I want us to be more than what we are." The tears began to fall, I couldn't stop them. "I was going through something during that time, Scott. I thought out of all people—"

"Jovi...you said nothing to me. All you said was your mood was off. How was I supposed to know?!" His voice went up a notch.

"How were you supposed to know?" I gave a humorless laugh. "You're absolutely right. How were you supposed to know? You're off the hook, you can go now."

"I've apologized, Jo." Scott took two large steps towards me, taking my hands in his. I glanced down at our intwined fingers; we still wore our wedding rings.

Scotts whole face scrunched together as if he just eaten a whole lemon. I automatically began to shake my head, trying to pull my hands out of his but he just gripped them tighter.

"You are not the boss, Jo. You can't decide when to start an argument and when to finish it!" He looked up to the ceiling. "I'm tired."

"I guess you're the boss?" I sneered in hopes that my indifference would put us out of our misery.

"Obviously, I'm not. If I was, this whole shit wouldn't be happening. We would still be together; I would be home with Clara waiting for you to come home from work."

"And we would still have the same problems."

"Maybe, maybe not."

"It's not that easy."

"Why not?!" Scott gave a deep, heavy sigh. "You know what? Don't even answer the question. You're tired. I'm tired. I'm going back home tonight. I don't know why..." he shook his head in disbelief, finally releasing my hands.

Scott turned towards the door and I began to panic.

Before he could fully open the door, I closed it. "I think you should stay," I said before I could rethink everything. I wiped the tears from my face because he was just a blur to me.

"Jo, you keep giving me mixed signals. Thank god, you're not a traffic cop because you would've caused a lot of damage."

"Get comfy, we're going to air shit out." It was like a switch went off in my head. We were both being stubborn, stuck in our views of what really happened but not seeing the other side. I wanted to see his side.

"Are you serious?" He raised an eyebrow in disbelief.

"Yes. Let's try to air everything out, but just so we don't kill each other, and the hotel doesn't send me a bill for cleaning out blood from the sheets, there will be rules," I said.

"Rules?" He folded his arms and waited for me to answer.

I took off my shoes, gave a quick nod. "As much as we might want to, there will be no shouting, no interrupting. We'll let each other speak."

"Will that be hard for you?" he asked. *He doesn't know me.*

I scowled in his direction and continued as if he didn't speak. "Also, we won't throw low blows."

"I can do that."

"Good." Scott didn't move from his spot. He looked as if he wanted to say something but he lips didn't move. "Yes?" I asked.

Scott rubbed the back of his neck, shifting his weight from one foot to the other; I found his nervousness endearing. "Jo, we tried to do this at therapy, what makes you think we can do this now?"

I paused to think about it. Scott was right. I was worried that this was a waste of time, but in order for me to trust him, we needed to do this.

"I don't want to spend every second with you being angry with…it's too exhausting to be this angry and not trusting your actions. I see you're trying…I need to try to," I confessed.

Scott's face softened. He walked over to the small sofa by the window, I took a seat on the bed right next to it.

My stomach had an uneasy feeling, hopefully it was the food and not some bad omen.

The next couple of minutes…were met with silence.

"Who's going to start?" he asked.

"I guess I will," I sighed.

"Don't be nervous."

"God, Scott. I'm not nervous. I just don't know where to start." I snapped, proving my statement false. *He didn't know me.*

"Jovi…"

"I know, Sorry. I'll watch my tone."

I knew that this was going to be hard for me; I was much more emotional than Scott.

"We already agreed that things started to change when Clara was born." I looked at him from under my lashes to see his reaction. Scott was always good with keeping his emotions under wraps. I continued. "I felt overwhelmed with everything. My body was hurting and tired. I was sleep deprived; I couldn't control my moods."

He nodded his understanding but said nothing. "I thought that you would know what to do because I didn't. When the doctor said it was sleep deprivation…I knew she was full of shit but I knew you thought I was a problem so…I didn't want to be the one to press it."

"I listened to the doctor because I didn't know what else to think," he admitted.

"I know."

"If I knew what was happening and that there was more going on, I would've done more. I wish I could've done more…I should've done more." I heard the emotion in his voice.

I nodded. "I know that now. I noticed that when you started doing more to help me. I don't want you to think I didn't notice you taking care of Clara, the house, the bills."

"Thank you...it felt like sometimes you didn't, it felt as if I was alone."

"I did notice, but I felt alone too. It was like having an evil step sister in my brain all day long. I was angry, sad...I felt hopeless."

"I'm sorry."

Scott took a deep breath, preparing himself for what he was about to say. We were hijacking our therapy sessions and trying to get to a breakthrough on our own. That was a lot of pressure. I could feel his nervous energy bursting out.

"I'm sorry, Jovi. Sorry that I didn't try to understand you...I think I was just overwhelmed to with trying to take care of Clara and—" I was about to interrupt him but was stopped by the slight raise of his eyebrow. "It's not a dig. You were trying your best, but I didn't know that then. When you went back to work, I thought it would make you feel better, but you came home more tired, angrier, moodier. That's when...I had that conversation."

My head fell back with a thud on the headboard. "The infamous conversation."

"Yeah, that one. I kind of thought I could scare you straight, snap you back. Just for the record, I never imagined myself with someone else. Ever."

"Why did you start texting with Kim?" I asked. I didn't want to leave any dysfunctional rock left unturned.

"I felt hurt that you and I weren't on the same wavelength...that was hard for me, Jo. No matter what was happening around us, WE were good."

I nodded.

"When you didn't feel good, I didn't know what to do...I didn't know how to fix it. It felt that every time I tried to bring it up, your mood would change, and I just didn't know who to turn to."

"What about Aaron?"

"Aaron always turned things into a joke or was very nonchalant about it. Then Kim texted me a question about work and that just turned into, what I thought was a friend texting another friend."

I snorted.

"Jovi..."

"Scott, you know how you said Remy always had a thing for me? Kim always had a thing for you too." Scotts mouth twisted in disbelief. "Yes! But I knew that you would always be mine. I wasn't worried."

"I didn't think she was going to send me a naked pic."

I sighed. "I was hurt. Not only did she have great looking boobs, a great looking face and her hair was always perfectly wavy! But what killed me the most was that she felt comfortable enough to send them to you." Oh god, the tears felt like hell fire as I tried to hold them back. "Did you sleep with Kim?" The question rushed out of me before fear won out.

Scott walked over, taking a seat next to me. The mattress sank from the weight of him as he reached for my hand. "Jovi, I had no intention of taking it further with Kim. I genuinely thought that she was being a friend. I did not kiss her. I did not have sex with her." I knew he was telling the truth. "I didn't even look at the picture, I erased it immediately."

I rolled my eyes. "Bullshit."

"Okay. I lied. I did look at it, but I erased it right away." I sucked my teeth at him, making him sigh in return. "I looked but I didn't text back. I didn't even talk to her when I went back to work...which was very hard because the school isn't so big. She's literally in the main office that's a few doors down from the gym. I've found ways to avoid that office."

Despite my melancholy, I laughed.

"It's not funny."

I shrugged. "It's a little funny."

"Why is it funny?"

"I just imagine you living like the boy in the plastic bubble." A comfortable silence fell around us. "Scott, I just think that sometimes...people grow apart."

"We're not people, Jovi."

I looked up at him. "What are we then?"

"We're us."

I squeezed his hand. "Scott, we can still be us just...not together."

"I want us to be together."

"I just—"

Scott linked his fingers with mine, staring at them he asked, "What are you afraid of?"

"That we are going to be back to this," I confessed.

"What? Us holding hands?"

"No! I'm afraid that if we got back together, we'll eventually end up here...having a heart to heart on how we ended up separated...for a second time."

His tilted his head at me in disbelief. "You think that if we got back together, we'd end up separated a second time?"

This felt like another argument, but I think this needed to be said. "I'd pray that it wouldn't, but we have big problems, and although it took both of us to break, we tend to say things to hurt the other...I was hurt, Scott," a few tears manage to escape. "You used to be the person I trusted the most."

"I'm sorry. You know that you're a great mom...I wish I had a mom like you growing up."

"Shut up, your mom was great...don't tell her I said that."

"I know...but she didn't throw disco parties before bed and she definitely didn't make me ninja stars out of cardboard so I could practice my aim."

I laughed. "Our kid is going to be so bad ass."

"She's already bad ass...you're a great mom and I'm an asshole, making you feel like you weren't."

Scott toyed with my hand. "Well, I'm sorry for not giving you a chance to help me," I said.

"I love you, Jo. If I knew how to help, I would've."

He tugged me towards him, laying a soft kiss on my lips.

"Scott...just give me time." I passed my hand across his chest, feeling the thump of his heart as I caressed back and forth.

We settled back against the queen size headboard; for the next couple hours the heart to heart turned from civil conversations to passionate argument about trivial things like; "Scott! You didn't put the seat down and I fell right in!" to more hardcore topics like "Jovi! I cook all the time! Even if I'm not watching her, I'm contributing to the household!"

The arguments kept building up until we laid on the bed in an exhausted heap; sore throats, red eyes, dried tears...we put in a lot of work today.

"Why are we like this?" The rasp in his voice revealing how tired he was.

"Because we have almost five years of pent-up anger and animosity towards each other."

"I'm just tired."

I turned on my side to look at him. "We did good today, forty-five minutes in Dr. Rubenstein's office isn't enough."

"She gave us work to do...that you refuse to do."

I rolled my eyes. "I know..."

"You know this is just the beginning," he said.

"I know."

"We still got work to do."

"I know."

"But maybe...tomorrow?" he asked.

"Agreed." I rubbed my eyes in an attempt to ease the burning that exhaustion and crying brought.

Scott reached out for me, settling me in the crook of his arm. "You mentioned that you started therapy, a book club...what else is going on?"

"Now?" I asked while my eyes were dropping.

Part of me wanted to sleep while another part wanted to keep talking.

"Is there a better time?" he asked.

In spite of myself, I smiled. "I guess not."

"So, tell me, I want to know."

I curled closer to him, placing a hand on his wide chest, feeling the rise and fall of it was soothing. My eyes were too heavy to open, but I wanted to keep revealing myself to this beautiful man. I wanted to take advantage of this time where we were talking, and I wasn't throwing something at this head.

I told him all about my therapy. I explained how I thought it was stupid idea until I realized it was helping me sort some things out; it helped me prioritize myself and my needs, which ultimately made me want to be present. I also explained that although I'm better, I still have to fight the dark thoughts that cloud my mind from time to time.

"I'm here to help you, Jo...you just have to tell me what's up."

I offered him a soft smile, that was all I could do to keep from crying.

With Scotts encouragement, I continued to tell him about joining a book club because some of the other moms in Clara's ballet class were standoffish. One of the other moms, upon seeing my misery suggested a book club that meets every Saturday while the kids were in class...which was moms drinking unlimited mimosas while discussing some raunchy book.

Scott talked about how his life was going because we've rarely talked about him.

Scott mentioned that he was playing baseball again during the weekends, he thought he might coach one of the teams. He was rediscovering one of his first loves; baseball. He continued telling me about the kids on his baseball team. He has a handful who never played the game; he was taking pleasure in teaching the sport and the technique that goes behind every position.

I was falling asleep, listening to the passion in his voice.

As the night went on, we laughed, we cried, and we talked.

For the first time in a long time, we began to learn about each other...again.

******

Scott

It was one of the best nights in a very long time.

It was tough earlier; We opened up to each other like we haven't in years, taking a huge weight off my shoulders.

I made it my mission to not fuck it up with sex. As much as I wanted to lay it down, especially seeing how turned on she was in the elevator, I also wanted to show her we can be more.

I wanted Jo to be confident in knowing that if we started something it wouldn't end up in our demise.

It killed me that she didn't trust me. I killed me that I didn't help her like I should have or how she needed. It also killed me how much I wanted us to go back to how we use to be knowing that we need to evolve.

We talked until our voices grew hoarse.

I stared at her as she told me another ridiculous story of how her family showed up to a restaurant during a work meeting and her mom couldn't stop gushing about the time Jovi played Dorothy in her fourth-grade production of *the Wizard of Oz.*

I laughed uncontrollably.

"Scott, for real! She just went on about how I was the best Dorothy anyone had ever seen, and that success is what lead me to be so confident!"

"Your mom is just so proud of you," I laughed.

"Yeah, but why can't she drop my fourth-grade accomplishment?"

"She really wanted you to be an actress."

Jovi let out a heavy sigh. "I sometimes think that she's a little disappointed that I'm not famous."

"Your moms just disappointed that SHE couldn't be an actress."

Jovi slapped my arm. "Damn, Scott! You sound smart. Maybe you should be a therapist."

"Where you think our daughter gets it from?" I quipped, I just wanted to hear her laugh.

"I know she gets her smarts from you; her bad ass-ness comes from me."

I shrugged. "I'm not even going to argue with that."

I laid with Jovi, who was snuggled up in my arms with her eyes closed. Her chest slowly rising and falling as she dozed off.

"Jovi," I whispered.

"Hmmm?"

"Tell me something else that I don't know."

A faint smile graced her lips. "I started sleeping with a frying pan in my bed," she whispered.

"What?" I glanced down at Jovi, her dark hair spread across my chest.

"Scott don't make it seem like it's a weird thing," she snuggled in deeper into the nook of my arm, as if what she said was something normal.

"Oh, no, because it's perfectly normal to sleep with a frying pan in your bed...just in case you feel the need to fry an egg."

Jovi let out a big yawn. "No! it's for a burglar or murderer."

I shook her a little bit to get her to open her eyes and focus on me. "Have there been any burglaries or murders since I left?"

She had this amused look on her face, like I should know better. "Of course not, doesn't mean I shouldn't be prepared." She closed her eyes, settling back down in the nook.

"Oh, so a frying pan would suffice as a weapon?"

A tired sigh escaped her lips. "Scott, what am I supposed to do? Buy a gun? Sleep with a machete under my pillow? At least with a frying pan, Clara can pick it up."

This woman was insane.

"So, in the hypothetical case that a burglar or murderer makes it into your apartment, our four-year-old can whack them with a frying pan?"

"You say it like it's a far fetch idea." Jovi's eyes closed.

Her breathing was full and relax...*did she fall asleep?*

"Promise me if something happens, you will call 9-1-1 or at least try to swing the pan first," I whispered.

Jovi smirked. "Fine, I promise."

After agreeing to my small request, Jovi fell asleep; giving me a chance to stroke her smooth hair and admire her face without her getting upset or embarrassed.

I wanted to treasure this moment.

It's different when you have another body next to you; especially if it was a curvy body and your hand just fits the groove of her waist perfectly, as if it were made just for me.

The cave man in me was relishing in the softness of this woman.

I held her tighter, saying a silent prayer before finally finding solace in sleep.

It's funny how time works. The night seemed to last forever, allowing us time to air out some of our issues, while the morning seemed to come in seconds.

The sun peeking in through the curtains should have woke me up, instead it was the light knock on the door that did.

I looked over to Jovi, she was out like a light. I tried my best to roll out of the bed and not wake her.

There was another firmer knock.

I swung the door open, ready to give whoever it was on the other side a piece of my mind.

"Remy," I sighed.

I heard it! The disdain in my voice that Jovi accused me of having whenever I said his name. I cleared my throat. "How can I help you?" I looked back to make sure Jovi was still asleep.

Remy stood there wide-eyed and slack jawed looking slightly horrified; like he just seen his mother naked. "Um...just came to see if Jo was already up. I wanted to see if she wanted to get breakfast with me."

"She's still sleeping," I replied, crossing my arms. This was one of the times that I was thankful for my tattoos; people always found them intimidating.

We continued to stare each other down. When he didn't do or say anything, I raised my eyebrow.

"Was there anything else, Remy?"

"Nope, I'll be back later to pick her for the interviews." he began to back away.

"I'll make sure to tell her you stopped by," I said politely. But, before he could leave, I stopped him. "Remy, before you go, can I ask you a question?"

"I don't know. Are you going to try and fight me?"

"I can't promise anything, it depends on your answer," I answered honestly. Truth was, I wanted to punch him in the face for showing up at Jovi's door. He pushed his glasses up his nose as he waited for my question. "Why are trying to get with Jovi?"

The prick had the nerve to smirk. "Because you were dumb enough to let her go."

I wanted to pound his fucking face in; instead, I closed the door.

I quietly walked back to the bed; when I started to climb back in, Jovi began to stir. "What time is it? Who was at the door?" she asked, her voice was muffled by the pillows.

"It was Remy, he wanted to see if you wanted to get breakfast."

Her head was still buried in the pillow which made it difficult for me to see her reaction. "I'm too tired for breakfast," she mumbled to herself.

Relief passed over my body...no argument about not waking her, no passive aggressive behavior...maybe last night wasn't a fluke.

She sat up slowly; her hair standing on all ends. "Do you..." she tried her best to smooth her mane down, choosing to look everywhere else but at me. "Do you...are you hungry?"

I looked around the room, as if she were talking to someone else. "You want to get breakfast with me?"

She rolled her eyes. "I know, shocker, right? Um...so breakfast? You in?"

"Are we good, Jo?"

With a slight tilt of her full lips she answered, "No, we can't make everything right in one night."

I sat down next to her. "You think we'll be good after breakfast?" I asked. I was so eager to move on.

Starting over was my main objective.

Jovi dropped her head into her hands. "Scott, you're really annoying me."

"What I do?"

"Of course, we won't be good after breakfast...breakfast is a way of getting caffeine in my system and giving us a better chance to be okay."

I pried her head out of her hands and made her look at me. "Are you going to brush your teeth before we go?"

She nodded.

"Good because even under the pillows, your breath is kicking."

She laughed and threw a pillow at me. "Yours is worse!"

I wrestled her to the bed; I felt powerful with every giggle that escaped her lips. Eventually awareness won out, in an instant the laughter stopped.

This was old school Jovi and Scott.

I kissed her on the nose.

"Scott," she whispered.

"Yeah?"

"Go brush your teeth."

I laughed pulling her along with me.

At breakfast, we laughed easily while talking more about work and what we were looking forward to during our free time and eventually talking about Clara and her shenanigans. The thing about being a parent is that after a while you want time away from your kid so you can be a grown up and do adult things like drink beverages that are more flammable than fruit base; but when you get the chance to be away, all you seem to talk about is your kid.

Jovi and I were no exception.

We talked about our kid until our monstrous breakfast made it to the table. "You know her teacher says that she's been a bit more emotional at school. She cries over everything," Jovi explained.

"Yeah, I know."

"It just adds to the guilt I feel about everything else. What's happening with us is really affecting her."

I reached out for Jovi's hand. "She'll be okay. Our girl is strong."

"It's not about being strong, it's about us being there to help her. I just want her to be a happy, healthy, well-adjusted kid."

My heart pounding against my chest. I wish I could make things better with a wave of my hand, but I couldn't. "We can figure it out when we get back."

She nodded with the dust of tears saturating her eyes.

When we were done stuffing our faces with banana nut pancakes, Jovi looked at me over the rim of her coffee mug. "I have interviews this afternoon."

"I know, Remy told me." I didn't care if I sounded like a jealous kid.

"Are you sticking around?" she asked, she ignored the edge in my voice.

"No, I have to head back. I need to take care of things before I head back to work tomorrow." She nodded her understanding. "The school is throwing a dance. We're trying to get donations for the baseball team, maybe a sponsor. You can come by if you want. We could dance awkwardly...hands where the chaperones can see. I'll even get you a corsage."

Jovi shook her head. "No, it's your thing, I don't want to put a damper on things."

"Why would you?"

"I don't know, we had one great night and then I show up at your work party?" she shrugged.

"I'm still trying to find the issue," I said.

"If someone asks a question about us...what do we say?"

"Nothing, it's no one's business."

"What about Kim?" Jovi sat back in her seat, waiting for my answer.

"I already told you, it's no one's business. Jovi, I want you there."

"I'll think about it," She said quietly.

Her answer, although not a definite yes, made me feel like we were on the mend; in the deepest corner of my mind and my heart, I wanted it to be true.

18

Jovi

Last night felt like THE night.

The night that people make a big deal about in movies; where a couple stays up all night talking about their hopes, fears, and embarrassing stories that they've never told anyone.

It was the kind of night where one might begin to think that maybe she made a mistake.

There was no denying that we had great chemistry. We had a history. No matter what I told myself or how much I tried to fight it, one thing was for sure...Scott knew me.

But it was only one night, Jo.

I wanted to punch the voice inside me. I knew she wanted to protect me, but I also wanted to be happy.

Scott does make me happy...most of the time...when we're not arguing.

Plus, he told the truth. He didn't sleep with Kim. I knew he wasn't lying. There was something in the way he denied it that made me believe. There was this glimmer of hope deep in my soul that made me believe.

And Santa Clause is real.

I took a deep breath, hopefully that was enough to stop the negative thoughts from coming.

"You okay?" Remy asked from behind me, where he was packing up his equipment.

"Yeah, I'm good."

"I came by your room this morning."

I felt dread begin to ice my veins. I was too chicken to have this confrontation right now. Remy wasn't even my man! Scott was!

Whoa...Scott was my man?

I distracted myself with putting my stuff away in my tote bag; I really didn't want to talk about this. "Yeah?" Me, forever the queen of avoidance.

"Scott opened the door...I think he said you were sleeping." Remy looked up expectantly.

I gave a quick laugh to make it seem like it wasn't a big deal. "Yeah, he came to visit me," I said, hoping that short reply would do.

Remy stood straight with his bag hanging off one shoulder. "So...are you guys back together?" he asked.

Well, he cut right to the chase.

"No," I replied automatically.

My answer left a bitter taste in my mouth. First off, I didn't owe Remy an explanation. Second, Scott and I were not back together, but last night felt like we might be.

He pushed his glasses up his nose. "He made it seem like you were."

"Really? What he say?" I tried to play it cool, even though I was very close to snapping at
him for prying.

"Nothing much." He nodded towards the door and we both began to walk out. "He did ask me why I'm trying to date you."

"What did you tell him?"

"I told him because he was dumb enough to let you go."

I bumped into a table, knocking down a vase, causing people to look at us. I picked it up and walked faster.

I looked down in embarrassment. If Scott was dumb enough to let me go, was I dumb to take him back? Did Remy think that I was that type of person to go back into a shitty relationship?

Why do you care what Remy thinks?!

Remy gestured for me to get in the rental car. “So, you guys aren’t together?”

I shook my head. “No, we’re just being friendly. We’re co-parenting.” The words I had rehearsed for anyone bold enough to inquire about my relationship did not settle well.

“He came all the way here to co-parent?”

Now, I was getting mad.

Remy noticed my death glare and quickly backtracked. “I’m sorry for prying. I just don’t want to step on any toes, especially since I like you and you guys have a history. Just be honest, Jovi. What do you want?”

I laughed nervously, that was the same question Scott asked me. Funny how the universe works.

“Remy...” I put my big girl panties on and took a deep breath. “...I’m trying to work things out with Scott.” I saw the disappointment on his face.

“Uh...yeah...sure...” he began to stammer. “I'm happy for you, Slick." His soft smile warmed my heart. Hr began to fumble with his bag. "Um...you want to ride back to the city together?”

“No, Scott and I are riding together,” I lied.

I knew Scott had already headed back home. I didn’t want to drive three hours with Remy and his unrequited feelings. I didn’t see the point in sitting in the car for that long trying so hard not to be awkward which would make it feel that much more awkward.

Plus, I added an extra night to my hotel stay. After last night,

I wanted some more time to myself to sleep and...figure out what I really wanted with Scott.

Remy pursed his lips, not saying a word.

We made it back to the hotel, giving Remy a quick hug before rushing to the elevator. I was ready to be holed up in my room with wine and a romantic comedy.

I turned the corner to begin walking down the hallway to my room, stopping short when I saw Scott sitting in front of my door playing on his phone.

When I got close enough, he looked up, flashing a warm smile causing me to smile in return.

I felt the spark of excitement; could this mean there was a possibility for another great night together?

I began to rummage through my purse to give myself time to think. It's crazy but the muffled sounds coming from inside the rooms as I continued my walk of uncertainty put me at ease.

"What are you doing here?" I asked.

He reached out his giant hands out and I helped him up. "I knew you were working so I came to wait for you instead."

I turned to open the door. "I thought you left already."

"I was supposed to, but I...I wanted to see you."

I felt myself blush like a schoolgirl.

I put my bags down, right before picking them u again and setting them back down. I was trying to keep myself busy because I just didn't want my mind to get in the way; my emotions always seem to get the best of me.

"Hey, you okay?" he asked.

I stopped. "Yes!" I squealed. I cleared my throat. "I'm good. Why?" I huffed.

"Well, because you picked up that bag like twenty times and I still haven't done anything."

"Done what?" I asked. I was so distracted with my thoughts that I didn't hear a word he said.

His eyes widened. "Why are you on edge?"

I want your body, is what my mind screamed. Instead I deflected and asked, "What did you tell Remy this morning?"

Scotts playfulness disappeared; his jaw immediately clenched. "Why?"

"He asked me if we were back together."

"And what did you tell him?"

"No," I whispered.

His shoulders sank down as if he were finally defeated. "Listen...I...don't know what I expected to happen. I'm done."

I reached out to him. "Scott, I'm not done. I don't want to be done. I need time to figure this out! My mind is a ball of confusion."

Scott yanked me towards him.

He lifted my chin up, aiming for my lips.

I rose on my tip toes as best as I could, losing my foot and kissing him on the corner of his mouth.

He grinned at my spastic behavior, wrapping his arms around my waist.

My arms automatically made its way up his shoulders, wrapping around his neck.

"Let's try it again," he said with a smirk.

This time, his lips crashed onto mine and I melted into him.

The minute our tongues met I felt the wildfire of arousal begin to spread; I pulled away.

"Wait, Scott. What are we doing?"

"I think they call it making out."

I stepped back from him. "But we're separated!"

He ran a hand down his face. "I know this."

"What does this mean?" Arousal clouded my already confused mine. I wanted this man in my bed. That was not the issue. The issue was, could I trust him with all of me when I only trusted him with my body? My head, body and heart were at odds.

"What does what mean?" he folded his arms, clearly frustrated with the analytical turn that my mind took.

"This kiss, last night...breakfast."

Scotts eyes turned into saucers with every word that came out my mouth. "Why are you overthinking everything."

"How can I not?"

His hands were on his hips, accentuating his shoulders. "What do you want, Jovi? You said you wanted me. We're not fighting, so now you're fighting with yourself." He took a deep breath. "At this exact moment what do you want?"

What did I want?

My eyes glanced at the sex toy I had discarded the day before. He glanced over, and his frustration transformed into cocky arousal. "Do you want me to fuck you?" Scotts question came out in a rasp. It turned me on to the point where I felt goosebumps break out all over my body and he hadn't even touched me. "That toy didn't get that pussy wet?"

"Touch me," I whispered to him.

His hand reached out and cupped my breasts, squeezing it gently. My head fell back as I pushed my chest out. He growled as his lips found my neck.

I stepped out of his embrace and I began to unbutton my blouse.

Scott fumbled with the hem of his t-shirt; trying to yank it off like an excited teenager.

I took off my pants while biting my lip to keep from laughing at the sight of him in his boxers looking so eager.

"Wow, you're fast," I said with a raised eyebrow.

He stood straight, doubt shadowing his face. "Tell me you took your shirt off because you want to have sex."

"No, I usually take my top off for men when I just want a cup of coffee." When he didn't react to my sarcasm, I snapped. "Of course, I want to have sex!"

He reached out and snapped me back into his arms. His mouth took mine with the aggression and eagerness of one who's been deprived; parting them with an expertise that came along with time.

We both nipped, sucked and savored.

There was a hint of desperation but we both tried our best to take our time. He lifted me up, carrying me to the bed. I felt like Scarlett O'Hara when Rhett carried her up the stairs to have his way with her.

I laid back, automatically parting my legs for him.

"You're so fucking beautiful, Jovi." I felt myself blush at his praise. He laid between my legs, pressing his hardness against me.

His lips began to travel down; I stiffened. "What's wrong?" he asked.

"Don't leave hickies."

"I won't. Trust me."

He bent his head; continuing their journey down. My fingers found their way through his hair, tightening around his strands as his lips found my nipples.

I let out a strained moan; I hated that I loved this so much.

He knew the push and pull of my body. Where to rub his fingers while he continued sucking. My entire body flushed with desire.

Scott knew how the calluses on his fingers turned me on; strong, rough. Those same fingers made it to my wet slit, saturating themselves before entering me.

God!

This is what heaven felt like.

I wanted to feel his touch deeper. "Please..." I begged.

I heard his low chuckle before he slid his fingers out of me. I quickly opened my eyes. "What are you doing?" I asked.

Scott reached over to the night stand to retrieve the discarded sex toy. He held it out to me. "Spit on it," he commanded.

I did as I was told.

"Good girl." The buzzing seemed louder than usual. His cocky grin was mesmerizing as he spread my legs wider and settled between them. "I'm going to lick your pussy and fuck you with this, any objections?"

I couldn't answer verbally. I just shook my head.

His entire mouth covered my pussy, licking it before sucking my clit. That alone would have sent me over the edge...then I felt the dildo enter, I stretched around it, arching my back to take it in. "Is this what you wanted? Is this what you needed."

He began to lick me again as he fucked me slowly with the toy. "Yes...yes..." I couldn't speak. There were no words. I felt my nipples harden as is the combination of his tongue and the toy; the warm build up was too much.

Scott began to work the toy faster, his tongue lashing out; sucking and licking...

In a matter of minutes, I came without warning.

I stretched as the sensation rained all around me; too much for me to keep my eyes open. Before they fell, I saw the glaze on his face from my climax. The image forever ingrained in my mind.

I felt his manhood rubbing all over my juices before pressing his way in.

I arched my back, trying to take all of him in; I looked like something out of the exorcist! Scott has always been a big boy; my body needed some time to adjust.

When I felt comfortable enough, I moved my hips; giving him the signal to move.

He wrapped me in his arms; I turned my head, my lips looking for anything to take a hold of.

As he pumped harder, I bit his tattooed arm to muffle my moans.

His big hands released me to take a hold of my waist, digging into me; holding me in place as he continued his beautiful assault on my body.

I cried out as the waves of pleasure crashed around me again. My lips sucked his neck making him moan and pump faster into me.

The beads of sweat drenched our bodies; although my body was sensitive and still humming with satisfaction, my hips continued to match his rhythm.

Scotts head found the crook of my neck, groaning as he found his release as well.

I wrapped my arms and legs around his body, holding him close.

We laid like that for a while. At that moment I didn't want to let him go.

I continued kissing his shoulder and neck as laid in exhaustion trying to catch our breaths.

"I wanted to have a quiet evening," I whispered.

Scott groaned against my neck. "That was before I dicked you down."

I laughed.

I wiggled beneath him trying to break free from under his body.

"Woman, that's not the way to get me off of you."

He bit and licked my shoulder before rolling off of me, taking all the warmth with him.

It was as if the cold air splashed a bucket of reality on me. I immediately rolled in the opposite direction; standing to get away from Scott and calm my nerves down.

Scott sat up, a frowning. "Why are you running, Jo?"

"I'm not running," I quickly answered.

"You literally ninja rolled off the bed."

"No, I didn't," I scoffed.

"So why are you over there?"

"I...this...is a lot," I confessed.

"I know, I thought I would last a little longer," he joked. He noticed how serious I was. "But we don't have to analyze it right away," he added.

"I know but I don't want us to go back home and be awkward. I don't want us to argue all the time."

Scotts head fell back against the headboard. "You are a frustrating woman." He whispered.

I looked at all six foot, five inches of him reclining back; Every tattoo, every muscle, every ripple...I walked slowly to him.

This is the man who I was obsessed with from the first minute I laid eyes on him.

I ruined this moment for us. I climbed into the bed, not thinking about anything except only bringing him pleasure.

He slowly lifted his head out his hands, his face a bundle of confusion. "Jo..."

I didn't say anything.

My knees sunk into the soft mattress as I kneeled down and settled between his legs. I licked the trail beginning at his belly button down to his dick that began to harden, licking the shaft before taking it all into my mouth; I tasted me...us, all over him.

His groan hyped me up.

Scotts hands reached out and grabbed fistfuls of my hair, holding me in place as I took him as deep in my mouth as best I could.

"God, Jovi...that fucking mouth...that pretty fucking mouth..."

I looked up, the vision of him with his head back, eyes closed as I'm sucking him off would be one of the most erotic things I've ever seen.

He tasted of pure masculinity and salty goodness.

His pumps were growing more erratic, I didn't know if I could handle his thrusts; my eyes began to water from strain, but I continued to suck.

I knew he wanted to come; My hands managed to grab his ass, giving me leverage to help him stroke into my mouth better.

With one hard stroke, Scott finally let go of my hair; allowing me to catch my breath as he climaxed.

I began licking everything up as best as I could.

Scott fell back onto the pillows— his eyes closed; his body drenched in sweat.

I felt his arms reach out for me, he brought me to his lips, kissing me lightly.

After what we just did, it felt silly that he would kiss me that way, but it was...perfect.

My head found the familiar nook.

I melted into the peace.

******

Scott

I felt myself jerk awake.

I looked around the dark hotel room, confused.

Then I sat up as I remembered that Jovi and I have been having sex all night long. I looked around the room hoping that she hadn't left me behind like last time.

I took a second to control my temper which had begun to go hot at the idea of her leaving me again.

That's when I heard the shower go on.

What did tonight mean?

Jovi freaked herself out with that question, now I wanted to know the answer.

To me, it felt like we were finally moving past our mistakes.

Tonight, we just let go of everything.

I wanted to scream with joy. I saw the fear in Jovi's face when I was storming out. It was the same fear I felt when she confronted me and asked for the divorce. But I was wise enough to know that Jo was probably in the shower talking herself out of reconciling— telling herself that what we did was bad and that it should and would never happen again.

I opened the door slowly, the steam from the shower rushing out. I stood there admiring the blurred image of her through the glass doors of the shower.

I knew every mark, every scar on her body. I was proud in the fact that I was one of the few that experienced how generous she could be with her body.

My wife is beautiful.

"You just going to stand there or are you coming in?" she asked.

She didn't have to tell me twice! I practically jumped into the tub.

This was a good sign; she sounded playful.

She passed me a bar of soap. "Wash my back?"

"Yeah." I took my time washing her back, down her spine to her ass cheeks, squeezing as I passed the soap over it.

"Hey!" she giggled.

She turned around and wrapped her arms around my neck.

"You good?" I asked.

Although it was just two words, we both knew what I asked was a lot heavier.

I wanted her to tell me what was going on in her mind so I can banish all the dark thoughts. The water cascaded around us, making me wish it could wash all our issues down the drain.

She had a faint smile on her lips. "Yes," she whispered.

"I was afraid that you left me alone in bed again."

She sighed. "Scott—"

"Jo, don't overthink it...please." I rested my forehead against hers.

"It's hard not to."

"Do you want to be together?"

She rolled her eyes. "Scott."

It was hard not to feel frustrated when we kept going around in circles. “I know I sound like a broken record, but I want us to be together.”

She gave a slight nod that lit a small beacon of hope inside of me.

“What does that mean?” I asked, afraid that she was going to change her mind.

“It means, we don’t say anything to anyone...for now...maybe date? Let's get to know these new versions of us and see if it works.”

My heart was ecstatic.

I wanted to jump for joy, scream at the top of my lungs.

Deep in my soul I knew that we were meant to be together; I wanted her to know that too.

I kissed her as if it were the last time because even though she agreed to try, in the back of my mind I had a sinking feeling she would try to find a way out.

I felt her lips kiss back; I pulled her closer to me. The water washed over us as I dug my hand in her hair, our tongues mingling.

I needed to be inside her again.

I backed her into the tiled wall, picking her up with ease. Her legs wrapped around my waist. Jovi was still slick from our moments before. I slid inside her, a moan slipped from her lips. "Scott..."

"I'm going to keep fucking you, just to hear you say my name like that."

"Harder."

I fucked her hard.

It's what I needed. It's what she needed.

I wanted no doubts in her head.

19

Scott

The drive home was full of laughter; Jovi's hands traveled to places that made me stiffen with desire and because I take traffic violations very seriously, I reluctantly removed her wandering hand, enveloping it within mine.

The lightheartedness of the car ride did little to settle the crippling heart palpitations that seemed to begin when we hit the George Washington Bridge.

It was that queasy feeling you get when you come off a roller-coaster; heart pounding, dizzy, thrilling but a little bit terrifying.

Within the confines of our car bubble, father time was working against us because before we knew it, we were parked in front of the apartment complex.

With only the sound of the heater around us, I squeezed Jovi's hand.

"You okay?" Jovi's voice trembled.

I wondered if she could smell the sweat and nervousness oozing out from my pores.

"Jo...I know we had a good time this weekend, but I want us to keep going." My eyes examined each one of her fingers as I held onto them for dear life.

"I know," she answered, her free hand came around, smoothing my beard before tilting my head up.

Her lips formed a hard line while her eyebrows came down hard. "I have something to tell you."

I leaned my head against the headrest and closed my eyes. "I don't like the sound of this."

When she didn't spill the news right away, I slowly opened my eyes. I felt her fingers twitch and I loosened my hold. "You're scaring me, Jo."

"I wrote about us," she confessed.

"You wrote about us."

"And I want to submit it to the paper."

"And you—"

"Stop repeating everything I say!"

"I'm sorry, Jovi but I'm trying to process what you're telling me," I explained. "You didn't turn it in?"

"I wanted to talk to you about it. They want to turn our story into a full-length book. I really think—"

"No."

"I just think—"

"Jovi, no."

Her face flushed and I could see the flash of anger in the dimness of the car. "Why?"

I felt her try to shake out of my hand, but I refused to let go. "Because I have a life...a job that I don't want to lose."

"Why would you lose your job?"

"Believe it or not but people read your stuff...it could get back to me, it may come off as not professional. I work at a school; parents don't want their kids surrounded by scandal." she stared at our interlocked fingers in silence. I leaned to give her a kiss. “Please understand, Jo.”

She smiled but it didn’t quite reach her eyes. “I understand.”

I wanted Jovi to be successful in her career, but I didn’t want it to put my job in jeopardy.

I could feel the cold radiating of her body. I leaned in to kiss her; I felt her lips soften, giving into me before she pulled away quickly.

I sat back, looking out. “Is Clara upstairs?”

Jovi opened the passenger door, nodding as she exited.

I exited the car and made my way around, reaching for Jovi, pulling her into my arms.

I placed a quick peck on her forehead. “Jo, please don’t be mad.”

Seconds passed before I felt her sigh, her hands wrapping around my waist. “I’m not mad, just...disappointed,” she said against my chest.

I gently shook her shoulders. “Are we good?”

“I’m afraid to fight with you,” she confessed

“Are we fighting now?” I gave a small laugh.

“We never fought before...now it seems ever since I yelled for a divorce all we do is fight.”

“Just because we’re home doesn’t mean we’ll fight all the time,” I explained.

“But we’ll fight.”

“Isn’t that what normal couples do?”

“We aren’t normal,” she laughed.

“I mean...our fighting could just the bad before the good.”

“You think?” she asked hopefully.

“I hope so...I don’t want you throwing my clothes out the window again.”

“That was some of my best work,” she giggled.

Jovi was the only person that could throw a pot at me or my clothes out the window and I would still find her irresistible.

"Do you trust me, Jo?"

All five feet three inches of her stood on tippy toe to reach my lips. I felt the heat pass between us. If the streets were empty, I would've done a lot more than just squeeze her ass.

With one final kiss, I lead the way to her place.

Before we were able to unlock the door, it opened.

"Well, well, well...if it isn't my sister and the sperm donor," Liz greeted cheerfully.

I narrowed my eyes in her direction.

"Liz be nice," Jovi warned.

Jovi didn't tell me to be nice. "Well, well, well...if it isn't—"

"Mommy!!! Daddy!!!!" Clara came running to the door, making me swallow the insult that I was about to throw at her aunt.

I held Clara in my arms, being careful with her cast, while Jovi laid kisses all over her head.

We walked into the living room where Tommy and his family were seated waiting for us. "Oh good, Jovi's here."

"Hey, Scott," Frank greeted from the couch.

"What's going on?" Jovi asked.

"I invited Eddie over and Tommy invited himself." Liz's eyes traveled from my toes to my head; I could see her mind trying to figure out where to attack first.

"Goody, so I get to meet him too," I said with feigned excitement.

"He's not staying." Liz pointed to me and stomped her foot like a petulant four-year-old.

I answered before Jovi could say anything. "Actually, I'm visiting my daughter so I think I will stay."

Tommy and Frank clapped from where they sat as they took in the drama. "That's right, Scott. Stand up for yourself," They cheered from the couch.

I felt Liz approach me and spun around to face her when I felt my phone begin to vibrate. I held a finger at Liz, taking out my phone.

"You better put that finger down," she growled.

"Scott, stop provoking her," Jovi sighed.

I looked down at my message, knowing how much angrier Liz would get.

It was Aaron.

Hey, want to hang out tonight?

I replied:

Sure, Come meet me at Jovi's, I want to spend time with Clara.

I put Clara down and followed her and her cousin to the bedroom. I could feel three sets of giant eyes burning holes into my back. I heard the mumbles and whispers begin as soon as I turned the corner.

"I can hear you!" I yelled and they settled down.

I knew all of them like the back of my hands. They all would pepper Jovi with questions about this weekend.

I decided to ignore the siblings and enjoy teatime with the girls.

Fifteen minutes later, heavy knocks sounded on the door.

I sat waiting for the sounds of murder to break out, thinking it was Aaron who showed up.

When I heard no such sounds, I excused myself from teatime.

Liz was holding hands with a tall, bulky man with ray bans on. He was dressed in the tightest sweater and jeans that I've ever seen in my life.

"Guys, this is my fiancée Eddie," Liz said.

I was surprise that I didn't see hearts shoot out her eyes. According to Jovi, Liz was evolving in a way that she didn't think would ever happen. She was cooking, cleaning, empathetic.

"This explains a lot," I heard Tommy whisper.

From where I stood in the corner, I could see Jovi force a smile that was all teeth.

"Well, nice to finally meet you Eddie, I ordered pizza for everyone." Her words came out slow as if she were talking to a child.

"I don't really eat pizza; I have to maintain this body for work. I have a shoot tomorrow so no dairy," Eddie replied.

As Liz dragged him onto the couch, Tommy asked, "What exactly do you do?"

"I—"

"He manages nightclubs..." Liz cut him off.

Beads of sweat began to form on her upper lip. Something was up.

Jovi folded her arms, her eyes in a hard squint. "How did you meet?" Jovi knew something was off, she was just too polite to say something.

"Liz, had a little too much to drink—"

"Surprise, surprise," Tommy rolled his eyes.

"Shut up, Tommy!" Liz's cheeks flushed.

"We danced...continued the night at my place and she hasn't left."

The heavy silence that filled the room was amplified by the knock that sounded on the front door.

Jovi jumped from her spot, zooming to answer the door. "That must be the pizza!"

When Jovi came back with Aaron instead of the pizza, Liz immediately began to have a shit fit. "What the hell are you doing here?" she asked, hands on her hips.

"Hello to you too." Aaron turned to look at Eddie.

"I'm Aaron," he held out his hand.

"Eddie."

We all held our breaths as they shook hands at a leisurely pace. "Oh, so you're the guy—" Liz leaped over and punched Aaron in the arm.

Eddie had about a couple inches and almost fifty pounds on Aaron.

"If she's holding you against your will blink twice," Aaron joked.

I grabbed Aaron by the shoulders. "Okay, we're headed out."

"Eddie, don't be afraid to call the police if necessary, they already know Liz—"

"Okay, that's enough, buddy." I patted Aaron on the back.

"Yes, please, take him away!" Liz snatched back Eddie's hand, wrapping herself in his arms.

I gave my daughter a kiss goodbye before turning to Jo.

What do I do with Jo? Do we kiss? Hug?

I was very aware that all eyes were on us.

Jovi's eyebrows rose up as I bent to kiss her lips. At the last second, I decided to kiss her cheek and pat her shoulder like she was a dog!

"I'll call you tomorrow?" I asked.

Her eyes darted to her siblings; she cleared her throat, bobbing her head fast. "Yeah, sure...whatever you want," her cheeks flushed an attractive rose color.

Her gestures made me feel as if we were in high school; brand new, almost forbidden even though we were married.

As Aaron and I began to head out, Aaron sighed with each step down the stairs.

"What the hell's wrong with you?" I asked as I unlocked the car.

Aaron looked at me from over the car. "Things went well with Jo?"

"Seriously?" I turned the car on, prepared to leave Aaron behind.

"Well, what happened?"

I looked at my best friend of almost thirty years. "I wooed her."

A slow smile spread across his face. "You woo'd her...like dinner? or intimate?"

"I'm not talking about it."

He began to laugh. "So, this is it. You got her back!"

"No."

He pursed his lips as he assessed me. "No?"

"We're going slow."

"Did you not do it right?" he asked.

I turned to face him. "Do what right?"

"You know, the sex...you didn't do it right or you probably were a minute man—"

"What?! No!"

"It's understandable, you were probably too eager."

I stared at him for a minute; this guy was out of his mind. "I'mma fuck you up."

"So, if it's not the sex, then why take it slow?"

"She doesn't trust me," I sighed. With that admission, Aaron fell silent. "She doesn't trust me because...I let her down with the whole Kim thing...she's afraid I'll do it again."

The look of sympathy that Aaron gave me just made me angry. I needed my wife to commit to me again; I didn't need the sympathy of a man that was in a volatile relationship with a woman who was engaged to a boy band reject.

"You know what you need?" he asked.

I was afraid to answer him.

"You need to show her she can trust you."

I rolled my eyes. "Duh, no shit. Why are you trying to sound like Obi-one? You're not doing much better than me!"

"I'm not in a relationship and I don't want to be in a relationship."

"Keep telling yourself that."

******

Jovi

"Well, what happened?" Tommy asked.

Tommy, Frank and I left the others in the living room under the pretense of getting drinks.

"Nothing happened." I was still processing and wanted to do it alone. I didn't want everyone's opinion to taint my thoughts.

Frank raised his eyebrows. "Something happened."

"Why you think that?" I handed him cups to fill.

"Because we all saw you the other night at your parents, you were ready to kill each other and now…you're practically melting…and then that weird goodbye…y'all are fucking," Frank pointed out.

"Oh, please!" I felt my body flush as my mind went back to last night.

"We know that he laid it down and now you don't know how to act," Tommy said.

"You don't know that," I admonished.

I left them in the kitchen just in time to see Eddie get up from the couch. "Jovi, I'm sorry but I have an early call time tomorrow."

"He means…opening…opening a new club and they need him, so…he's going."

I narrowed my eyes at the both of them; they were hiding something, but I didn't know what.

"I think I know you from somewhere…you look so familiar," I began to say.

Eddie began to fidget with his phone, looking at Liz who began to shake her head. "I don't think we've met before, goodnight everyone," he stomped away without a backwards glance, Liz skipped behind him.

"What was that about?" Tommy asked.

"Oh. My. God!" I gasped.

It just hit me.

Liz returned with grin on her face. "You see guys, he's real—" which evaporated once she noticed the look on mine. "What?" she asked.

"Your fiancée is a porno star!" I yelled.

Frank and Tommy let out loud gasps that would put any novella star to shame.

I could tell I was right by the sheer fact that Liz lost all her color in her face as if she seen a ghost.

"Jovi, how do you know?" Frank asked.

I felt myself flush. "Because I...I may have..."

"Oh my god! Did you get off watching a porno Eddie was in?" Tommy whispered, looking back to make sure our daughters wasn't in the room. He was practically foaming at the mouth.

"That's not the point!" I looked at my baby sister who had her mouth open like a dead fish...a pale dead fish. "Elizabeth..." only when her eyes connected with mine did I continue, "Is Eddie, Edward cock-in-hands?" I felt my face burning as I kept my voice low.

Tommy and Frankie squealed in pleasure. "Is that his porn name or just a character?"

"How do you know this?" Liz squeaked.

I cleared my throat. "I...um...I...kind of...saw the video..."

"Oh my god!" Tommy howled. "You really saw him?!" he immediately pulled out his phone.

Liz jumped on his back, knocking the phone out of his hand.

I heard the children run out the room, eyes wide. "What is Titi doing?"

We all froze like statues, taking in these two wide-eye innocent girls.

Liz let go of Tommy. "We were...um...playing," Liz said as she tried to catch her breath. She sounded if she ran a marathon.

Even at their young age, the girls knew better. They shrugged their shoulders and walked to where the pizza was.

I pulled Liz towards me. "Why the hell are you dating a porn star?" I whispered.

Liz's wide eyes darted from each one of us. "I was asked to work on set—"

"What?!" my heart jumped to my throat.

"As a make-up artist, geez." She looked over to the girls. "and he was working." Her frown turned into an accusatory gaze as she pointed a finger at me. "Why are we talking about me when it's obvious you're back with Scott?"

"We're not talking about me—"

"Yes, we are!" Liz stomped her foot.

I tilted my head as one question popped up. "If he's a porn star, why aren't you guys having sex?"

She sighed. "I don't feel comfortable...yet."

"What?"

She sheepishly looked at the three of us who were attentively waiting for her answer.

"I just don't want it to be about sex. I know he has sex all the time for work...I want to be different."

"Tommy, why are your sisters such a mess?" Frank asked with a mouth full of pizza.

"I don't know, babe. Just be thankful that I'm the normal one."

"What's going on with you and Scott?" Liz crossed her arms.

I let out a heavy sigh. "We had sex. We're going to try to work things out."

Everyone's smirk told me they already knew, they just wanted me to confirm the information.

I mimicked Liz's stance. "What about you? What's the deal with the porn star?"

Her eyes began to well up. "I want to end it so bad, but the perks are so good!"

"I'm done!" Tommy threw his hands up in the air, taking a seat with the girls.

I nodded for Liz to continue. "I need this to last. I've already been with everyone and they've all ended up in disaster."

"What are his benefits?" We both turned to Frank who asked it from his seat on the couch.

"I can get into any club,"

"Honey...you're thirty-one...is that where you really want to be?" Frank asked.

Ignoring him, Liz continued. "I just want to have a relationship like...You guys."

I let out an unlady like grunt. "Like who?!"

"Tommy and Frank love each other so much they want to raise an entire family. You and Scott—"

"Are a mess! Liz...I'm getting divorced," I hated the crack in my voice.

"Are you?" her eyebrows shot up out of her head.

"Yes!" then I shook my head. "No...maybe...I don't know!"

"So, why keep going to therapy or let him sex you up or why do you let him make you so angry if—"

My heart began to race. "That's not love...that's insanity."

"Love is insanity, Jo! It makes you do amazing and fucked up things! Jovi, you love, Scott."

"But you don't love Eddie," I said.

The moisture in Liz's eyes made her eyes bigger. "Liz don't keep it going if he's not who you want," Frank added.

I walked her to the couch, both of us melting into the suede.

I took her hand in mine. "Scott invited me to this school dance in at the end of the week. I think I'm going to go."

She nodded. "You should. I don't like Scott; he's always seemed like he disapproves of us...like he's better than us."

"You think he doesn't approve of you," I clarified.

"Yeah."

"Well, shit, Liz...admitting that could've probably saved us fifteen years of drama," Tommy said from his spot at the dining table.

"I thought you were over all of this," Liz shot daggers in his direction.

He smirked and turned back to the girls.

"Go, support and party with your husband," Liz encouraged.

"I think you should come with me."

"Why?"

I knew better than to meddle..."So you can be with the one you want."

She rolled her eyes. "I don't want Aaron."

"Keep telling yourself that."

We all fell silent. Eating our slices and trying to figure out why our lives are so fucked up at the moment.

I cleared my throat.

"God, Jovi, if you have something to say just say it!" Tommy yelled.

"Oh my god, you're pregnant," Liz said.

"No! I want to submit a book proposal about my marriage, Scott is against it." I blurted out.

All the grown-ups in the room looked at each other. "If he said no then you can't really do anything can you," Tommy was always the voice of reason.

"I think you should do it! This is a great thing for your career!" Liz exclaimed.

Frank shrugged his shoulders, and I was still at a loss. "I want to just submit it and see if they want to move forward...they reached out to me first."

Liz cocked her head to the side. "Jovi, you're a grown ass woman, I think you should be able to do what you want, don't you think?"

I let out a heavy sigh; not because I didn't know what I wanted to do but because sometimes doing what I think is right might not seem that way to others.

I knew deep down in the bowels of my soul what I had to do.

I turned my head to look at Liz. "So, what you going to do with the porn star?"

We all waited with bated breath for an answer that we knew would never come. The children playing at the table filled the silence.

"What are you wearing to Scott's work thing?" Liz asked, avoiding my question.

I groaned as I got up from the couch.

I needed a drink.

20

Scott

A week later, I was supposed to be filling out student progress reports to hand in by the end of the day. After that I was going to reach out to local businesses to see if they would be willing to sponsor the baseball team. Instead, I found myself looking up a flower arrangement to send to Jovi.

Since the hotel room, it's been like old times; we were sneaking away every free moment we had to fuck, we would sneak away to talk over drinks on the days...I had what I wanted and we were happy.

She had been busy these last couple of days and I wanted her to know I was thinking about her.

Jovi was not materialistic; I got her an engagement ring and wedding band, but she still preferred to wear the dinky ring I got when I unofficially proposed to her on an impulse trip to Six Flags.

The sun had long gone down; when we reached the top of the Ferris wheel, I had the urge to ask her to marry me. I remembered, she was a little sun burnt from walking the park, her natural curls were a mess from all the heat and sweat, and her smile could light up New York City in the dark—I couldn't resist. She jumped on me as best she could.

When we got down, we found the arcade and played games until I had enough tickets to get a cheap ring.

The following week, after asking her dad for her hand, I proposed during a the family's Fourth of July BBQ.

A knock sounded on my door bringing me out of my happiest memories; I began to type absentmindedly on my computer.

"Sorry, Scott but I was told to check in with you on the food arrangements for Friday's dance."

Kim came in, keeping her eyes on her note pad, and tapping her foot.

She was angry about something. Before I could stop myself, I asked her, "Are you okay?' I continued to pull up the catering service information that I had compiled.

"Yes."

I was going to let it go but she rolled her eyes and tapped her foot aggressively. "You don't seem okay."

She raised a sharp eyebrow. "What do I seem like?"

"Hostile."

Her mouth fell open in shock and I immediately regretted my word choice.

"Oh, so now that I'm not fawning all over you, you think I'm hostile?" she snapped.

I exhaled out, calming myself; talking to her was like walking through a field of land mines.

"I didn't say that," I said slowly. I wanted to be calm, I didn't want to cause anymore problems. "I was just asking if you were okay because you seem angry."

"Why'd you lead me on?"

My heart dropped.

I looked at the office door that had remained wide open; I was afraid that someone would walk by and hear this conversation.

"What?!"

She pointed one long acrylic nail at me. "Don't act innocent. You know I broke up with my boyfriend for you."

I felt sick to my stomach. I really wanted her to leave. "I didn't ask you—"

"You didn't ask me, but you kept talking to me and flirting with me."

I shook my head in disbelief. In what parallel universe..."Flirting with you? How? I thought I was talking to a friend."

"You told me about the problems with your wife." She shrugged her delicate shoulders. "Why would you tell me this if you didn't want to be with me?"

Kim's face was flushed with rage.

I was caught off guard with the whole confrontation. "I thought we were friends, I thought I was talking to a friend. I was venting because I was hurt."

Her eyes began to well up.

I was lost for words; I didn't know what I could do to console her. Kim was not my wife. Kim was nothing to me. I wanted Jovi; always have, always will.

"I sent you—" Kim began but I immediately shut it down.

"I know what you sent me." She bit her full red lips, her eyes watery with unshed tears but I ventured forward. "Kim, I'm sorry if I lead you on, that wasn't my intention. I love my wife. I'm in love with Jovi." With a final click I sent my notes to print. "I sent the papers to your printer."

Kim pursed her lips, clicking her tongue at me. "Do you love your wife? Because all you did was complain about the things she wasn't doing."

My stomach did a flip; I felt like I was going to be sick. Did I really make it seem I was so miserable with Jovi? "Are you and Jovi back together?"

I wanted to say yes, but I told Jovi it wasn't Kim's business, so I didn't answer.

"I read her story online...and she made it seem like you guys aren't together."

That damn story. My worst fear was starting to materialize. *That's old news, we're over that,* I told myself. "Yeah, I know...that was before we decided to work it out."

"Really? Because this one was just posted." All I heard was the click, click, click of her heels as she slammed the door behind her.

I sat stunned. *Just posted?* I began to type on the keyboard so hard I thought I was gonna break the damn thing. I pulled up Jovi's latest article online. I felt my chest go tight; it was getting harder to breath with every word I read.

Reading the entire article in a matter of seconds, there was ringing in my ears.

I know that she was reluctant to work things out but to write about it and tell the whole world her inner most thoughts. Her words was her sword and she finally killed me.

Even on the good days, divorce was inevitable.

I read that line over and over again until my eyes grew sore.

We had a therapy session later on today.

What was the point of going if I was the only one making an effort to save us? What was the point if she was moving forward with the divorce?

Did she laugh with her brother and sister when she talked about me?

I silently seethed as I reread her depictions and view of our therapy sessions; I'd admit, if I wasn't one of the parties involved, I would find this binge worthy. Jovi's writing was that damn good.

I heard a ding of my work email.

Aaron had sent me a copy of the article. I felt my phone vibrate.

"What, Aaron?"

"I was sent this by a jilted secretary," he revealed.

"You got to be kidding me." I felt a migraine coming on. I can only imagine who else got this article.

******

Jovi

I waited anxiously in the bond-esque waiting room of Dr. Rubenstein. The butterflies in my belly were alive and well as I waited for Scott to show up. It's been a week since we returned home, and I heard not one peep from him.

We've been having sex non-stop but apart from that, we've been talking again. We were starting to have a friendship again and I saw us working out. I had high hopes.

I figured he was just as busy at work as I have been. These past couple of days he hasn't come over for a visit; not text, no calls...I was starting to worry but after talking to Tommy, I began to realize he needed space.

I didn't want to pressure him.

I'd be lying if I said I hadn't missed him. I expected him to show up late like usual; every time someone came into the office, I'd look up expecting to see him, only to be disappointed.

"Jovi Garcia?"

"Hey, Doctor...Scott's not here yet...I don't know if—"

"Oh, he just called to say that he's not coming today."

My steps faltered as I followed Dr. Rubenstein to her office. With each soft click of her loafers with prescribed arch support, the little voice in the back of my head kept getting louder, telling me that there was something wrong; but for once, I tried to suffocate that voice with a little bit of optimism.

I took my place on the loveseat, checking my phone. "I didn't know that Scott wasn't coming today...I don't have any miss calls."

I looked up to see Dr. Rubenstein, blinking her owl eyes at me.

"We can reschedule this session," I said. When she didn't immediately agree with me, my temper began to bubble to the surface. "Doc, we can reschedule. There's no point in couples' therapy if only half of the couple shows up."

"Actually, Scott will not be returning. But I thought it best to have a solo session with you. Usually when things get strained, I like to talk to each party separately."

I leaned in just to make sure I heard her properly. "Excuse me?"

"Scott asked me if we can take a couple of sessions to focus on you."

It was getting difficult to breath when all I wanted to do was tear this room to shit. "Why...why would we do that?"

"Scott mentioned that you were having trust issues and—"

"Well, if Scott mentioned that then maybe he should be here to confront it!" I yelled. Her eyes widened. "Dr. Rubenstein, I am so sorry for yelling..." I began to rub my eyes because I felt the sting of tears. "I just..."

I felt her gnarled hand on my shoulder and tried not to flinch as I looked up. "Jovi, it's okay to not be okay. I know there's trust issues because of the other woman. But have you given him a chance to redeem himself?"

"I thought I did!" I shrieked. "We had an amazing weekend. An amazing week up until this moment. I thought we were on the right path and now he doesn't show up to therapy."

"Sex doesn't fix much." I tilted my head in her direction "Well, do you think he may not trust *you*?" this bitch new something I didn't.

"Why wouldn't he trust me?"

"I'm not sure, have you spoken—"

"I haven't spoken to him in two days, which is weird because even if he didn't want to talk to me, he'd call to talk to Clara."

"Some of the exercises that can help with trust—"

"What do you know?" I asked through clenched teeth. If she didn't answer me, I was really going to tear this whole office apart.

She began to fidget in her seat as if she were sitting on hot coal. "I am not at liberty to discuss another client—"

My jaw dropped. "Are you serious?" I wanted to jump across the room and tackle her, but prison was not the place for me.

"Let's—"

I didn't give her a chance to finish. I grabbed my things and stomped out of the room.

I stomped my way through the glass doors, slamming them open and letting out a shriek, causing another patient to jump out of her skin.

"Sorry but my husband is driving me crazy," I quickly apologized before stomping away.

In the blink of an eye, I sat in my car, willing myself to relax before I confronted Scott. In my rage I don't know how I made it to my mother in laws house, but I did.

I rang the bell.

No one came to the door.

I began to pound on the door so hard that I was sure my knuckles would bleed.

"Jovi?"

Scotts mom looked at me as if I had two heads.

"Hello Caridad, where's your son?"

"He's in his room."

I pushed past her and practically ran to the room. I opened his door without a knock.

"Why weren't you at therapy?" I asked.

He was reclined on his bed with a headset on and a game controller in his hands.

"I was busy."

Without a second thought, I grabbed the controller and threw it into the hallway. Caridad came running. "What is wrong?"

"I'm sorry Cari, but I need to talk to Scott alone." I closed the door, locking it.

"Aaron, I need to go," he said into the headset.

"So, this is what has you busy?" I asked after he took the headset off.

"What does it matter to you, Jovi?" The hard set of his jaw told me he was ready for a fight.

"Are you serious right now?" I sneered.

He shook his head. "No, Jovi, are *you s*erious right now?"

"Me? I'm not the one who skipped therapy to play video games in my childhood bedroom that still has Yankee wallpaper border like I'm ten!"

"Oh, you're so funny. You really want to know why I didn't go to therapy?"

"Duh, Scott! Why else do you think I'm here?"

"You wrote about us! Again!"

"What?" I was so confused. "What are you talking about?"

He crossed his arms. "Stop the fucking act. I saw the article."

"Scott, I really don't know what you're talking about."

My heart was racing. What was he talking about? I didn't submit anything to my editor. I was working it out all in my head; all the emails I sent, the stories I submitted...nothing rang a bell.

"You know what hurts the most, Jovi? is that through all of this...therapy, the fights, the sex, the talking, the weekend...I thought we were finally getting better."

"We were," my throat hurt from the emotion that was on the verge of spilling out.

I was at a loss.

Scott began to pace in the small, crowded room. "Then I read the article and you tell the whole fucking world that although your husband is putting all his effort into this relationship, even with therapy...*even on the good days, divorce is inevitable*!"

Oh. My. God. "Scott, I didn't send that in."

"I was always fighting for nothing!" He yelled, the echo making the room vibrate.

"It wasn't for nothing Scott! I want us! We can fix it!" I began to yell out of desperation.

It's weird how you don't know how bad you really want something until you can feel it slipping from your grasp.

This felt like the end. No matter what I said, Scott looked as if he hated me. I couldn't stand it. While his face was flushed red, his pulse throbbing as if it was about to jump out of his neck; I was a blubbering mess.

"Scott, I didn't send it in. I didn't write it for people to read it."

"But you wrote it, Jo. And people read it."

As the tears continued to pour out, my chest began to hurt from the gulps of air I was trying to take in.

After minutes went by, my breathing and crying came back down to an acceptable level.

"Was I a joke to you? Was this all a way to get revenge?" Scott asked, his voice barely above a whisper.

"No, Scott."

He shook his head; his eyes were dark and cold. There was no laughter or flirtation.

"I don't believe you," he growled. "You won, Jovi. You want a divorce? I'll give it to you."

21

Scott

Jovi ran out in tears.

I wanted to run after her but I fought against that desire.

Hours passed since Jovi left; a soft knock sounded on my door.

Without any encouragement, my mother unlocked my door.

When I raised an eyebrow, she laughed. "This is my house; you think I don't have a key for every door?" I laid back down, throwing an arm across my eyes hoping she get the hint. I felt the bed sink as she sat down. "Are you okay?"

I raised my arm slightly. "I'm just a ray of sunshine."

She smoothed her hand on my chest. "Papi, I know you love Jovi but maybe you're not meant to be together," she sighed.

"Are you trying to make me feel better? Because you're doing one hell of a job."

She lightly smacked my chest. "Watch your tone...I'm your mother."

"Sorry," I mumbled.

"You guys had a good run and a beautiful baby girl...maybe this was all part of God's plan."

When I didn't respond, she rubbed my chest. "Are you hungry? I made Mangú with salami and cheese...I know that's your favorite."

I offered her a small smile and I nodded. "Okay, give me a minute."

When she left the room, I began to think about all the things that went down with Jovi.

Everyone read her inner most thoughts. She never saw us getting back together, it was all some mind-fuck revenge plot to drive me insane.

It worked.

I was sitting at home embarrassed because my wife of fifteen years played me dirty. I had teachers coming up to me, offering me unsolicited advice along with phone numbers to divorce lawyers.

The parents didn't say anything. Some gave me looks of sympathy, others looks of hatred...how could I cheat on the mother of my child? Fuck them, they didn't know the full story. They didn't know what really happened. And thankfully they didn't know that Kim was somehow involved.

Jovi cried during our fight, maybe she was being sincere.

Or maybe she's just a really good actress. She's probably home having a good laugh with Liz, talking about how we had sex and then how eager I was to get us back on track.

I'm such a fucking idiot.

I asked her not to write about us and she went and did it anyway!

She didn't trust me?! Well, I didn't trust her!

I sat through dinner in silence, sitting and stewing in my thoughts.

The doorbell rang, my mother got up to answer. When she returned, Tommy and Aaron were right behind her.

"Want to get some wings?" Tommy asked.

"Hell, yeah."

"And what about all this food?" My mother pointed out.

"Leftovers for tomorrow?" I grabbed my jacket and kissed my mom on the way out. "Don't wait up."

A half hour later, we sat in *the Dirty T*, waiting for our order.

It was a Wednesday night, so we were one of the few sitting at the bar.

"What happened with Jovi?" Aaron cut to the chase.

"How you know something happened?'

Tommy and Aaron exchanged a knowing look. "Dude, you took off the headset, but you didn't turn off the system, I heard everything!"

"Yeah, then he called me," Tommy added.

"Have you spoken to—" I began to ask.

Tommy shook his head. "No, she went to moms with Clara, she's meeting Liz there...I think they're spending the night."

A dancer, wearing only pasties and a G-string approached the table. "Hello, boys. Quick dance?"

"No," Tommy said.

"Sure, a quick one won't hurt," Aaron answered.

She straddled him, gyrating against him, suffocating him with her breasts.

I sat back and drank my beer.

"Oh, no this isn't uncomfortable at all," Tommy joked but continued to stare.

Aaron looked over. "Might as well enjoy the entertainment while waiting for the food."

"Okay...Scott, back to you, what's up with you and my sister?"

I shrugged. "It's over...for real this time."

The waitress dropped the wings off at our table. Through the rising steam I could see Tommy's expression.

"What?" I asked.

"You really think it's over?" Tommy asked.

The stripper finished her dance. "It's not over," Aaron added as he tipped the dancer.

"I told her not to write about us for the paper and she did it anyway."

"A woman sent you a picture of her tits...I think you can let this go," Tommy pointed out.

I shook my head. "How can she say that she doesn't trust me when I can't trust her?"

Aaron and Tommy looked contemplative as they took bites of their wings.

Normally, I would've devoured the wings, but I didn't have much of an appetite.

When the guys didn't answer, I asked, "How can I continue to make an effort now that I know that she had no intention of reconciling? I was a fucking joke."

"But she said she was in it...maybe she changed her mind?" Aaron said.

Was he right? Did she change her mind?

"Ooooo, look, he's thinking about what you said," Tommy chuckled at Aaron. "Something you said had an effect on him."

Aaron shrugged. "Sometimes I amaze myself."

"Shut up, I'm trying to think!" I yelled at them over the hip hop music.

Tommy placed a soft hand on my shoulder. "Listen, I think that you need to give each other a little space...a lot was said and maybe you guys just need to cool off for a bit."

Tommy was right.

Jovi and I needed some time to think; I should've given her time to think from the second she asked for a divorce. I was just scared of losing her forever.

I lost her anyway.

I got off the bar stool. "Listen, I gotta go...I can't stay here."

Aaron and Tommy exchanged looks. "But you didn't eat anything," Tommy said.

"Not hungry. I honestly feel...tired. I just want to go to bed."

Aaron gestured for a waitress. "Sure, let's wrap this up and I'll drive you home."

"No, don't worry about it, I'll just take the train."

"It'll get better!" Aaron yelled over the deafening sounds of Drake playing over the speakers.

******

Jovi

Liz caressed my head while I cried like a newborn baby.

Clara was in Tommy's old room sound asleep while Liz and I were in our old room.

When I called Liz earlier, she immediately went to pick Clara up from after-school and met me at our parents' house.

My eyes felt like they were burnt to the point of no return; I'd be surprise if I still had vision after all this.

Liz smoothed my hair back. "Tell me what happened," she soothed.

"I want him...I don't know...what happened," I hiccuped.

"I thought you guys had a great weekend." I sat up, making my baby sister gasp at the sight of me. "Oh my god, Jo!"

I wiped my nose along my sleeves. "What?"

"You look...like a mess."

I did my best to wipe the tears and snot from my face. "I just can't believe that it's really over."

"Isn't that what you wanted?"

"Yes...no..." I hiccuped again.

"I don't know how to help you."

I laughed. "Funny...at one-point Scott said the same thing."

"What did he say to you?" Liz reached out for my hand, holding on to me, knowing that I was on the verge of another meltdown.

"He missed therapy, when I went to his mom's house..."

Liz's eyes narrowed. "Did he have another girl there?"

I reached for the tissues. "No, he was playing video games with Aaron."

"Aaron was there?'

"No, he was on the headset."

"Fucking asshole," she spat out.

"Aaron?"

"Him too! But I'm talking about Scott."

Even though I felt like shit, a hiccuped laugh snuck out. "You don't even know what happened."

"I know but if he was stupid to hurt you so bad that you're sleeping at moms house looking..." I raised my eyebrow, she shrugged. "Let's be honest, Jo...you're not looking so hot."

"Gee, thanks," I mumbled.

"So, tell me...I need to know so I can help."

"I don't know how...but remember I mentioned to you that the paper wanted to run a series about the divorce? I wrote a piece about our first therapy session but after talking to Scott, I never handed it in...now, it's online for the world to see...I just, I don't know how."

The silence that followed let me drift into my thoughts again; every scenario or digital glitch that may have sent the article to my editor instead of a drafts folder.

Did I send it by accident thinking it was another article? There was no other explanation.

After minutes of silence, Liz made no attempt to vocalize her opinion.

"You okay?" I sniffled.

Liz looked as if she were in some kind of trance, looking off into nothing. She shook her head. "I have something to tell you," she licked her lips and tucked a curl behind her ear, the same way she did when we were kids and she fucked up.

"Elizabeth..." my heart began to race.

She looked up to the ceiling. When her eyes began to well up, I began to panic. "Jovi I...it was me." When her eyes came down so did her tears.

"You what?" I hate to fight against the lump in my throat.

There was that feeling that I knew what she was confessing to.

"I was the one who sent the story in."

She squeezed my hand as I pulled away from her. "But how? Why?"

Liz began wiping the tears away as she continued her confession. "You wanted the book deal so bad and you and Scott were so all over the place I didn't think you would care—"

I looked around the room, the only way out was the door...I didn't want to wake Clara up. I felt the rage in my body rise up. "It's my marriage, Elizabeth! Of course, I cared!" I yelled.

"Jovi, I'm so sorry," she sobbed.

Her face was just as blotchy as mine.

I thought I felt betrayed when I saw Scott and Kim's messages; this was on a whole different level. This was my sister, my blood. I tell her everything and even though her life was a little more colorful than I would like it to be, she was still one of the closest people to me.

"How could you?" I asked.

"I thought I was helping you. I knew you wouldn't send it in yourself because Scott told you not to...but I wanted you to have that book deal."

"I made a choice, Liz. I chose to respect my husband."

"But at what cost?"

"Shut up, Liz! Don't try to sound philosophical when all you're doing is making an excuse for a shitty thing you did!" I began to pace the small room, still with *NYSNC and Backstreet Boys posters still on the wall.

She began to pace along with me. "I know what I did was shitty, but I thought I was helping! Jovi, I thought you needed help!"

I spun around fast, almost knocking her over. "Liz! don't try to fix my life when yours isn't any better!"

Her hands went on her hips. "What does that mean?"

"You're engaged to a porn star!"

"And?!" she shrugged her shoulders defiantly.

"But you're in love with Aaron!"

"I am not!" Her face scrunched together and her lips pursed as if she tasted something sour.

"I give it a week before you call it quits, I'm surprised Eddie stuck around this long."

"Shut up, Jo."

"You use them and throw them away cause—"

"Shut up, Jo!" she shrieked, pushing me onto one of the beds.

We slapped each other like we did when we were kids! Two-grown ass women...a mess!

Liz slapped me one good time, bringing me out of my rage. "Liz! Stop!" I yanked her hair, making her freeze.

"Okay, okay," she huffed.

We both froze; hair clenched, mid slap, breathing heavy. "Lower your hand and I'll let go of your hair," I bargained.

She lowered her hand slowly and I let go. We both fell back onto the mattress, starring up at the ceiling; our breath slowly going back to normal.

"I was happy." I closed my eyes, just tired of fighting with everyone.

"I'm sorry, Jo." She rolled over, pulling me into her arms. "I really thought I was helping."

"I know," I sniffled. "He fought for us and in the end, I broke us...and it's over."

Liz wrapped me I her arms, rubbing my back. "No, Jovi. If he fought for you guys this whole time, it's because he loves you...love doesn't just disappear like that."

"He was so mad."

"Babe, he's mad now but just give him space...he'll calm down."

I felt the tears again.

I asked Scott for time to think. How crazy that now I needed to give him space? I was afraid that time would not work in my favor. I was afraid that he would realize that we were better apart.

I knew that sleep would never come but Liz held me until I grew too exhausted to cry.

22

Scott

These last couple of days was the longest I've gone without talking to Jovi; I felt like hell.

Instead of calling Jovi's phone to speak to Clara, I called the landline. No one ever called the landline. The landline was for apocalyptic emergencies...or parents who couldn't figure out how to work a cellphone.

I just figured she would see my name on the caller ID and let Clara pick up.

I'm not going to lie, it hurt that she didn't take that chance to talk to me, but I told myself it was for the best.

There was no doubt in my mind, I loved Jovi with everything I had. but at this point it was just a matter of self-preservation; I needed to survive.

I kept telling myself that I would survive this even though it felt like I wouldn't.

I was expecting any day now to get served with official divorce papers.

Is that what happens? Does one get served with divorce papers? Does someone come disguised as a delivery guy just to sneak attack you with divorce papers or does it come in the mail? I didn't want to find out.

I wanted to make love to Jovi until all this was behind us. I wanted to kiss her until she trusted me again. I wanted to hold her until she loved me again.

Because I wasn't talking to Jovi or her family, I threw myself into working, praying that the distraction would help get over everything. I made sure the decorating committee had what they needed, the catering was set, one of the teachers who moonlighted as a DJ was ready, I made sure teachers and parents signed up to be chaperones...I was doing it all.

Our school was in a festive mood; and although I was planning it all, I wanted no part of it. After checking everything, I would always end up in my office hiding from everyone.

A light knock sounded on my office door. I stood up quickly at the sight of a ball of curly hair; my heart was pounding so hard that I for sure thought I would have a heart attack any minute thinking it was Jovi sporting her natural curls...then Liz poked her head in.

"I can see you're excited to see me," she grumbled.

I felt my shoulders slump and I couldn't help the grimace that appeared on my face. "You're not the person I was expecting," I answered.

"If you're expecting to see Jo, you're shit outta luck."

"Why the hell are you here Liz?" I snapped.

For the first time ever, Liz looked nervous. She began to fidget, touching her necklace, earring, tucking a stray curl..."Well, what is it?" My patience was wearing thin.

She sighed. "I was the one who sent the story in."

"You...were the one..." my mind couldn't wrap itself around what she said.

"That sent the story in," she finished. She licked her lips and clasped her hands in front of her, waiting patiently for my reaction. I wanted to ring her neck.

I was at a loss for words. "Why?"

"Because she was miserable!"

As she yelled, I turned to look out. I jumped up and slammed the door to my office. "You need to lower your voice, you're at my place of work," I snapped.

Liz had the audacity to roll her eyes. "Scott, I'm here to say that it was me who sent the story in. Jo had a big opportunity, and you were going to ruin it for her."

"Liz...I really hate that you're here. Do you know what I hate more?" When she crossed her arms, I continued. "I hate that you think you know best for everyone but yourself!" My voice had a mind of its own. I felt my blood pressure rise, only these Rivera women could get me to lose my cool.

"I already had this conversation with Jo...I know I fucked up." Liz held her hands to her chest. She looked sincere but I wasn't born yesterday.

"Big time!"

Liz turned to look out the office. "You need to lower your voice...where at your place of work."

"Okay, Liz...you came here to tell me that it was you, it doesn't help that she wrote it. Those where her real thoughts."

Liz shook her head. "Why are men so stupid? She wrote it before you guys started working it out."

"And?"

"She loves you, stupid. I don't know why, but she wants you."

I didn't want to have this conversation with Liz. "I need you to leave."

"I'm going to go...I just...this really broke her. I love my sister and I...don't like seeing her like this."

"It broke me too. She asked for the divorce...she put no effort into trying. But no one cares how I feel. How I felt."

"My sister could be stupid sometimes too," Liz shrugged. "Being with you for so long turned her that way."

I shook my head. "Now's not the time for your verbal abuse, Liz. You're the one who fucked up."

She looked down, playing with a giant ring on her finger. "I know...I'm sorry," she mumbled. She shook her curls out and huffed. "Scott, I told her to give you time to think."

"Stop giving people advice."

Liz pursed her lips. "I'll remember that for next time, but I think you need to forgive her...just like she was starting to forgive you for cheating on her."

"I didn't—"

Liz held up her hand. "I don't care, it's not my business."

Before I could vocalize my smart reply, there was a knock on the door; forcing both of us to turn.

Before I could answer, Aaron showed himself in. "I thought I saw Medusa here. I thought I'd come in to help you out."

"I was on my way out anyway," Liz waved him away.

She passed Aaron, exchanging a look that I couldn't decipher and frankly I didn't want to.

"Liz, I heard about the porn star."

"Problem?"

"No princess, it's your life...if you want to contract herpes again, you're on the right track."

"I hate you so much," she hissed. "Scott, I think both of you are being dumb...as much as I hate to admit it...you guys belong to each other."

She smiled at Aaron, flipping him her delicate middle finger before finally leaving the office.

"What did the devil want?" Aaron asked as he took a seat.

"She says that Jovi didn't send the article in...it was her."

Aaron began to clap. "That's great! Now you can go get your woman."

"No."

"No, what?"

"She didn't hand it in, but she wrote it...that's how she really feels." Aaron stared at me as I went on with my ramblings. "What if we say okay, let's try again and that's not what she really wants."

"I think we both know that Jovi does what she wants. Damn, these women for being independent and free," he joked.

I ran a hand down my face, I needed to clear my head but my mind kept reeling...I loved Jovi; I would wait a million years for another chance.

I rushed to grab my jacket only to stop and drop it back down; maybe she needs time.

I picked my jacket up again; maybe she'll talk herself out of trying.

I dropped the jacket back down.

"Are you having a breakdown?" Aaron asked.

"I don't know what do," I admitted.

"Want my opinion?"

"Not really." I just wanted to go get my wife.

"I think you should give it a couple days. You guys are emotional right now."

"Liz told Jovi the same thing."

Aaron shrugged. "For once she said something smart."

"I don't know if it's the best thing to take advice from you and Liz...you guys are a fucking mess."

Aaron had a look of amusement. "We're a mess? We aren't married with a kid and playing mind games with each other."

I scoffed. "What you guys are doing isn't mind games?"

"No."

"That's really funny."

"We don't want to be in a relationship with each other and we are happy just being each other's form of release—"

"Gross."

Aaron shook his head. "No, not gross, just realistic."

I finally sat down behind my desk, slumped because it took too much effort for me to use proper posture. "You know what? The balls in her court now...I'll give her until the end of the week to make a move."

"And?"

"And if she comes to me, I'll know she wants me."

"That's dumb but okay."

There was the voice in the back of my mind asking, *what if she didn't make a move?*

Was I prepared for the consequences of waiting for Jo to make a move?

My anxiety began to kick up a notch, but I kept it under wraps until I got home and immediately dialed Jovi's phone.

With each unanswered ring I was beginning to lose my nerves...and then her voicemail came on. I dialed one more time because you never knew, she could have been busy with work or Clara or...putting pins in a voodoo doll that kind of looked like me.

Instead of the incessant ringing, it went straight to voicemail!

That only means one of two things; her phone ran out of batteries or she deliberately sent my call to voicemail.

Knowing Jo...it was the latter.

She saw my name pop up on her phone and she dismissed me. I thought about hanging up, but I held out hope.

"Jovi, it's me...I know we have a lot of things to work on but I...I love you and I want to keep making us better...I need you." I was unsure of what to say next. "I have that event at work I was telling you about, I want you there...it would mean the world to me. It's on

Friday night, party starts at five. I'm sorry for the long message, I just didn't want to wait."

I hung up the phone and stared at it, willing it to ring; it never did.

23

Scott

Getting the dance together, baseball practices starting...along with the regular curriculum—I was working non-stop. Before I knew it, Friday was here.

I heard nothing from Jovi which would make this the longest we've gone without speaking to each other.

I wanted to go to the apartment myself and tell her it was going to be okay; then I reminded myself that the balls in her court. I made every effort; I made the last call...there's been nothing but crickets in return.

I looked up at the clock; time to get ready for the dance.

******

Jovi

"You need to shower, Jo." Tommy's voice barely penetrated the fog that I've had around me for the past week.

"I've showered."

"When? When was the last time you showered?" he was annoyed.

This was the time that I wished that my glare could shoot lasers.

“Mommy showered Wednesday,” my daughter answered innocently.

“Jovi! you need to set a good example for our daughters! A shower a day keeps the bugs away.”

The girls giggled as they ate the pizza that I had delivered...yet again.

My brother starred me down making me sigh. “Tommy, I’m just exhausted.”

“From?!”

I glanced to where the girls sat, taking all the adult drama. “Do you guys want to go watch a movie? I can put on *the Little Mermaid*.” I wiggled my eyebrows playfully so that the kids would get excited.

“Yay!!!” They both shouted.

I took my time setting the girls up in the living room because I didn’t want to deal with Tommy's nagging.

When I finally made it back to the kitchen, it was as if Tommy hadn’t move from his spot. “I don’t want to talk about this stuff in front of the girls, it was hard for Clara and the teachers are saying she’s getting better.” Tommy nodded. “And just for the record, I am exhausted from thinking about Scott.”

“What do you want, Jo? Because we’re all getting a little crazy for you to make up your mind.”

“I want people to stop asking me what I want," I muttered.

"Make a decision then! Get out of this rut! You have the power to do whatever you want!"

I snapped. "I want him! I know it’s crazy but—”

“It’s not crazy, relationships are a crazy thing but what you’re feeling is not.”

Tears began to surface. “Ugh! I hate that I’ve been crying non-stop for the past week!” Tommy stood there, letting me vent. “What kills me was that I was ready to forgive him for everything...I think I was okay with moving on from all that...now, he’s being so hardheaded...not one call, not one text...no carrier pigeons, smoke signals...”

"Okay, you're going off on this weird tangent, bring it back."

I sighed. "I just thought that he would forgive this, I...I thought he wanted me no matter what."

It was Tommy's turn to be flabbergasted; he threw his hands in the air. "Well, shit, Jovi. He's been trying to make it work, only to see that you went into therapy with failure already in mind."

"But—"

"He doesn't know if it's worth fighting for if you're not invested."

"But I'm invested!"

"Now you are, but did *he* know this? Does he know this now?!"

My siblings knew how to get me; we were so close that they knew how my mind worked better than I did and at this moment I wasn't into it.

Without a backward glance, Tommy left me in the kitchen. "Thank you for abandoning your baby sister when she's in the middle of a breakdown!" I shouted after him.

"God, Jovi, relax! I went to get your phone." He rolled his eyes. "You're so needy," he groaned as he walked back into the kitchen.

I scowled in his direction. "Excuse me for going through a divorce."

"Jovi! you are not going through a divorce. People going through a divorce would have been divorced by now. You and Scott are in some weird cosmic funk that you guys are not sure how to get out of."

Could it be that we've been so perfect that the universe decided to fuck us up enough to get a divorce?

Scott was my best friend, the one that knew absolutely everything about me, and I was positive that he would say the same thing about me.

"Uh...Jovi?"

I looked at Tommy who was busy staring at my phone.

"What?"

"You have a two-day old message from Scott."

I snatched the phone out of his hand; eager to see what he had to say.

"Why is his number on silent?!" I asked, my heart being a mile a minute.

"I don't know, just listen and see what he has to say!" Tommy yelled right back at me.

"Honey, I'm home!" Liz yelled as she let herself in.

"Shhhhh!" I silenced her as I listened to the message.

Liz paused at the entrance of the kitchen, listening in on the message with us.

"That's rude," she pouted.

"She's listening to a missed call from Scott," Tommy filled her in.

My heart began to beat with excitement that finally Scott and I were on the same page.

"Why didn't the phone ring?" I asked myself.

"Oh, because I silenced his number for you so you can think about what you want with no distractions," Liz said with a giant smile.

My whole body went cold. I should've known that Liz had something to do with this.

Sensing that I was about to explode, Tommy ran to stand between us. "Jovi! he wants you too! So, let's go get your man!" he clapped.

But I was having none of it. "Liz."

My tone made Liz to stand up a little straighter. "Jovi?" she tilted her head to the side, waiting.

That set me off.

Without warning I ran to jump on my sister! There was this rage that I could not control.

Liz did her best to run from me, choosing to hide behind the small breakfast table. "Jovi! are you out of your mind?!"

Tommy stood in front of me, thinking that he could probably stop me from killing our sister. "I was! But now I'm thinking clearly, I'm going to kill you!" I growled, running to the side of Tommy, pulling my arm out to yank Liz to me so I can do some damage.

"Jovi!"

I was able to get a couple of slaps in before Tommy pulled us a part. "Jovi! Liz was only trying to help!"

"Yeah, I just didn't want you to be sad anymore!" Liz said in her own defense as she straightened herself out.

"I wasn't sad until you started to meddle! You can keep fucking up your life all you want, it's your life! But stop fucking up mine!"

Liz's eyes flashed red. "Jovi, you were miserable, and we kept having to hear about how much you hated Scott and then you guys were banging and then the next you hated him...make up your god-damn mind!"

"How about you?!" my voice was so sore from all the yelling, but I couldn't stop myself.

"What about me?" she crossed her arms, preparing for a fight.

"Engaged to someone who fucks for a living when the whole fucking world knows you want Aaron so bad that it makes you so bitter!"

"Me? Bitter? Don't get that twisted. Aaron and I are nothing."

"And it kills you, doesn't it?" I spat out.

The kitchen fell silent.

The tick, tick, tick of the clock and our heavy breathing was all that could be heard.

"Jovi, I'm sorry." Her voice cracked. "I thought I was helping."

Tommy still held on to my arms. "I think we all need to take a minute to relax...emotions are high."

"Liz." I tried to shake my greasy hair out of my eyes. "I need you to let me borrow that ruched black dress and drive me to the school dance."

Liz looked at Tommy with confusion clouding her big eyes. "Does that mean you forgive me?"

I pinched the bridge of my nose just so she can see how frustrated she made me. "Liz, you're my baby sister and I love you but don't mess with my marriage again."

I wanted the steel in my voice to set her straight; telling by the apologetic way her puppy dog eyes looked at me told me that she was regretful.

She took me in her arms, hugging me close; practically suffocating me with her hair.

"I love you, Jovi."

Just as quickly as she hugged me, Liz let me go and ran out the kitchen. "I'll be back with the dress!"

Tommy clasped his hands in front of him and raised an eyebrow. "Now will you take a bath?"

24

Scott

"Scott! this is great!" Aaron and some of the other teachers called out to me; I walked over to make small talk.

The school gym was filled to capacity with students, parents, supporters from the community who wanted to be involved. I looked around the room and everyone was in light-hearted mood; I wanted to join in the festivities, but my impending divorce was taking up too much space in my mind.

There was only one person I wanted to celebrate with.

"Scott?" Kim called my name from behind me.

I felt the chill down my back; I needed to tell myself to relax and stay cool; there's no reason to be on edge.

Aaron and the rest of the group stopped the conversation, waiting for my response.

I counted to three and turned around. "Yes, Kim?"

She was dressed in a white dress that hugged all her curves; the only thing that made that dress work appropriate was the cardigan that she wore over her shoulders.

"Can I talk to you for a minute?"

I wanted to say no but before I could answer, Aaron saved me.

“Actually, I was about to take Scott to talk to the owner of Tom’s sports shop.”

Kim’s annoyance bubbled o the surface briefly before she smashed it down. “Okay, we can meet in your office in about ten minutes?”

I was well aware that everyone in our circle was looking at us; they were probably thinking that there was something going on...which was what I was feared.

“Sure,” I finally answered.

I walked off with Aaron. “Shit, what do you think she wants?” Aaron asked nodding towards Kim.

“I don’t know, and I don’t care.”

“You look like shit man,” he whispered.

“I put on a nice shirt, I got a shape up, I made an effort.”

“Yeah, but you have that mopey look and to be honest you’re bumming a lot of people out.”

My head shot up at the mere mention of parents having a problem with my attitude, or a potential donor catching wind of a scandal. “Someone said something?”

“It’s me. You’re bumming me out.”

“Sorry that I’m so fucking pathetic.” I began to walk away but Aaron reached out, grabbing onto my arm.

“Listen, I was joking man, I just don’t want you to be in this rut.”

“My marriage is over; I think I’m allowed to feel like shit.”

Aaron began to nod slowly. “Okay, so we’re going to have a pity party.”

“I called Jovi, left her a voicemail and heard nothing...not a peep from her," I said through gritted teeth. My anger bristled to the surface and I snatched my arm out of his grasp.

“Just give her time, man.”

“How much time should I give her? I told her I love her, and I want us together and...nothing.”

"Maybe...she didn't get your message," Aaron said quietly.

"Key word is maybe...maybe she did get my message but just didn't want to talk to me."

Aaron looked too cool for school, placing his hands in his pocket and shrugging. "Fine, go, cool off and wreck your brain thinking about the worst-case scenario."

I stomped away from Aaron with no real destination in mind.

As if she smelled my loneliness, Kim saddled up beside me. "Can we talk now?"

"We can talk here." I folded my arms and stood my ground. I was so over everyones bullshit. I wanted to be left alone. Correction, I wanted to be with Jovi.

"In your office."

"Let's go outside," I suggested, knowing full well that being alone with this woman would do me no good. Outside there were parents, faculty and kids; the chances of her making a scene outside was low. Regardless of what I told myself, my eyes still darted around the room hoping Aaron, or anyone, would come over for a chat...I was left to fend for myself.

We walked to the front of the school. The noise from the party oozed out into the cool crisp night.

"What did you want to talk about?" I found no need in beating around the bush.

Color rose to her cheeks, deepening the blush she had applied, she secured my wrist in her delicate hand and pulled me to the side of the building. "I just wanted some alone time, just to be with you."

She waited for my reaction. I wanted nothing from her so I began to back away. "I don't think you want me Kim."

Her hold on my wrist tightened.

"Kim...I don't think you want to do this."

She was standing close. I was drowning in her perfume. She let go of my wrist, her hands slid up my abdomen, making me flinch against her touch. She wrapped her arms around my neck. Beads of sweat began to form around my temples. What was I to do? I couldn't push her; she would most likely scream bloody murder.

"I think you need a little persuading." She leaned in, pressing her curves against me.

My hands instinctively landed on her hips as I attempted to gently get her off of me.

She persisted, this time standing on her tip toes and placing a kiss firmly on my lips. I felt my eyes grow to saucers at her brazen attempt at seduction.

My lips did not move. I kept them as tight as possible; no tongues mingling, no spark, no nothing.

Kim pulled back. "What's wrong with you?"

"I'm in love with my wife. I'm in love with Jovi," I told her.

Something just past her shoulders caught my eye.

My eyes connected with Jovi. She shook her head at me and turned to run away.

"Jo!" I yelled, I prayed that my voice would slow her down. Kim's arms finally gave way, allowing me to run to Jovi.

I made it to the front of the school, scanning the area for any sign of Jovi. Fuck. I went inside bumping into Aaron.

"Hey, Jovi was here. She checked your office, you weren't there. I told her maybe you went outside for air."

I looked around the room in a frantic panic. "She saw Kim kiss me."

"Dude, you have no luck at all."

I kept scanning the room, Kim stomped towards me. "I threw myself on you—" her voice dripped with disdain.

"Kim!" My outbursts drew stares, I lowered my voice. "Kim, I've said this before, I had no intention of being with you. There's only one person I want and that's Jovi and now it's all gone because she saw you kiss me."

Kim looked away; her cheeks flamed red. "I'm sorry." Her voice cracked and she made her way out the dance.

I turned back to Aaron. "I need to find Jovi. I don't care how long it takes but we're going to be together again. Wrap this dance up for me?"

"You got it," Aaron assured me.

I stalked out the party, not caring whether it looked bad to people. I had one goal in mind and that was to get my wife back once and for all.

******

Jovi

I can't believe that after everything, this is how it ends; with Scott making out with Kim. I waited until I parked my car to let out the tears.

It hurt.

It hurt to know that the person I loved was moving on with the person who helped break us up. The glow from my living room was a bright beacon calling me in; I knew the minute I walked in, Liz would bombard me with questions I didn't want to answer.

I needed a moment to not be okay...alone.

I was tired of crying; of not feeling good enough—I was sick of being a failure.

My head laid on the steering wheel when someone tapped on my car window. The one person I didn't want to see was peering in.

"Jovi, can I talk to you?" Kim's soft voice immediately made me want to rip her to shreds.

Kim's eyes were perfectly lined and although it was clear she had been crying, she still was one of the most beautiful women I have ever seen in real life.

I didn't move right away.

"Jovi, can I get in the car?"

I sighed, unlocking the door. I don't know why I did it, I was curious to hear what she had to say.

At the sound of the click, Kim skipped to the passenger side. "I thought you wouldn't let me in," she said as she adjusted herself.

"It was either let you in or run you over...I think letting you in was a safer bet."

"I'm sorry, Jovi." Her lips trembled and she began to cry.

I felt the ball in my throat. "For what?"

Her long nails traced along her toned legs which were exposed in her dressed. "I know that I was the reason why you and Scott are getting a divorce."

I looked straight ahead because my tears began to form, and I didn't want her to witness my breakdown. "You're one of the reasons, but not the only."

"Jovi, he loves you!"

I laughed. "Does he?"

"I thought he wanted me but...I think that was wishful thinking on my part," she explained. "Every time I tried to get closer, he pushed me away because...he loves you." I heard her sniffle and my tears quietly fell.

Kim's hand reached out for mine; I congratulated myself for not flinching. "I sent him the picture because I thought if I did that, he would leave you for me," she confessed.

I snatched my hand out of hers. "Why would you do that?" my anger erupted.

"Because I'm not a happy person."

"*I'm* not a happy person!" My voice rose along with my anger; I no longer had control.

"I'm sorry, Jovi!" she wailed.

"Kim," I rubbed my eyes, getting rid of the moisture and most likely messing up my mascara and liner. "Why?" I had so much I wanted to say to her but only that simple question made it passed my lips.

"I was jealous...of what you guys had."

"That gives you the right to steal my husband?!" I screeched.

"No, no Jovi, it wasn't like that. I was not in a good head space...I'm trying to get better but...he was the first guy that actually listened to me."

"But he wasn't yours, you were stealing another woman's husband."

She kept her eyes on her shaking hands. "I know and if I could go back and just be a real friend, I would."

I shook my head, no longer caring how crazy I must look now. "You are beautiful, smart, kind and a lot of other things I don't think I am, maybe that's what he went looking for."

"No, Jovi, you're beautiful, comfortable in your skin, smart, talented...he wanted you all along."

The sounds that came out the both of us were gross; like feral hyenas or something just as scary. Under normal circumstances I would have kicked her ass out, but I was over all the drama.

We should be able to talk everything out like normal adults.

Yeah, but the hussy admitted to trying to steal your husband; kick her ass, Jovi.

The devil on my shoulder was very loud while making a few good points, still this beautiful woman was just a hot mess as the rest of us.

Kim wiped her nose with the palm of her hand. "Every time I invited him out or tried to flirt, he'd always bring you up. I don't think he meant for all this to go down...guys are just dumb sometimes."

That made me laugh. "Kim, why are you telling me all this?'

"Because he really loves you and...someone should be happy."

I cleared my throat, prepping myself to give the woman who tried to steal my husband some sound advice. "You need to make yourself happy before you go into a relationship and expecting for that person to make you happy...that's something I found out recently."

Kim's perfect lips began to tremble. "But it gets really lonely."

"There's beauty in the silence. You get to know yourself a little better. I think I put too much pressure and weight on Scott. In my mind he had to fix me. It led us to all this."

"I think I need to figure out what I want," she sighed, falling back into the seat exhausted.

"Scott enhances my happiness...you need to find out what makes you happy and find someone who enhances that...preferably someone who isn't married."

"You're smart," Kim said, as she wiped her nose against her palm again.

She reached across to me, but I leaned away from her.

"I know we're bonding but you're using your hand as a tissue and I don't want any part of it."

Kim laughed big and it was...nice.

"Jovi, I'm sorry."

"I'm angry but...I'm sorry, too." I let out a heavy stream of air.

Her lips set in a grim line. "What are you going to do now?"

I shrugged. "I have no clue."

25

Scott

I drove straight to Jovi's without a second thought; I needed to make things right.

I parked right next to her car, jumping out and only stopping when I noticed the shadow sitting on the stoop.

"What are you doing out here?" I asked.

"Waiting for you," Jovi answered with a small smile.

It threw me for a loop; I for sure thought we would break out into a melee. I ran through every scenario to convince Jovi to talk to me.

I didn't foresee her actually wanting to speak to me.

"Can I sit next to you?"

She scooted over, giving me room to sit. "Scott, what happened to us?"

"I fucked up."

She shook her head. "*We* fucked up."

To my surprise, Jovi reached out for my hand. "I shouldn't have been texting another woman."

"I don't want to be the type of wife who checks your phone because she doesn't trust you."

"I don't want to be the type of husband who can't make you happy."

Jovi squeezed my hand. "You were the one thing that made me happy, my mistake is that I let other things cloud that."

I felt the emotion coming up. "What are you trying to say, Jovi?"

"I love you, Scott. From the first time I spotted your afro..."

A big ball of laughter came out of me.

"...even at this moment, when things seem impossible...I love you."

"I love you too, Jovi."

A gust of autumn chill settled around us, Jovi moved closer to me. "I think we should keep going to therapy because no matter how messy and scary Dr. Rubenstein is, I kind of like her."

I nodded in agreement. "We need to be honest with each other, Jo. If there's something that's bothering you or going on with you, you need to let me know."

"Agreed. We need to have date nights, or just spend real quality time together because I missed that. You're my best friend and...I felt like all that disappeared." Her eyes shone against the night; her nose was red.

The pain in my chest that I got from the knowledge that I made her cry was excruciating.

I wrapped my arm around her, bringing her closer to me. "Jovi, it seems like you're trying to work this out."

I'd be lying if I said my hopes weren't sky high.

"It seems that way because that's what I want."

My heart was pounding so hard from happiness; I was surprise it didn't just pop out of me. "What about Kim? She practically jumped me right when you came by."

"I wouldn't worry about Kim."

"Why? What'd you do?" I was afraid if I walked to the trunk of her car, I would find Kim's body.

"We came to an understanding."

My eyebrows shot up. "Understanding?"

I felt her body shake from laughter. "Just don't be stupid and think all women want to be your friend...some do but then there are others...with darker intentions."

"I'm sorry, Jovi. That should have never happened. It was my fault for leading her on—"

I felt Jovi's soft sigh as her hand reached up to pull my face closer to hers. "I know."

"You know?"

"I know you're sorry and yeah, you shouldn't have led her on, but I am also to blame...it took both of us to break us."

"Are we good?"

Her eyes connected with mine; for the first time since she asked for a divorce, I felt genuine hope.

"We're on our way to good," her smile was breathtaking against the moonlight.

I couldn't resist anymore, I kissed her with all the love I had for her. She kissed me back and I felt a huge weight evaporate.

She stood up, holding her hand out to help me up. "Want to know what attracted me to you in the beginning?" she asked. I nodded, prompting her to go on. "It was your eyes."

"Really?"

"Yup, I was drunk, but I noticed your eyes in the mirror; soft, kind...I knew then and there that you were mine...then on the first date I realized how innocent you really were," she laughed.

I pulled her into my arms. "Wait until we get upstairs." I growled as I nipped her lip.

She giggled as she squirmed against. "Clara and Liz are upstairs."

"Just the mention of your sister gives me heart burn."

Jovi rolled her saucer eyes. "I already spoke to her about everything."

"For some reason that doesn't ease my anxiety."

"She just did what she thought was right."

"I guess," I mumbled as I followed my wife into the building, knowing that whatever direction we were going was the right one.

26

Epilogue

One year later

Jovi

If someone would've told me that I would be dressed in a beautiful polka dot dress, ready to renew my wedding vows, I would've have laughed in their face before crying hysterically from my marital failures.

It was only last week when we decided to do it.

I had gotten the news that my editor wanted to give me my own column about marriage successes, hardships and advice.

I was afraid to take it on, but I was up for the challenge. I was also told that a big publishing house wanted to move forward with a memoir about the demise and rise of my marriage.

Scott gave me his blessing and reassurance; he had no qualms about me writing about us. Realizing that he was loved at the school and they would defend him.

Especially since his baseball team won their first championship last spring. The parents and kids were excited about it all that any small hiccup that our marriage caused was instantly forgotten.

Scott turned out to be my number one cheerleader.

He was there when I got the call about the column and the book, suggesting that we celebrate everything positive that has been going on in our lives.

So, here I was, in my parents' house getting ready to reaffirm our commitment to the love of my life.

I felt the butterflies in my belly.

"You ready?" Liz asked from behind me.

I've been checking myself out in the mirror, amazed at how beautiful I looked in my crème-colored satin halter dress, with white polka dots scattered about.

"Are you okay?" I asked.

Where I've been lucky at love, Liz has had one terrible relationship after another. The porn star was ancient history; two weeks ago, she just got of a relationship with a woman who was so jealous, she had problems with Liz speaking to me.

"I'm fine. Janice is holding some of my things hostage."

"Why do you always date the shadiest people?"

He shrugged nonchalantly. "They're the most fun."

"Maybe you should be dating a certain bearded man who drives you crazy?"

"I would but I think Jason Mamoa is married."

I rolled my eyes. "You know I meant Aaron." I hated that Liz refused to see that Aaron was her person.

She looked up to the ceiling. "God help me."

"What?" I asked.

"Aaron and I just use each other."

"He brought a date," I said, hoping that by goading her she would make a move.

"I don't care."

Our spat was interrupted by Tommy and the screaming baby in his arms.

"Oh no, what's wrong with him?" I asked.

Tommy placed the baby on the bed. "I just have to change him."

"Where are the girls?" Liz asked.

"Waiting like angels' downstairs with Frank." Tommy turned to address Liz. "You know Aaron brought a date?"

"Ugh! I'm waiting downstairs."

Tommy and I exchanged knowing looks.

I continued to twirl in front of the mirror as Tommy changed his son's diaper.

"How are you feeling?" he asked.

"Nervous." I ran a hand down to smooth my dress.

"For what? You've done this before...with the same guy!"

I laughed. "Can't a girl just be nervous."

"Are you happy?"

"Very."

I took a minute to really think about it. With the help of therapy, Scott and I have learned to communicate productively and efficiently. We learned to open up to each other in a way that was reminiscent of our earlier days.

Taking care of Clara has become a team effort, we were running like a smooth machine.

The tears began to well up, but I held them at bay because I didn't want to ruin the makeup that Liz had meticulously applied to my face.

"Hey, I left my socks in here," Scott came in, bare foot and dapper in his grey suit.

"Scott! you can't see the bride, it's bad luck," Tommy scolded.

He shrugged. "I don't believe in bad luck."

“Hey, did you hear from Kim?” I asked.

“She says sorry she can’t make it; she’s been working non-stop at her new job and couldn’t take the time off.”

Tommy sucked his teeth at us. “I can’t believe you guys invited her.”

“Why not? She’s my friend,” I explained.

I know it’s crazy! Within the last year, Kim and I have become good friends. She decided to leave the school, putting her marketing and advertising degree to good use.

The baby started crying again. “Time to feed baby.” Tommy bounced his son as he made his way out. “You guys look great by the way,” he said as he closed the door, leaving us alone.

Scotts eyes darkened with arousal as a slow grin appeared on his face.

“Scott! no, we can’t—”

“Of course we can, it’ll only be ten minutes,” he laughed as he kissed my neck.

I giggled. “No!”

“How about we sneak some booze up here and have some drinks—”

“I would love to, but I can’t.”

Scott tilted his head. “Why can’t you?”

I was going to wait until the day was over to drop a bomb.

“Scott, I love you.” I wrapped my arms around his neck, making sure not to get any makeup on his suit.

“I love you, too.”

I smiled. “There was a lot of things I didn’t think I want...”

“Like?” he kissed the tip of my nose, I grew nervous.

“Like couples’ therapy...that air fryer...kids,” I said softly.

I felt him tense up at the mention of kids. “Jovi what are you saying?”

“I’m saying I didn’t know I wanted anymore kids...”

I could see him process the information; it was a slow process. “So, you want kids?”

I nodded.

“I thought you were going to tell me you were pregnant,” he chuckled into my hair.

“I was...I mean I am.”

He stood back; I felt his eyes land right on my belly.

“You’re pregnant?” he whispered.

“Why are you whispering?”

“I don’t know,” he laughed nervously, passing a hand down his face. “Jovi, are you pregnant?”

“Yes,” I answered firmly.

Scott picked me up as if I were a ragdoll, hugging me tightly.

I held on to my dear sweet husband.

We stood like that for what felt like an eternity. I heard his sniffles and pulled away slightly.

“Scott? Are you crying?”

His tan face turned red and blotchy, as he cried and laughed at the same time. “I’m just really happy.”

“Me too.”

My face started to hurt from how much I’ve been smiling; but I didn’t care.

Scott kissed me, not caring that he was going to have red lipstick all over his face.

“Jo?”

“Yeah?”

“Thank you for loving me again.”

Just a girl from the Bronx living her best life.

J.L. is a wife, mother, and now author with her debut novel *The lawyer & the thief.* After years of working in the fashion industry, J.L. is turning her lifelong dream of writing into a reality. She hopes to inspire readers and make them laugh with her unique sense of humor, one-of-a-kind characters, and hilariously adventurous stories. J.L. currently lives in Connecticut with her son, husband, and extended circle of friends, all of whom help to inspire her everyday!

J.L. enojoys reading romance novels, watching *Gilmore Girls* for the millionth time, hanging out with her friends and family and pretending to be a pop star while singing karaoke.

CPSIA information can be obtained
at www.ICGtesting.com
Printed in the USA
BVHW071017200922
647501BV00001B/79